The Mamur Zapt and the Donkey-Vous

The Mamur Zapt and the Donkey-Vous

A Suspense Tale of Old Cairo

Michael Pearce

THE MYSTERIOUS PRESS
New York • Tokyo • Sweden
Published by Warner Books

A Time Warner Company

First published in the United Kingdom by
William Collins Sons & Co. Ltd.

Mysterious Press books are published by Warner Books, Inc.,
1271 Avenue of the Americas, New York, NY 10020

A Time Warner Company

The Mysterious Press name and logo are trademarks of
Warner Books, Inc.

Printed in the United States of America

First U.S. printing: July 1992
10 9 8 7 6 5 4 3 2 1

Library of Congress Cataloging in Publication Data

Pearce, Michael, 1933–
    The Mamur Zapt and the donkey-vous / Michael Pearce.
       p.   cm.
    ISBN 0-89296-486-3
    I. Title.
  PR6066.E166M26   1992
  823'.914—dc20   91-50848
                                                        CIP

The Mamur Zapt and the Donkey-Vous

1

Owen arrived at the hotel shortly afterward.

McPhee came down the steps of the terrace to meet him.

"Thank goodness you're here!" he said.

A cobra stretched lazily in the dirt at the foot of the steps stirred slightly. McPhee paused in his descent for a second and in that second its charmer thrust out a bowl at him. McPhee, flustered, dropped in a few milliemes.

"For heaven's sake!" protested Owen. "You'll have them all on to us!"

The crowd surged over them. Hands reached out at McPhee from all sides. Owen found his own hand taken in soft, confiding fingers and looked down to see who his new friend was. It was a large, dog-faced baboon with gray chinchilla-like fur.

"Imshi! Imshi! Get off!" shouted McPhee, recovering. One of his constables came down from the terrace and beat back the crowd with his baton. In the yard or two of space so gained a street acrobat in red tights suddenly turned a cartwheel. He cannoned heavily, however, into the snake-charmer and ricocheted off into a row of donkeys tethered to the railings, where he was chased off by indignant donkey-boys. Taking advantage of the confusion, Owen joined McPhee on the steps.

"What's it all about?"

"You got my message?"

"You'd better tell me."

McPhee had sent a bearer. The man had run all the way and arrived in such a state of incoherence that all Owen had been able to get out of him was that the Bimbashi was at Shepheard's and needed Owen urgently.

"A kidnapping," said McPhee.

"Here?" Owen was surprised. Kidnapping was not uncommon in Cairo, but it did not usually involve foreigners. "Someone from the hotel?"

"A Frenchman."

"Are you sure it was a kidnapping?" said Owen doubtfully. "They don't usually take tourists. Has there been a note?"

"Not yet," McPhee admitted.

"It could be something else, then."

"That's what I thought," said McPhee, "at first."

"If it's just that he's gone missing," said Owen, "there could be a variety of explanations."

"It's not just that he's gone missing," said McPhee, "it's where he's gone missing *from*."

He took Owen up to the top of the steps and pointed to a table a couple of yards into the terrace. The table was empty apart from a few tea things. A proud constable guarded it jealously.

"That's where he was sitting when he disappeared."

"Disappeared?" said Owen sceptically.

"Into thin air!"

"Surely," said Owen, trying not to sound too obviously patient, "people don't just disappear."

"One moment he was sitting there and the next he wasn't."

"Well," said Owen, and felt he really was overdoing the patience, "perhaps he just walked down the steps."

"He couldn't do that."

"Oh? Why not?"

"Because he can hardly walk. He is an infirm old man, who gets around only with the aid of sticks. It's about all he can do to make it on to the terrace."

"If he can make it on to the terrace," said Owen, "he can surely make it on to the steps. Perhaps he just came down the steps and took an arabeah."

There was a row of the horse-drawn Cairo cabs to the left of the steps.

"Naturally," said McPhee, with a certain edge to his voice, "one of the first things I did was to check with the arabeah-drivers."

"I see."

"I also checked with the donkey-boys."

"He surely wouldn't have—"

"No, but they would have seen him if he had come down the steps."

"And they didn't?"

"No," said McPhee, "they didn't."

"Well, if he's not come down the steps he must have gone back into the hotel. Perhaps he went for a pee...?"

"Look," said McPhee, finally losing his temper, "what do you think I've been doing for the last two hours? They've turned the place upside down. They did that twice before they sent for me. And they've done it twice since with my men helping them. They're going through it again now. For the fifth time!"

"Sorry, sorry, sorry!" said Owen hastily. "It's just that..." He looked along the terrace. It was packed with people. Every table was taken. "Was it like this?"

"Yes. Everyone out for their tea."

"And no one saw what happened?"

"Not so far as I have been able to discover."

"You're sure he was there in the first place? I mean—"

"He was certainly there. We know, because a waiter took his order. It was his usual waiter, so there's no question of wrong identification. When he came back the old man was gone. Disappeared," said McPhee firmly, "into thin air."

"Naturally you've been along the terrace?"

"Naturally I've been along the terrace," McPhee agreed.

"Friends? Relations? Is he with anyone?"

"His nephew. Who is as bewildered as we are."

"He wasn't with him at the time?"

"No, no. He was in his room. Still having his siesta."

"There's probably some quite simple explanation."

"Yes," said McPhee. "You've been giving me some."

"Sorry!" Owen looked along the terrace again. "It's just that..."

"I know," said McPhee.

"This is the last place you would choose if you wanted to kidnap someone."

"I know. The terrace at Shepheard's!"

"About the most conspicuous place in Cairo!"

•   •   •

The manager of the hotel came through the palms with two men in tow. One Owen recognized as the Chargé d'Affaires at the French Consulate. The other he guessed, correctly, to be the nephew of the missing Frenchman. The nephew saw McPhee and rushed forward.

"Monsieur le Bimbashi—"

He stopped when he saw that McPhee was in conversation.

McPhee introduced them.

"Monsieur Berthelot—"

The young man bowed.

"Captain Cadwallader Owen."

Owen winced. The middle name was genuine enough but something he preferred to keep a decent secret. McPhee, however, had a romantic fondness for things of the Celtic twilight and could not be restrained from savoring it in public.

"Carwallah—?" The young man struggled and then fell back on the part he recognized. "*Capitaine?* Ah, you are of the military?"

"*C'est le directeur de l'intelligence britannique,*" said the man from the Consulate.

"Not at all," said Owen quickly. "I am the Mamur Zapt."

"Mamur Zapt?"

"The Mamur Zapt is a post peculiar to Cairo, Monsieur Berthelot," McPhee explained. "Captain Cadwallader Owen is, roughly, Head of the Political Branch. Of the police, that is," he added, looking at the Chargé d'Affaires reprovingly. He wasn't going to stand any nonsense from the French.

"*Politicale,*" murmured Monsieur Berthelot doubtfully, only half comprehending.

"We hold you responsible for Monsieur Moulin's safety," the Chargé said to Owen.

"I will do everything I can," said Owen, choosing to take the remark as referring to him personally and not the British Administration in general. The French had previously shared, under the system of Dual Control, in the administration of Egypt and had been edged out when the British army had come in to suppress the Arabi rebellion, something they unsurprisingly resented. "However, I doubt whether this is a political matter."

"*Politicale?*" The young man was still having difficulties.

"I only deal with political matters," Owen explained. "Assassinations, riots, that sort of thing. I suspect this will turn out to be a routine criminal investigation. The police," he simplified, seeing that Monsieur Berthelot was not entirely following.

"The police? Ah, the Bimbashi—"

"Well, no, actually."

Owen wondered how to explain the Egyptian system. The Egyptian police fell under one Ministry, the Ministry of the Interior. Criminal investigation, however, fell under another, the Ministry of Justice. When a crime was reported the police had to notify the Department of Prosecutions of the Ministry of Justice, the Parquet, as the Department was called. The Parquet would then send a man along who would take over the investigation from the police and see it through.

He looked at the Chargé for help. The Chargé shrugged his shoulders.

"It's like the French system," he said, "quite."

Egyptian criminal procedure was in fact based upon the Code Napoléon, a product of an earlier French administration.

"Ah!" Monsieur Berthelot was clearly relieved.

"Has the Parquet been notified?" asked the Chargé.

"Yes," said McPhee.

"I'd better get on to them," said the Chargé, "and make sure they send along someone bright."

He started back into the hotel.

"Tell them to send El Zaki," Owen called after him. "Mahmoud el Zaki."

"Thanks," said the Chargé, and disappeared indoors.

"And now, Monsieur," said Owen, turning to the bemused young man, "about your uncle..."

• • •

Monsieur Berthelot was in fact able to tell them very little. Like his uncle and in common with almost everyone else in the hotel, he had taken a siesta after lunch. His had been more protracted than his uncle's and he had still been in his room when the Assistant Manager had knocked on his door. He had gone at once to his uncle's suite but found that he had not returned there after going down to the terrace. He had then gone down to the terrace and walked right along it, thinking that perhaps his uncle, unusually, had been taken up by some acquaintances.

Unusually? His uncle did not care for companionship, perhaps? Well, it wasn't so much that, it was just that his uncle generally preferred to be on his own when he got up from his siesta. He was like that in the morning, too, preferring to breakfast alone. He was always, the nephew said, "*un peu morose*" after waking up. That was why he, the nephew, took his time about joining him, both in the morning and in the afternoon. It worked out better that way.

And he always went to the same table? Yes, that was part of it. He didn't like to make decisions when he was still waking up. He preferred everything to be "*automatique.*" Besides, that particular table was the one nearest the door of the hotel and he had less far to walk.

His uncle suffered from some disability? He had had a stroke two years previously which had left him semiparalyzed down one side. He was recovering, he was much better now than he had been, but he walked with difficulty. Twenty or thirty meters was all he could manage.

They didn't go to the bazaars, then? No, there was no question of that. They had seen some of the sights but always from an arabeah.

And always Monsieur Berthelot had gone with him?

Well, that was the point of him being there. His uncle liked to have someone perpetually by him whom he could call on for support. Monsieur Berthelot looked a little glum.

Had his uncle ever gone off on his own before? Never! The young man was adamant. Never once since they had been in Cairo! Again he seemed a little depressed.

And how long, in fact, had they been in Cairo? About six weeks now. They would have to go back soon or they would face the *"reproches"* of his aunt, Madame Moulin. The young man gave the impression that this was something neither of them viewed with equanimity.

This was, then, purely a holiday? Not entirely. Monsieur Moulin had business interests in Egypt too.

What sort of business?

Contracting. Monsieur Moulin represented, was indeed a director of, a number of substantial French firms with building interests. But the chief point of their stay was recreational. Owen suspected it was as much to get away from Madame Moulin as anything else.

Had Monsieur Moulin received any messages? From his business friends, perhaps? Monsieur Berthelot did not think so, but would check if the messieurs desired. In any case, though, the friends would have come to Monsieur Moulin and not vice versa. Monsieur Moulin did not like leaving the hotel. He found the heat of the streets and the density of the crowds oppressive. Shepheard's alone was where he felt comfortable, and Shepheard's he rarely left. The young man could not understand what had happened on this occasion. He was at a loss. Surely his uncle had not left the hotel without telling him! He would never have done so voluntarily. But perhaps he had not left voluntarily.

He turned luminous, slightly protuberant eyes on Owen.

The Bimbashi had spoken of kidnapping. Did Monsieur think—

No, no, no, no. Monsieur did not think. There was probably some quite simple explanation.

That was what he kept telling himself. He was sure Monsieur was right. Only... He suddenly buried his face in his hands.

They were in one of the alcoves of the grand central hall of the hotel. It had once been an open courtyard but had been roofed over with a magnificent glass dome. Traditional Moorish arches, painted and striped, gave on to recesses and alcoves screened off with heavily fretted arabic paneling. Inside the alcoves and scattered around the floor generally were thick Persian rugs, the predominant color of which, cardinal red, matched the deep red of the comfortable leather divans and chairs. Beside the divans were low, honey-colored alabaster tables and backless pearl-inlaid tabourets. Suffragis in spotless white gowns and vivid red sashes moved silently through the hall on errands for guests. Owen found the opulence rather oppressive.

McPhee stirred slightly and the young man jerked upright.

A thousand apologies! He was delaying them, and when there was so much to be done. Was there anything else the messieurs wished to know? No? Then...

As they left the alcove Monsieur Berthelot said, almost wistfully, that his uncle had always preferred the light of the terrace to the dark of the hall. "He came from the South, you see—the bright sunshine." And then there was always so much to see on the terrace!

• • •

A smartly dressed young Egyptian ran up the steps. "Parquet!" he said briskly.

The manager hurried forward.

"Monsieur..."

"Mahmoud el Zaki, Parquet." He caught sight of Owen and his face broke into a smile. "Hello!" he said. "Are you on it, too?"

"Not exactly," said Owen. "McPhee thinks it might be a kidnapping."

"A kidnapping? Here?"

"I know. But there are some odd features."

"They don't usually take foreigners."

"That's what I said."

"Odd!" He turned to the manager. "I shall need a room."

"My office." The manager hesitated. "I hope it won't be necessary to—to disaccommodate the guests."

"As little as possible. However, I may have to ask them a few questions."

The manager looked doubtful. "Of course," he said. "Of course, I was hoping—would you not prefer to talk to my staff?"

"Them too."

The manager shrugged but still looked worried. He led them to his office.

"I will send you some coffee," he said.

"How is it that Mr. McPhee is involved?" asked Mahmoud. "Surely they didn't send for you directly?"

"They did. A foreigner. They thought it important," said Owen.

He listened intently while McPhee brought him up to date. Then they went out on to the terrace. The tea things had all gone from the tables now, except for the one table. In their place drinks were appearing. It was already growing dark. Night came quickly and early in Egypt. The short period of twilight, though, when it was still light enough to see and yet the heat had gone out of the sun, was one of the pleasantest parts of the day and lots of people were coming out on to the terrace to enjoy the evening air.

All along the front of the terrace was a thick row of street-vendors pushing their wares through the railings at the tourists above: ostrich feathers, hippopotamus-hide whips, fly switches, fezzes, birds in cages, snakes coiled around the arms of their owners, bunches of brightly colored flowers—roses, carnations, narcissi, hyacinths—trays of Turkish Delight and sticky boiled sweets, souvenirs straight from the tombs of the Pharaohs (astonishingly, some of them were), "interesting" postcards.

The street behind them was thick with people, too. They could not be described as passersby since they had stopped passing. Mostly they gathered around the pastry sellers and sherbet sellers, who stood in the middle of the road for the convenience of trade but to the great inconvenience of the arabeah-drivers, and just looked at the spectacle on the terrace above them.

"With all these people looking," said Mahmoud, "you would have thought that someone, somewhere, must have seen something."

•　•　•

He went down the steps into the crowd. Owen hesitated for a moment and then decided to join him. McPhee turned back into the hotel to conduct yet another search.

Mahmoud went straight to the snake charmer and squatted down beside him. The snake charmer had rather lost heart and was trying to find an untenanted patch of wall against which he could rest his back. From time to time he played a few unconvincing notes on his flute, which the snake, now completely inert, ignored.

The snake charmer pushed his bowl automatically in Mahmoud's direction. Mahmoud dropped in a few milliemes.

"It has been a long day, father," he said to the charmer. "Even your snake thinks so."

"It needs a drink," said the charmer. "I shall have to take it home soon."

"Has it been a good day?"

"No day is good," said the charmer, "but some days are less bad than others."

"You have been here all day?"

"Since dawn. You have to get here early these days or someone else will take your place. Fazal, for instance, only he finds it hard to get up in the morning."

"And all day you have been here on the steps?"

"It is a good place."

"They come and go, the great ones," said Mahmoud.

"Yes, they all pass here."

"My friend—" Mahmoud indicated Owen, who dropped into a sympathetic squat—"cannot find his friend and wonders if he has gone without him. His friend is an old man with sticks."

"I remember him," said the snake charmer. "He comes with another, younger, who is not his servant but to whom he gives orders."

"That would be him," said Owen. "Have you seen him?"

"No," said the charmer, "but then, I wouldn't."

He turned his face toward Owen and Owen saw that he was blind.

"Nevertheless," said Mahmoud softly, "you would know if he had passed this way."

"I would," the old man agreed.

"And did he?"

For a long time the old man did not reply. Mahmoud

waited patiently. Owen knew better than to prompt. Arab conversation has its rhythms and of these Mahmoud was a master.

At last the old man said: "Sometimes it is best not to know."

"Why?"

"Because knowing may bring trouble."

"It can bring reward, too."

Mahmoud took a coin out of his pocket and pressed it into the old man's hand.

"Feel that," he said. "That is real. The trouble may never come." He closed the old man's fingers around the coin. "The coin stays with you. The words are lost in the wind."

"Someone may throw them back in my face."

"No one will ever know that you have spoken them. I swear it!"

"On the Book?"

"On the Book."

The old man still hesitated. "I do not know," he said. "It is not clear in my mind."

"The one we spoke of," said Mahmoud, "the old man with sticks: is he clear in your mind?"

"Yes. He is clear in my mind."

"Did he come down the steps this afternoon?"

"Yes." The old man hesitated, though. "Yes, he came down the steps."

"By himself or with others?"

"With another."

"The young one you spoke of?"

"No, not him. Another."

"Known to you?"

There was another pause.

"I do not know," said the old man. "He does not come down the steps," he added.

"Ah. He is of the hotel?"

"That may be. He does not come down the steps."

"But he did this afternoon. With the old man?"

"Yes. But not to the bottom."

"The other, though, the old one with sticks, did come to the bottom?"

"Yes, yes. I think so."

"And then?"

The snake charmer made a gesture of bewilderment.

"I—I do not know."

"He took an arabeah, perhaps?"

"No, no."

"A donkey? Surely not!"

"No, no. None of those things."

"Then what happened?"

"I do not know," said the charmer. "I do not know. I was confused."

"You know all things that happen on the steps," said Mahmoud. "How is it that you do not know this?"

"I do not see," protested the charmer.

"But you hear. What did you hear on the steps this afternoon?"

"I heard nothing."

"You must have heard something."

"I could not hear properly," protested the charmer. "There were people—"

"Was he seized?"

"I do not know. How should I know?"

"Was there a blow? A scuffle, perhaps."

"I do not know. I was confused."

"You know all that happens on the steps. You would know this."

The snake charmer was silent for so long that Owen thought the conversation was at an end. Then he spoke.

"I ought to know," he said in a troubled voice. "I ought to know. But—but I don't!"

• • •

The donkey-boys were having their evening meal. They were having it on the pavement, the restaurant having come to them, like Mohamet to the mountain, rather than them having gone to the restaurant.

The restaurant was a circular tray, about a yard and a half across, with rings of bread stuck on nails all round the rim and little blue-and-white china bowls filled with various kinds of sauces and pickles taking up most of the middle, the rest being devoted to the unpromising part of meat hashed up in batter. The donkey-boys in fact usually preferred their own bread, which looked like puffed-up muffins, but liked to stuff it out with pieces of pickle or fry. They offered some to Mahmoud as he squatted beside them.

"Try that!" they invited. "You look as if you could do with a good meal."

Mahmoud accepted politely and dipped his bread in some of the pickle.

"You can have some too if you like," they said to Owen. "That is, unless you're eating up there."

"Not for me. That's for rich people."

"You must have a piastre or two. You're English, aren't you?"

"Welsh," said Mahmoud for Owen.

"What's that?"

"Pays Galles," said a knowledgeable donkey-boy. Many of them were trilingual.

This sparked off quite a discussion. Several of them had a fair idea of where Wales was but there were a lot of questions about its relation to England.

"They conquered you, did they?"

"It was a long time ago."

"It's hard being a subject people," they commiserated. "We should know! Look at us!"

"The Arabs."

"The Mamelukes."

"The Turks."

"The French."

"The British."

"We've had a lot of rulers," someone said thoughtfully. "When's it going to end?"

"Very soon, if the Nationlists have it their way," said someone else.

That set off a new round of discussion. Most of the donkey-boys were broadly in sympathy with the Nationalist movement but one and all were sceptical about its chances of success.

"They're the ones with the power," said somebody, gesticulating in the direction of the terrace, "and they're not letting it go."

"They've got the guns."

"And the money."

"At least we're getting some of that," said someone else.

"You're doing all right, are you?" asked Mahmoud.

"Not at the moment we're not."

"When the next ship gets in we'll be all right," said someone.

"When a new lot arrive at the hotel," one of the donkey-boys explained, "the first thing they do is come down to us and have their pictures taken with the donkeys."

"For which we charge them."

"It's better than hiring them out for riding. You don't tire out the donkeys."

"Or yourself," said someone.

There was a general laugh.

"The children are best."

"It's a bit late in the year for them, though," said someone.

"Not too busy, then, today?" suggested Mahmoud.

"Busy enough," they said neutrally. The donkey-boys did not believe in depreciating their craft.

"There's been a lot of excitement up there today," one of them said.

"Oh?"

"They've lost someone."

All the donkey-boys laughed.

"It's easy enough for these foreigners to lose themselves in the bazaars," said Mahmoud.

"Oh, he didn't lose himself in the bazaars."

"No?"

"He lost himself on the terrace."

There was a renewed burst of laughter.

"Get away!"

"No, really! There he was, sitting up on the terrace as bold as life, and then the next minute, there he wasn't!"

Again they all laughed.

"You're making this up."

"No, we're not. That's how it was. One minute he was there, the next he wasn't."

"He just walked down the steps?"

"Him? That old chap? He couldn't even fall down them."

"He went back into the hotel."

"They can search all they like," said someone, "but they won't find him there."

"You've got me beat," said Mahmoud. "Where is he, then?"

"Ah!"

"Try the Wagh el Birket," someone suggested.

They all fell about with laughter. The Sharia Wagh el

Birket, which was just 'round the corner, was a street of ill-repute.

"If you don't find *him* there," said someone, "you'll find every other Frenchman in Cairo!"

"And Englishman, too!"

"But not Welshman," said someone kindly.

• • •

"They know something," said Owen.

"Yes."

Owen and Mahmoud were sitting wearily at a table on the terrace. It was after eleven and the hotel manager had just sent them out some coffee. The night was still warm and there were plenty of people still at the tables. Across the road they could see the brightly colored lamps of the Ezbekiyeh Gardens but here on the terrace there were fewer lights. There was just the occasional standard lamp, set well back from the tables because it drew the insects, which circled it continuously in a thick halo. Because of the relative darkness, the stars in the yet unpolluted Egyptian sky seemed very close, almost brushed by the fringed tops of the palms. The air was heavy with the heady perfume of jasmine from the trays which the flower sellers held up to the railings for inspection. Some women went past their table and another set of perfumes drifted across the terrace. In the warm air the perfumes gathered and lingered almost overwhelmingly.

Owen watched the light dresses to the end of the terrace. There was a burst of laughter and chatter as they reached their table and the scrape of chairs. Someone called for a waiter, a suffragi came hurrying and a moment later waiters were scurrying past with ice buckets and champagne. A cork popped.

The railings were still crowded with vendors and the

crowd in the street seemed as thick as ever. Every so often an arabeah would negotiate its way through and deposit its passenger at the foot of the hotel steps. Then it would join the row of arabeahs standing in the street. The row was growing longer. There were few outward journeys from the hotel now.

The donkey-boys had stopped all pretense of expecting business and were absorbed in the game they played with sticks and a board. They threw the sticks against the wall of the terrace and moved broken bits of pot forward on the board depending on how the sticks fell. The scoring appeared to be related to the number of sticks which fell white side uppermost. The dark sides didn't seem to count unless all the sticks fell dark side uppermost, which was a winning throw.

"Yes," said Mahmoud, "they know something. But how much do they know?"

"They know how he disappeared."

"Yes," Mahmoud admitted, "they might know that."

"They said he didn't come down the steps."

"They didn't quite say that. Anyway, I believe the snake charmer."

"The charmer said the old man had been helped down. We haven't been able to find anyone who helped him."

"Not on the hotel staff. It might have been a guest."

"We could ask around, I suppose. It won't be popular with the hotel."

"A crime has been committed," Mahmoud pointed out. When in pursuit of his duties, he was not disposed to make concessions.

"We don't know that yet."

"At least we could try the ones on the tables nearest him."

"If we could find out who they were."

"The waiters will have a good idea. They'll be intelligent in place like this. I've got them making a list."

"Even if we knew," said Owen, "would it help much? I mean, it might have been just a casual thing. Somebody saw him trying to get down the steps and helped him out of kindness."

"We'd know definitely that he came down the steps. It would confirm the charmer's story."

"And challenge the donkey-boys'."

"Yes. We would be back to the donkey-boys."

"But they're not talking. Why aren't they talking?"

"Why should they help the authorities? Especially if they're not *their* authorities."

"Well, hell, they're the only authorities they've got."

"The one thing Egyptians have learned over the centuries," said Mahmoud, "if they've learned anything over the centuries, is to keep clear of the authorities, never mind who they are. Anyway," he added, "there's probably another explanation."

"Which is?"

"They've been paid to keep their mouths shut."

"Like the charmer?"

"No. He's not been paid. He's just frightened."

"You think someone's frightened him?"

"Possibly."

"And paid the donkey-boys?"

"Possibly."

"So you think it was a kidnapping, then?"

"I haven't got that far yet. I'm waiting for the note."

• • •

It came just before midnight. McPhee emerged from the hotel and walked slowly across to them. He was carrying a slip of paper in his hand which he laid on the table in front of them. Owen read it by the light of one of the standard lamps. It was in the ornate script of the bazaar letter writer.

> Mr. Yves Berthelot,
> Greetings. This letter is from the Zawia Group. We have taken your esteemed uncle. If you want to see him again you must pay the sum of 100,000 piastres which we know you will do as you are a generous person and will want to see your uncle again. If you do not pay, your uncle will be killed. We will tell you later how to get the money to us.
>   Meanwhile, I remain, Sir, your humble and obedient servant
> > The Leader of the Zawia Group

"Zawia?" said Mahmoud. "Have you heard of them?"

"No," said Owen, "they're new."

"Taking tourists is new, too," said McPhee.

"Yes. It doesn't look like the usual kind of group."

"I take it you'll have nothing in the files?" said Mahmoud.

"I'll get Nikos to check. I don't recognize the name but maybe he will."

"How did it come?"

"It appeared in Moulin's pigeonhole. Berthelot found it when he went to check the mail. I've had him checking it at regular intervals."

"Presumably it was just handed in?"

"Left on the counter when the receptionist was busy."

"He didn't notice who left it?"

"No."

Mahmoud sighed.

Owen looked along the terrace. The conviviality at the far end had developed into quite a party. Corks were popping, people laughing, suffragis bustling with new bottles. The general gaiety spread far out into the night. At the intervening tables people were sitting more quietly. They were mostly in evening dress, having come out into the cool air after dinner. They looked relaxed, confident, immune. But from somewhere out in the darkness something had struck at these bright, impervious people: struck once and could strike again.

2

"Even if it is a kidnapping," said Owen, "there's no need for me to be involved."

"Oh?" said Garvin. "Why not?"

Garvin was the Commandant of the Cairo Police. It was an indication of something special that he was taking an interest in the case. Normally he left such matters to his deputy, the Assistant Commander, McPhee.

"It's not political."

"If it's a Frenchman," said Garvin, "then it *is* political."

    •   •   •

"Zawia?" said Nikos. "That's a new one. It's not the usual sort of name, either."

Most of the kidnappings in Cairo were carried out by political "clubs," extremist in character and therefore banned, therefore secret. It was a standard way of raising money for political purposes. The "clubs" tended to have names like "The Black Hand," "The Cobra Group," or "The Red Dagger." Owen sometimes found the political underworld of Cairo disconcertingly similar to the pages of the *Boy's Own Paper*. There was in fact a reason for the similarity. Many of the "clubs" were based on the great El Azhar university, where the students tended to be younger than in European universities. In England, indeed, they would have been still at school, a fact which did not stop them from kidnapping, garrotting, and demanding money with menaces but which led them to express their demands in a luridly melodramatic way.

"Zawia?" said Owen. "I don't know that word. What does it mean?"

"A place for disciples. A—I think you would call it—a convent."

"A place for women?"

"Certainly not!" said Nikos, astonished yet again at the ignorance of his masters. Nikos was the Mamur Zapt's Official Secretary, a post of considerable power, which Nikos relished, and much potential for patronage, which Nikos had so far, to the best of Owen's knowledge, not thought fit to use. "It is a Senussi term."

The Senussi were an Islamic order, not strong in Egypt, but strong everywhere else in North Africa.

"It also means corner, junction, turning point."

"Turning point?" said Owen, alert to all the shades of significance of revolutionary rhetoric. "I'm not sure I like that."

"I'm not sure I like it if it's a convent," said Nikos. "Particularly if it's a Senussi one."

•   •   •

Midway through the morning Nikos put a phone call through to him. It was one of the Consul-General's aides. Since the British Consul-General was the man who really ran Egypt Owen paid attention. Anyway, the aide was a friend of his.

"It's about Octave Moulin," his friend said.

"Moulin?"

"The one who was kidnapped. I take it you're involved?"

"On the fringe."

"If I were you I'd move off the fringe pretty quickly and get into the center."

"Because he's a Frenchman?"

"Because of the sort of Frenchman he is. His wife is a cousin of the French President's wife."

"The French Chargé was 'round pretty quickly."

"He would be. They know Moulin at the Consulate, of course."

"Because of his wife?"

"And other things. You know what he's doing here, don't you?"

"Business interests?"

"The Aswan Dam. He represents a consortium of French interests who are tendering for the next phase."

"I thought it had gone to Aird and Co.?"

"Well, it has, and the French are not too happy about that. They say that all the contracts have gone to British firms and they wonder why."

"Cheaper?"

"Dearer, actually."

"Better engineers?"

"We say so, naturally. The French have a different view. They say it's to do with who awards the contracts."

"The Ministry of Public Works. Egyptians."

"And with a British Adviser at the head."

Most of the great ministries had British Advisers. It was one of the ways in which the Consul-General's power was exercised. In theory Egypt was still a province of the Ottoman Empire and the Khedive, its nominal ruler, owed allegiance to the Sultan at Istanbul. Earlier in the last century, however, a strong Khedive had effectively declared himself independent of Istanbul. Weaker successors had run the country into debt and exchanged dependence on Turkey for dependence on European bankers. In order to retrieve the tottering Khedivial finances, and recover their loans, the British had moved in; and had not moved out. For twenty-five years Egypt had been "guided" by the British Consul-General: first by Cromer's strong hand, more recently by the less certain Gorst.

"There's a lot of money involved."

"That's what the French think. They've made a Diplomatic protest."

"And got nowhere, I presume."

"It's a bit embarrassing all the same. So we might give them something to shut them up. There's a subcontract to go out for constructing a masonry apron downstream of the dam sluices to protect the rock. We might let them have that. That's where Moulin comes in. At least we think so. There are a lot of French interests jostling for the contract."

"So what do you want me to do?"

"Find him."

"That's a bit of a tall order."

"And quickly. Before the contract is awarded. You see, the French think we might have had a hand in it!"

"In what?"

"The kidnapping."

"They think we kidnapped him? That's ridiculous!"

"It's too well organized for us to be behind it, you mean? I tried that argument on the Old Man but he doesn't like it."

"Why would we want to kidnap him?"

"To affect the bidding. The French think we are still

determined to influence the result. They have an inflated regard for our duplicity."

"That's because they are so duplicitous themselves they can't believe anyone else would act straight."

"I'll try that one on him too."

"However," said Owen, "I wasn't really planning to get involved in this one."

"I think you ought to revise your plans. The French are holding us responsible for Moulin's safety."

"In a general way, of course..."

"In a particular way. They say that the Mamur Zapt is responsible for law and order in Cairo. The kidnapping of a French citizen is a matter of law and order. Therefore the Mamur Zapt is responsible for Monsieur Moulin. Personally responsible."

"Ridiculous!"

"They think you've got you, boyo. If I were you I wouldn't stay on the fringe."

• • •

The Press had asked for a conference.

"They'll just be wanting a briefing. You handle it," Garvin had said.

Owen, whose duties included Press censorship, was used to the Press. But that was the Egyptian Press. The conference included representatives of the European Press and he was not used to them.

"Would the Mamur Zapt show the same lack of urgency if Monsieur Moulin were a British subject?" asked the man from *Paris-Soir*.

"I am not showing a lack of urgency. I am treating the matter with extreme seriousness."

"Then why haven't you been to the Hotel today? Surely the investigation is not complete?"

"The investigation is being carried out, as is usual in Egypt, by the Department of Prosecutions of the Ministry of Justice, the Parquet. It is in the capable hands of my colleague, Mr. El Zaki, who, I am sure, is giving it all his attention."

"Are you treating this as a routine criminal investigation?"

"Yes."

"Is it routine for someone to be kidnapped from the terrace at Shepheard's?"

"No."

"Would the Mamur Zapt agree that security is lax when a prominent foreign visitor is kidnapped from the terrace of one of the world's most famous hotels?"

No, the Mamur Zapt would not agree.

"Are you worried about the effect on tourism?" asked an American correspondent.

"No. Tourists are quite safe provided that they don't do anything stupidly reckless."

"Like having tea on the terrace at Shepheard's?" asked the man from *Paris-Soir*.

Owen saw Garvin standing at the back of the room. When the conference was over he came forward.

"Political enough for you?" he asked unkindly.

•   •   •

The waiters had provided a list of guests who had been in that part of the terrace at the time Monsieur Moulin disappeared and Mahmoud had spent the whole morning working through it. He had just reached an English family when Owen arrived. It consisted of a mother and daughter, and a young man with straight back and ultra-smart clothes whom Owen at once identified as an army officer.

"An elderly gentleman?" the mother was saying. "No, I don't think so."

"He always sat at the same table, the one at the top of the stairs."

"No, I'm afraid not."

"Of course you do, Mummy!" the daughter said sharply. "You pointed him out to me yourself. An old man with droopy moustaches and sticks."

"'A gentleman' I think Mr.—ahem, the Inspector, said."

"Well, he was a gentleman of sorts. Foreign, of course."

"Not much of one," the young man put in heavily. "It's my belief that he took that table so that he could ogle all the girls as they went in and out."

"Oh, come on, Gerald!" the girl said, laughing. "He's about ninety-five! Mind you," she added, "that didn't stop him pressing up against me in the foyer the other evening."

"Did he really?" The young man's neck turned red with anger.

"I was encouraging him, of course."

"Lucy! That is quite enough! I think Mr.—ahem, Inspector, you have had your answer. We have no knowledge of this, ah, person. Gentleman or not."

"But, Madame, your daughter—"

"Thank you. And now, Lucy, I am afraid it is time for us to prepare for lunch." She gathered her things and began to get up.

Mahmoud half rose and then sat down again determinedly.

"I am afraid I have not quite finished, Madame. A moment or two longer, *je vous en prie*."

"I don't think that will be necessary," said the young man, jutting his jaw.

Mahmoud looked at him coldly.

"This is a criminal investigation, Mr. Naylor. Would you mind leaving us?"

The young man stared at him unbelievingly. "What did you say?"

"I said would you mind leaving us."

The young man's face flushed crimson.

"Gerald!" said the mother warningly.

Gerald leaped to his feet. "I'm not putting up with this," he said. "Not from a bloody Egyptian!"

"Gerald!" said the woman very sharply.

The young man turned to her. "I'm sorry, Mrs. Colthorpe Hartley," he said, "but there's really no reason why you should be exposed to this sort of thing. This fellow—"

"Excuse me," said Owen.

The woman looked up. He addressed himself to her rather than to the man.

"Mrs. Colthorpe Hartley?" He put out his hand. "Captain Owen." He seemed to be always using his rank these days. Perhaps it was something to do with Shepheard's. "I am afraid Mr. El Zaki is quite right. It *is* rather important. Although—" he smiled—"perhaps not so important as to risk sacrificing your lunch. I wonder, though, whether your daughter could spare us a moment? It won't be longer, I promise you. I'm sure you wouldn't mind, would you, Miss Colthorpe Hartley?"

"Well, no, of course," said the girl, slightly flustered. "I haven't met you at any of the balls, have I?" she asked, recovering.

"Not yet," said Owen, piloting her firmly away into another alcove and leaving mother and young man floundering. He sat her down on a divan and pulled up a chair for himself leaving the one opposite for Mahmoud.

"Mr. El Zaki is an old friend of mine."

"Is he? You speak English jolly well," she said to Mahmoud.

"And French too," said Owen.

"I wish I could," said Lucy. "The people here speak French, don't they? As much as English, I mean."

"It's a great mixture."

"Have you been in Egypt long?" she asked Owen.

"Two or three years."

"You look so brown!"

"I was in India before that."

"Were you? Gosh, I'd like to go to India. Only Daddy says it is too expensive."

"Where is your father?" said Owen, looking 'round.

"Having a drink, I expect. He can't bear to come shopping with us."

"Was he on the terrace too?" asked Mahmoud.

"He joined us out there."

"About what time was that?"

"Four o'clockish. Mummy always likes her tea about then."

"That was when your father joined you?"

"Yes. He was a bit behind us, as usual. He always takes ages over his shower."

"When you came out on to the terrace was Monsieur Moulin already there?"

"You mean that old man with sticks?"

"Yes, that's right."

"I sort of noticed him, I think, though I couldn't swear to it. Wait a minute, yes, I did notice him. He was looking around. I thought perhaps he'd lost that girl of his."

"What girl of his?"

"You know, that girl who's always hanging around him. His bit of fluff."

"Bit of fluff?" said Mahmoud, completely lost.

"Yes." Lucy frowned in concentration. "His *petite amie*. That's what you would say, isn't it?" She smiled at Mahmoud.

"Well, maybe," said Owen. "That would depend on the

circumstances. Can you tell us about this lady, Miss Colthorpe Hartley?"

"Well, she's—well, first of all, I think my mother would say she's not a lady. Not just foreign, I mean, but definitely not a lady."

"She's French, is she?"

"Yes, I think so. She's blonde, not dark like they usually are, and it's real blonde too, not dyed. Although she's common, she's also quite sophisticated, if you know what I mean, at least that's how she strikes me. She's terribly well dressed. It must have cost a fortune. If only Daddy would let *me* spend that amount of money! That's sugar-daddy sort of money, not daddy sort of money. I say, that's pretty good, isn't it! I must tell Gerald that."

"Would he understand?" asked Owen.

Lucy laughed merrily. "He's not as stupid as all that," she protested. "Well, not quite as stupid. You don't like Gerald much, do you, Captain Owen?"

"Not much."

Why was he saying that? This was supposed to be a formal investigation, not party chit-chat. He must have caught it from her.

"But are you sure she's Monsieur Moulin's *petite amie* and not Monsieur Berthelot's?" Mahmoud intervened.

"Monsieur—?"

"Berthelot. The young man who accompanied Monsieur Moulin. His nephew."

"Oh, I know the one you mean. The one with the bulging eyes. Well, no, I don't think so, though you often see them together."

"Does she come out on the terrace too?"

"Only in the evening. I expect," said Lucy acidly, "that she doesn't have time. It takes her so long to make up."

"Then why," asked Mahmoud, "when you came out on

to the terrace yesterday afternoon and saw Monsieur Moulin looking around, did you think he had lost her?"

"My goodness!" said Lucy. "You *are* sharp! He's caught me out, hasn't he?" she appealed to Owen.

"He has."

"I don't know why I said that. It's my silly tongue running away with me again. What *did* I mean?" She thought hard.

"Well, it's true," she said after a moment, "or it might have been true. She's always hanging around him. It's so blatant. I should think he jolly well might have felt lost when she wasn't there for once."

"And she wasn't there?"

"No. And it *is* true that you don't usually see her on the terrace in the afternoons. Not till later. *I* think," said Lucy, giggling, "that she finds it hard to get up. Perhaps she's worn out!"

Lucy shrieked with laughter. Mrs. Colthorpe Hartley, sitting obediently outside the alcove but not abandoning her post, looked at her disapprovingly. The young man beside her stirred unhappily.

"So she definitely wasn't on the terrace yesterday afternoon but he definitely was?"

"Yes, that's right. You've got it."

"And you're sure about that? About him being there, I mean?"

Lucy thought again. "Yes, I'm pretty sure." She tossed her head. "No, I'm definitely sure."

"And that would have been about fourish. You're not able to place the time more precisely?"

"About five to four. We're always *on* the terrace by four."

"And then you had tea. Was Monsieur Moulin having tea?"

"No, I don't think so."

"He was just sitting at the table?"

"Yes."

"Looking around for someone? As if he was expecting them?"

"Yes. Of course, now I think about it, it might have been her."

"And then what?"

"Well, then we finished our tea."

"And did you notice Monsieur Moulin any more? Did you see him leave his table, for instance?"

"No."

"Go down the steps?"

"He might have been ogling me," said Lucy with a toss of her curls, "but I wasn't ogling him."

"You stayed on the terrace for about how long?"

"About an hour."

"And when you left, was Monsieur Moulin still at his table?"

"No," said Lucy.

"That's definite, is it?"

"Yes, because I can remember seeing the tea things on the table and wondering why the waiters hadn't cleared them. They're very good here, you know."

"One last question, Miss Colthorpe Hartley," said Mahmoud. "You said your father joined you later?"

"A bit later."

"Thank you. In fact, thank you very much for being so helpful."

"I'm glad I've been helpful," said Lucy. "I'm not usually. Daddy says I'm scatterbrained, but I'm not really. I just sometimes *choose* to be scatterbrained."

She got up to go. Mahmoud rose too.

"You're very nice, aren't you?" she said to him. "You've got such sweet brown eyes. But such a sad face!"

• • •

"I haven't got a sad face, have I?" asked Mahmoud.

They were having lunch 'round the corner. By the time they had finished with Miss Colthorpe Hartley, it was nearly noon. The heat had driven everyone off the terrace and back into the cool of the hotel, first to lunch and then to the darkness of their bedrooms.

Owen normally worked till one-thirty and then went to lunch at the Sporting Club, but today it was too hot even to do that, so he and Mahmoud found a small Turkish café in one of the side streets near the hotel. Even that was nearly deserted. Although there were one or two tables outside, none of them was taken. The few customers had retreated with the proprietor into the dark depths of the interior where the sun never penetrated. A small boy served them with cups of Turkish coffee and glasses of iced water. They would eat later.

"No, I don't think so." Owen considered him. "No, I don't think so at all."

Mahmoud if anything looked very bright and alert. Miss Colthorpe Hartley must have been misled by his Arab looks.

"Sometimes I feel depressed," said Mahmoud. "I felt depressed this morning when I was talking to the old lady and the man."

"Don't take any notice of him. He's just a stupid bastard."

Mahmoud shrugged. "He's just Army, that's all. I'm used to people like him. But the old lady was different. She was very polite but she made me more depressed, if anything. She reminded me of Nuri."

Nuri Pasha was a common acquaintance and the father of what might have been called, if anyone had dared risk the description since there was nothing petite about Zeinab and she was a forceful person, Owen's own *petite amie*.

"It's because they're the same generation and have similar social backgrounds," said Owen. "She put my back up too."

"She's rich, of course. She must be, to be at the hotel."

"It's not just that."

"It's the way they look down on you."

"I wouldn't let it bother you."

"It's easier for you."

"Not much."

"Being British, I mean."

"We escape some things, but don't escape others."

"You feel about her the way I feel about Nuri?"

"More or less."

Mahmoud thought this over. Then he said: "Of course it adds to it when they're foreign. I sometimes feel quite pleased when something like this happens."

"A kidnapping?"

"When a Moulin gets kidnapped."

"You've got to take action."

"Oh, I know that. And I do." He suddenly cheered up. "Though not in the hottest part of the day. There's no point in going back now. I'll go back about four. He'll be up from his siesta then."

"He?"

"Mr. Colthorpe Hartley. He came out on the terrace later, remember. He may have seen something."

• • •

"Fellow with long moustaches and sticks?" said Mr. Colthorpe Hartley. "Yes, I saw him. Always sitting there. Same table, same time. Looking as if he's growing there."

"You're sure it was yesterday?"

Mr. Colthorpe Hartley considered a moment.

"Yes. Definitely. Saw him when I came out of the hotel.
I was a bit behind the others, you know. Had a longer
shower than usual. Bit damned hot just at the moment,
isn't it? You need a shower even when you've just been
lying down."

"And you definitely saw him?"

"Oh yes. Exchanged nods. Don't know the chap, of
course, but you sort of know him when you see him every
day. We pass the time of day. I say something, he says
something back. Nothing much. I don't think he speaks
much English. And I certainly don't speak French."

"He didn't say anything yesterday? I mean, nothing
particular."

"No. Hardly noticed me. Seemed a bit preoccupied.
Mind on other things. Didn't stay there long."

"Did you see him go?"

"Did I see him go? Let me think. No. I don't think I
saw him go. Saw he'd gone, but that's not the same thing."

"Can you pinpoint when that was? About how long
after you'd got to the terrace?"

"Well, I must have got to the terrace about four. Saw
him then. Nodded to him. Sat down. Had tea. Noticed he
was a bit fidgety. Then when I next looked up he had
gone. Say about twenty minutes. Between twenty past
four and half past four."

"But you didn't actually see him go?"

"No."

"You didn't see him go down the steps, for instance?"

"No. Don't think he would have gone down the steps.
Not by himself. A bit too shaky on his pins."

"With someone helping him?"

"Oh, he could have managed it then, all right."

"But you didn't see anyone?"

"Helping him? No."

Mr. Colthorpe Hartley rubbed his chin and stared

thoughtfully into space. A suffragi hurried past with a tray of coffee. The aroma came strongly across the room.

"Saw someone else, though," he said suddenly. "One of those chaps. Or not one of those chaps, one of the others. He was speaking to the Frenchman. Then he went across to the railings. Spoke to someone. As if he was on an errand for the Frenchman. Buying something for him."

"*Did* he buy anything?"

"No. Just came straight back."

"To the Frenchman?"

"Yes."

"Spoke to him?"

Mr. Colthorpe Hartley hesitated.

"Think so. Stopped looking. Can't go on watching a chap forever, you know. Bad form."

"So you looked away."

"Yes."

"And when you looked again, the Frenchman had gone?"

"That's right."

"Just one thing more, Mr. Colthorpe Hartley," said Owen. "You spoke of seeing a suffragi. Or one of the others. One of the others?"

"One of the other chaps from the hotel. The ones who go out with parties. Take you to the bazaar."

"A dragoman?"

"That's right. A dragoman."

"Would you be able to identify him if we paraded the hotel dragomans before you?"

"These chaps all look alike to me," said Mr. Colthorpe Hartley.

• • •

Mahmoud established with Reception the name of Monsieur Moulin's *petite amie* and sent a note up asking if she could see him. Madame Chévènement replied that she was still indisposed but would make an effort to see him on the following morning at eleven o'clock.

● ● ●

Nikos was going through Owen's engagements for the week. He had not included the Moulin affair. When Owen drew attention to this he shrugged his shoulders and said: "You're not going to be spending much time on this, surely?"

"Garvin wants me to. He says it's political."

"It will all be over by next week. They'll pay, won't they?"

"Probably. Though whether we ought to let it go at that's a different matter."

"There's not much else you can do, is there? They won't want you interfering."

"Yes, but it's the principle of the thing. If you let Zawia get away with it once, they'll try it again. And again. Until they're caught."

"In the end they'll make a mistake and then we'll catch them. Until then there's no sense in bothering about them."

"If we don't work on the case how will we know about the mistake?"

"Your friend El Zaki is working on the case, isn't he?" Nikos disapproved of too warm relationships with other departments. "Why don't you leave it to him?"

"It could blow up in our face. That's what Garvin's worried about."

"The French are quite efficient at this sort of thing."

"They're the ones who are on to me."

"Well, obviously they're not going to miss a chance to

make trouble. Anyway, if they can take it out on you they won't feel so bad about paying."

"We don't know they *will* pay yet."

"Of course they'll pay. Incidentally, has the follow-up message got through yet?"

"About paying? No, I don't think so."

"It probably has. They'll keep quiet about it."

"I think I'd have heard. They'd have warned me off."

"Perhaps it hasn't, then." Nikos considered. "If you're so worried about it," he said, "I could ask our man at the hotel to keep an eye open for it."

"*Have* we got a man at the hotel?"

"We've got a man at all the hotels. The main ones. It doesn't cost much," he assured Owen, thinking he detected a shade of concern and assuming, naturally, that the concern was financial and not moral.

On becoming Mamur Zapt Owen had inherited a huge information network, which Nikos administered with pride. What was striking about it was not its size, since a highly developed political secret service was normal in the Ottoman Empire and the British had merely taken it over, nor its ability to find informers, since people came cheap in Cairo: rather, it was its efficiency, which was not at all characteristic of the Ottoman Empire. It was, however, characteristic of Nikos, who brought the pure passion of the born bureaucrat to his work.

"Where is he?"

"At Reception."

"That might be useful."

"It was where the first message was left."

Owen thought about it. "If we could get a look at it—"

Nikos nodded. "That's what I thought. Note the contents and pass it on."

"It could all go ahead."

"They would pay."

"Moulin would be released."

"And with any luck," said Nikos, "we would be watching and could follow it up."

"I'd go along with that," said Owen, "I'd go along with that."

● ● ●

Later in the morning, Nikos came into Owen's room just as he was about to go out to keep his appointment with Mahmoud and Madame Chévènement.

"I've been checking through the files to see if I could find anything on Zawia. There's nothing on any group of that name."

"It's a new group," said Owen.

"Yes. But often new groups are re-forming from members of old groups, so I looked through to see if there were any references to groups with associated names."

"And did you find any?"

Nikos hesitated.

"Well," he said, "this kind of stuff is just conjecture. But what about the Wekils?"

"The Wekils?"

"Came on the scene last year. Two known kidnappings. One, a Syrian, notified to us in June. Case went dead, family left the country. My guess is they paid and got out. No point in us going back over that case. But we might look at the other. A Greek shopkeeper, taken about six months ago. Again the case went dead, so they probably paid. But I think the family is still here, so we might be able to find out something."

"Why is 'Wekil' an associated name?"

"It's a Senussi name. The Wekils are those Brothers who take charge of business matters and so are permitted to have dealings with Christians. As I said, it's just conjecture."

• • •

Mahmoud was waiting for him at Reception.

"Room 216," he said.

They climbed the stairs together. The door of 216 was open and suffragis were coming out carrying suitcases. Mahmoud and Owen went straight in. A row of already packed suitcases stood by the bed. The doors of the wardrobe were hanging open. It was quite empty. A man was bending over the suitcases. He turned as they came in. It was the French Chargé d'Affaires.

"Madame Chévènement?" asked Mahmoud.

The Chargé spread his hands apologetically.

3

But she's a material witness," said Mahmoud.

"Sorry!" said the Chargé.

"You can't do this!"

The Chargé shrugged.

"I—I shall protest!"

"We will receive your protest. If it's made through the proper diplomatic channels."

Mahmoud looked ready to explode.

"She's not really a material witness," said the Chargé. "She doesn't know a thing."

"Then why are you removing her?" asked Owen.

The Chargé looked at his watch.

"Look," he said, "perhaps I owe you something. How about an apéritif downstairs?"

Mahmoud, furious, and strict Moslem anyway, refused. Owen accepted. The Chargé ordered two cognacs.

"And a coffee for my friend," he added.

He led them over to an alcove.

"Sorry about this," he said. "I can assure you it was necessary. Absolutely necessary."

"Why?" asked Owen.

The Chargé hesitated.

"Well," he said, "it's like this. We heard the wife was coming. The old lady. Madame Moulin. I ask you: would it be proper for her to find...? Well, you know."

"You did this out of a sense of propriety?"

The Chargé looked at him seriously.

"Yes," he said. "We French are very proper people."

"Monsieur Moulin too?"

"Sex doesn't come into it. That's quite separate."

"Well, where have you put her? Can we talk to her?"

"I'm afraid not," said the Chargé. "She's on her way home. With a diplomatic passport."

"For reasons of propriety?"

"For reasons of state."

"Reasons of state?"

"Madame Moulin's a cousin of the President's wife. That's quite a reason of state."

"Come on!" said Owen. "Why did you do it?"

"That's why we did it. I've just told you. We couldn't have the French President's wife's cousin coming out and finding some floozie in her husband's bed. It wouldn't be decent. The President would get to hear about it and we'd all get our asses kicked. The last thing I need just now, I can tell you, is a posting to the Gabon. I've a little friend of my own here."

Mahmoud fumed.

The Chargé patted him on the knee "Don't worry about it! These things happen."

"That's why I worry about it," said Mahmoud sullenly.

The Chargé signaled to the waiter. "Another two co-cognacs," he said. He looked at Mahmoud's coffee. "I wish I could put something in that."

"No, thanks," said Mahmoud.

The Chargé sipped his cognac and put it down.

"Didn't I know your father?" he said. "Ahmed el Zaki?
A lawyer?"

"Yes," said Mahmoud, surprised. "That's my father."

"I met him in a case we had when I first came out here.
He acted for us."

Owen was surprised too. Mahmoud had never spoken
about his father.

"How is he?" asked the Chargé.

"He died three years ago."

"Ah. Pardon. These things happen." The Chargé shook
his head sadly. "I'm sorry to hear that. He was a good
man. You're very like him in some ways." He finished his
cognac.

"I've got to go. Look, I'm sorry about all this. We're
thinking of the family. That's all. Reasons of the heart,
you might say."

"You might," said Owen.

•   •   •

The shop was in the Khan-el-Khalil, the part of the
bazaar area most familiar to tourists. Some of Cairo's
best-known shops were there, places like Andalaft's or
Cohen's. The Greek's shop, however, was not in their
class. It was one of dozens of smaller shops all catering in
their different ways for the tourist trade. Most of them
sold a mixture of old brassware, harem embroideries,
lacework, enamels and pottery. In the height of the
season the Khan-el-Khalil would be packed with tourists,
though the extent to which they made their way to a
particular shop would depend on the extent to which the
proprietor had greased the palms of the dragomans with
piastres. It was now past the peak of the season but there
were still plenty of small parties of tourists, each guided
by a knowing dragoman. Traffic was growing less now,

though, and this was the time when greasing was all-important. Some of the shops were almost deserted while others still hummed with business.

The Greek's shop was one of the latter. As Owen ducked through the bead curtain he almost collided with an English couple, a mother and daughter, who were just emerging.

"Why, it's Captain Owen!" said Lucy Colthorpe Hartley delightedly.

Her mother looked at Owen with less pleasure and would have gone on if Lucy had not firmly stopped.

"Look what I've bought!" she said, and showed Owen her purchase. It was a small heap of turquoise stones. "Aren't they lovely? I'm going to have them made up when I get back. Or would I do better to have them made up here?"

"Here, but not in one of these shops. Get Andalaft to advise you."

"I like them because they're such a beautiful Cambridge blue. Daddy went to Cambridge. Did you, Captain Owen?"

"No."

"Gerald didn't, either. He's rather sore about it."

"Lucy, dear, we must not detain Captain Owen. He has business, I am sure."

"Business among the bazaars. What *is* your business, Captain Owen? It's obviously something to do with the police, but Daddy says you're not a proper policeman. Gerald says you're not a proper soldier either. So what are you, Captain Owen?"

"Obviously not proper."

"He is the Mamur Zapt," said the dragoman, who had just followed them out of the shop.

"So I gathered," said Lucy. "But what exactly, or who exactly, is the Mamur Zapt?"

Owen hesitated.

"I see," she said. "You don't want to tell me."

"It's not that," he said. "It's just that it would take some time."

"Which just now you haven't got."

"I'm afraid not."

"Then you must tell me some other time," she said. "This evening, perhaps?"

Mrs. Colthorpe Hartley turned determinedly away and Lucy was obliged to follow her. She gave Owen a parting wave over the dragoman's shoulder.

"Tonight at six," she called.

The shop was dark and cool and full of subtle smells from the lacquered boxes, the sandalwood carvings, heavy embroideries and spangled Assiut shawls which lined its walls. As Owen's eyes became used to the light they picked out more objects: flat, heart-shaped gold and silver boxes set with large turquoises and used to hold verses from the Koran, old Persian arm amulets, Persian boxes with portraits of the famous beauties of Ispahan and Shiraz, old illuminated Korans. The precious stones and jewelry were kept in an inner room, better lighted and down a step. A gentle-faced Copt looked up as Owen entered.

"Où est le propiétaire?"

"Elle est en dedans."

Elle? A silver-haired woman came out of an inner recess.

"Madame Tsakatellis?"

"Oui."

"Are you the owner?"

"Yes."

"I was expecting to speak to your husband."

"He is dead."

"Dead? I am sorry."

"It was a long time ago."

Light began to dawn.

"Of course! You are the elder Mrs. Tsakatellis. I am so sorry. I think the person I am trying to see is your son."

"My son is dead too."

"The Monsieur Tsakatellis who owned the shop?"

"Both have owned the shop."

"The second one stopped owning the shop only a short time ago?"

"That is correct."

"I am the Mamur Zapt. I have come about your son."

"It is a little late."

Owen acknowledged this with a slight inclination of his head.

"I am sorry. I did not know. Did not the police come?"

"They came," said the woman dismissively, "and did nothing."

"I am sorry."

"Now you have come," said the woman. "What is it you wish to know?"

"I want to know what happened."

"Why do you want to know? It is not," said the woman bitterly, "for Tsakatellis's sake."

"It has happened again. And it may be the same people."

"So now you take an interest. How many people have to be taken," the woman asked scornfully, "before the Mamur Zapt shows an interest?"

"There are, alas, many such cases in Cairo. I cannot follow them all. I had thought Tsakatellis might have been restored to you."

"Why should he have been restored?"

"Have you not paid?"

"No." The woman looked him straight in the face. "I do not pay. Even for my son."

"Most people pay."

"If you pay they will come again. If not to you, to another."

"All the same," said Owen gently, "it is hard not to pay. When it is one's own."

The woman was silent. Then she said: "For the Greeks life is always hard."

She called to the Copt.

"You wished to know what happened. Thutmose will tell you."

The Copt came down into the room and smiled politely at Owen.

"Tell him!" the woman directed. "Tell him what happened the night your master was taken."

"I wish to know," said Owen, "so that I can help others. I am the Mamur Zapt."

"There is little to tell," the Copt said softly. "That night was as other nights. We worked late. It was nearly midnight when we closed the shop. There was a little book-keeping to do so I stayed behind."

"You have a key?"

"The master left me his key."

"He must have trusted you."

The Copt bowed his head in acknowledgement.

"And then?"

"And then I did not see him again, nor suspected anything till the servant came knocking on my door."

Owen looked at Madame Tsakatellis.

"When Tsakatellis did not come home," she said, "at first we thought nothing of it. He often works late. When he had not come home by one I began to wonder. When he had still not come home at two I went to his wife and found her crying."

"She knew something," asked Owen, "or she guessed?"

The woman made a gesture of dismissal.

"The woman has silly thoughts. She thought Tsakatellis might be with another woman. What if he was? A wife has to get used to these things. In any case, Tsakatellis was not like that. I sent a servant in case he had stumbled and fallen or been attacked and was lying in the road. The servant came back and said he had found nothing. I sent him out again to wake Thutmose."

"I knew nothing," said Thutmose. "I came at once."

"We went out again," said the woman, "and walked by every way he might have taken. When the dawn came we began to suspect."

"The letter was delivered to the shop," said Thutmose. "When I saw it, I guessed."

"Who delivered it?"

"A boy. Who ran off."

"You have the letter?" Owen asked Madame Tsakatellis.

She went back into her recess and came back with a piece of paper.

> Greetings. We have taken your man. If you want to see him again you must pay the sum of 20,000 piastres, which we know you will do as you are a loving woman. If you do not pay, you will not see your man again. Wait for instructions. Tell no one.
>
> The Wekil Group

"Who was the letter addressed to?"

"It was meant for her."

"But Thutmose brought it to you?"

"I took it from her. She was useless. I sent a man to tell the police. A man came from the Parquet."

"He found nothing?"

"He did nothing. After a while he went away and we

did not see him again. Nor anyone else. Nor you, until now."

"And did the instructions come?"

"No." The woman lifted her head and looked Owen levelly in the eyes. "They must have known I had sent for the police."

"It may not be so."

"It is so. I killed him. That is what she thinks."

"They take fright," said Owen, "for many reasons. That may not have been the reason."

"It would have happened anyway," said the woman, "for I would not have paid."

There was little more to be learned, as the man from the Parquet must have found. He would have made inquiries to check if anyone had seen Tsakatellis on his way home, but the streets would have been deserted and even if someone had seen him it was unlikely that they would come forward. Cairenes did not believe in volunteering themselves for contact with the authorities. He would ask Mahmoud to check the Parquet records but he thought it unlikely that whoever had conducted the initial investigation had found anything of interest.

One last question.

"Did Tsakatellis have enemies?"

The woman made a crushing gesture with her hand.

"The world," she said.

Sometimes people used kidnapping as a way of settling old scores.

"But no one particular? Who had sworn revenge?"

"Tsakatellis had no enemies of that sort."

"A husband, perhaps?"

"No," said the woman definitely.

The only question, then, was what had brought Tsakatellis to the notice of his potential kidnappers. Some display of wealth, perhaps? Unlikely. The Greeks kept themselves to themselves. They worked hard, made money and did not flaunt it.

"What else did Tsakatellis do?" he asked. "Apart from work?"

"Nothing."

"Church?"

"Ah, well, but—"

"Did he serve on committees?"

"No."

"Do things for the community?"

"What community?"

"Are not the Greeks a community?"

"We have friends," the woman said, "but not many. Tsakatellis's father had been ill for a long time before he died. The business had to be nursed back. Tsakatellis worked long hours. Had done so since he was a boy. He had no time for other things."

"I was wondering how they came to hear of him."

"I have asked myself that. Why Tsakatellis? Why not Stavros or Petrides?"

"And what answer did you come to?"

"I came to no answer. Except this. There is no reason. You lead your life. Then one day God reaches down and plucks you out. And throws you into the fire!"

"It is not God who does these things. It is man."

"That is a comfort. With man there is always the possibility of revenge."

•　　•　　•

Nikos was waiting for him when he got back to the office.

"It's come," he said.

"What's come?"

"The second note."

"Telling them the arrangements for paying?"

"Yes."

Owen hung up his sun helmet and poured himself a glass of water from the pitcher which stood in the window where the air would cool it.

"What does it say?"

"They're to put the money in a case. Berthelot's to take it to Anton's at about midnight and check it in to the cloakroom. He's then to go on into the salon and stay there for about two hours. While they're counting, presumably. When he comes out they'll give him a receipt. On the receipt will be an address. That's where he'll find Moulin."

"Anton's. Is he in it?"

"Probably not. They're just using his place, but the cloakroom people have got to be in it."

"They'll only be in part of it, though, the money-passing bit. Still, that's responsible."

"Incidentally," said Nikos, "they don't tell Berthelot how to get to Anton's."

"They know he already knows?"

Nikos nodded.

"Interesting. I thought that young man didn't get around."

"He gets around and they know it."

"That, too, is interesting."

"Yes. They're usually well informed."

"It doesn't sound like a student group."

"Nor an ordinary Nationalist group either," said Nikos. "Certainly not a fundamentalist Nationalist group. These people know too much about tourists."

Owen drank another half glass of water. One glass was really his ration. When it was hot you needed to take in a little liquid often, not a lot at once. He put the glass down and went on through into his own office. Nikos followed him in with an armful of papers.

"Are you going to leave it alone?" he asked.

"Why not? I want the poor bastard free as much as the French do. It's only money, after all."

"Well, yes," said Nikos, "but..."

"I know what you're going to say. Sometimes it's not just money. It's just money only if you're willing to play ball. If you're not willing it gets nasty. As in the case of the other poor bastard, that Greek shopkeeper, Tsakatellis, whom they killed."

"That's not what I was going to say," said Nikos. "What I was going to say was that this is the first time they've taken a tourist. If you let them get away with it, it might become a habit. And then a lot of people might get interested."

Nikos always took a detached view of cases which were merely individual. On the other hand, he had a keen eye for political essentials.

• • •

Six o'clock that evening found Owen himself on the terrace at Shepheard's waiting for Lucy Colthorpe Hartley. Quite how he came to be there he was not certain. He had not had time to say no when Lucy had made the appointment; and would he have said no if he had? On the grounds that he was poor and they were tiresome, he made it a general practice to steer clear of the fishing fleet, as the young ladies were called who arrived in scores for the Cairo season in search, it was alleged, of husbands from among the ranks of wealthy young army officers. Besides, he considered himself more or less bound to Zeinab. On the other hand, meeting Lucy Colthorpe Hartley for a drink was hardly work, although he had said that it was when Zeinab had suggested he pick her up at six after her visit to the hairdresser's. He decided to salve his conscience by asking Lucy some work questions when she arrived.

If she arrived at all. It was already five minutes after six, which by Owen's standards was being late for an appointment. Perhaps she wouldn't come, in which case he would feel a complete fool. He hoped no one would see him.

At that moment his friend, the Consul-General's aide-de-camp, went past with a visiting foreign worthy. He gave Owen a wave behind the worthy's back. Owen returned the wave half-heartedly.

Garvin went past talking to an Adviser from one of the Ministries. He interrupted his talking to give Owen a smile of recognition. Some hope, thought Owen bitterly, that no one would see him. Out here on the terrace he was as conspicuous as—

Well, as Moulin must have been. And how the hell had he disappeared from the terrace without anyone seeing anything?

Owen looked down the steps. There was the snake charmer as on the day of Moulin's kidnapping, squatting so near to the steps as to be virtually sitting on them; there were the donkey-boys playing one of their interminable games within two yards of the foot of the steps. If Moulin had gone down the steps they *must* have seen him.

And if he hadn't gone down the steps? The only place he could have gone was back into the hotel. To do so he would have had to pass the Reception clerk and the people on the desk swore that he hadn't. There were two of them, they were some of the brightest people on the hotel's staff, the desk was public and busy, they had to be and were alert—hell, one of them was even on Owen's own payroll!

All the same, they could have missed him. It was a busy area and they might have been busy. Also, they could only see what passed them. Reception was actually inside the hotel, in the foyer, and the people on the desk couldn't see out on to the terrace itself. Suppose something had happened between the table where Moulin was sitting and the entrance to the hotel: Reception would not have seen it, the snake charmer couldn't have seen it, and donkey-boys, well, they might or might not have seen it.

But, surely, if anything had happened on the terrace *someone* would have seen it? Someone at a neighboring table? The tables were, after all, only a few feet apart. If there had been a struggle or anything of that sort—well, there couldn't have been. The Colthorpe Hartleys, who had been at the very next table, would certainly have seen it.

But suppose the incident, whatever it was, had been smaller in scale, apparently trivial? Suppose it had occurred at a time when their attention had been distracted, perhaps deliberately? That was a possibility. He would have to ask Lucy Colthorpe Hartley if anything like that had occurred.

Owen was sitting at a table a little further into the terrace than either the one Moulin habitually occupied or the one the Colthorpe Hartleys had been sitting at that day. The table was right at the front of the terrace, so close to the railing that the street-vendors touched his foot as they poked their wares through the bars. Hippopotamus-hide whips, splendid red tarbooshes, and filmy ladies' underwear jostled for his attention. A long brown arm with a snake coiled around it was suddenly thrust in his direction; and in an instant a whole pack of postcards of scantily dressed ladies fanned itself open in the air before his astonished eyes.

"Gracious, Captain Owen!" said Lucy Colthorpe Hartley. "I did not know you were such a connoisseur."

"Friends of yours?" he asked, recovering quickly.

"Intimate," she replied, sinking into a chair. "Abdul here greets me with a different nosegay every day."

A beaming vendor, rather darker than the others, laid a bunch of sweetly smelling flowers on the terrace beside her.

"They don't last long," she said, "but for a while they brighten up the room."

She fumbled in her purse for some token piastres.

"Allow me," said Owen.

Lucy put a restraining hand on his arm.

"Certainly not!" she said. "You are interfering with long-established custom. What you *can* do, though," she added, peering into her purse, "is help me count up the necessary milliemes as I seem to have run out of piastres."

"That's enough. A little money goes a long way here."

"You'd better have a talk with my father. He doesn't seem to think so."

"I'm sure he won't mind the flowers."

"No. But he did mind the turquoises. I took them in to Andalaft's as you suggested, Captain Owen, and he is going to find someone to make them up for me."

"Do you have other regulars among the vendors, Miss Colthorpe Hartley?"

"I have a faithful following," said Lucy, "which I attribute more to misplaced hope than to my personal charms."

"They follow you wherever you sit?"

"We usually sit in the same place."

"Which is at this end of the terrace, of course."

"It is exactly there," said Lucy, pointing. "How disillusioning! There I was hoping that what had brought you here was the attraction of my big blue eyes when all the time you are merely getting on with your work."

"I am combining work with pleasure. A little work and a lot of pleasure."

"At least you have the proportions right," said Lucy.

"You were, if you remember, going to tell me exactly what was your work, Mamur Zapt."

"Well..." said Owen.

"How fascinating!" said Lucy Colthorpe Hartley, resting her elbows on the table and her chin on her hands and gazing straight into his eyes.

•   •   •

"It didn't look like work to me," said Zeinab.

Zeinab, unfortunately, had passed by in an arabeah on her way home from her hairdresser's.

"I was asking her about the street-vendors."

"Oh yes," said Zeinab sceptically.

"Yes I was. I wanted to know if they were always the same. You see, if they were, they might have been there when Moulin was kidnapped and seen something."

"You were trying to see something," said Zeinab. "You were looking down the front of her dress."

"For heaven's sake! She was across the table. How could I?"

"She was leaning forward. Deliberately."

"Anyway she didn't have on that sort of dress."

"You see! You did try!"

"For God's sake!" said Owen, aware that he had lost yet another argument with Zeinab.

•   •   •

"Well," demanded Nikos, "are you going to do something about it or not?"

"I'm not going to stop it, if that's what you mean."

"That's not what I mean. The question is: do you want it watched? We don't have to interfere at all. We could let it all go ahead as they've arranged, let the money change hands, wait till Moulin is freed—and only take action afterward. That way we would get both Moulin and Zawia."

"Nice in theory, not so easy in practice. You'd have to be able to watch them all the way. Is that possible?"

"It's not easy," Nikos admitted.

Owen saw why when they made a reconnaissance that evening. The gambling salon was in a block of flats on the Sharia Imad-el-Din. It was on the first floor and was disguised as a scent factory. Nikos had been informing himself of its defenses.

"You get to it through the main entrance," he said. "There's a door on to the stairs which is kept locked and has to be opened by the porter. At the top of the stairs there's another door with a spyhole."

"Pretty standard."

"Yes. There's an electric bell downstairs by the porter's hand to give warning. Oh, and there's a consular representative across the street."

"Which nationality is Anton claiming this week?"

"Lebanese, I think."

Since under the system of legal concessions to foreign governments known as the Capitulations the Egyptian police did not have right of entry to premises owned by foreigners, most gambling houses had taken the precaution of acquiring foreign "ownership." To guard against misunderstandings—and misunderstandings were quite frequent as the police had often met the proprietor the week before when he was of a different nationality—the wealthier salons had taken to keeping a consular official handy on the permanent retainer for use in the event of an unexpected raid.

"We're not thinking of a raid, though," said Owen, "so it doesn't matter."

"We'll have to have someone inside."

Owen looked doubtful. "What good would that do? They'd have to be customers. They couldn't hang around the cloakroom. They'd have to go inside and play. They wouldn't be able to see anything. What's the internal geography of the place?"

"You go through the door into a sort of vestibule. The cloakroom—it's very small, barely room for the two attendants—is on one side. The tripot is on the other. You get to it through an arch."

"So you might be able to see something."

"You might. You'd be able to tell if someone left the tripot and went to the cloakroom. But my guess is that's not how it will happen, anyway. I've been checking on the attendants in the cloakroom. There are two of them. One of them goes off duty at about one-thirty and another man comes in. I reckon that the one who goes off duty will be carrying the money with him. The timing fits. Berthelot gets there at about midnight and stays till two. By then there will have been time to count the money and the attendant will have been gone half an hour—long enough for him to be able to pass over the money."

"How does he leave the building?"

"Through a side door. I'll have him tailed."

"He might not go that way this time."

"I think he will. They'll want to keep it as normal as possible. In any case, though, I'll put people all around the building. And on the roof."

"It's a block of flats. There'll be people coming and going all the time."

"At one o'clock in the morning? Carrying something? You'd have to have a bag or a case to carry that amount of money."

"I wish we could watch the cloakroom all the time."

"Can't be done."

"What's on the next floor up? Directly above the cloakroom?"

"A sewing shop. Try moving all those girls."

"Why don't we bribe one of Anton's people and ask them to keep an eye on the cloakroom?"

"They've got their jobs to do. They wouldn't be able to watch all the time."

"All the same..."

"As a matter of fact," said Nikos, "I already have."

•   •   •

Owen had men watching Monsieur Berthelot. The following afternoon they reported that Berthelot had been to the bank twice. The second time he had come away carrying a small leather case. On both occasions he had been accompanied by a member of the staff of the French Consulate.

On a hunch Owen checked steamer bookings. Two passages had been reserved under the name of Berthelot on a boat leaving Alexandria in thirty-six hours' time.

Mahmoud had heard nothing of any deal. Unlike Owen, he was dead against it.

"Do it once and you'll soon be doing it all the time," he said.

"But people *are* doing it all the time," said Owen.

He could get Mahmoud not to intervene only by telling him what he himself was proposing to do.

He went back to his office and worked late. Soon after ten he went home and changed into evening dress. He put a tarboosh on his head and slipped some dark glasses into his pocket. He would not be the only one wearing them. Others besides himself would have reasons for wishing to preserve their anonymity.

•   •   •

It was still relatively early in the evening in Cairo terms and there were only about thirty people around the table. Berthelot was at the far end intent on the play. The table was brilliantly lit up. All the rest of the room was in shadow.

Owen played standing up, reaching an arm in when it was necessary. In that way he could keep out of the light. He wasn't sure how effective his disguise was. He was still relatively new in Cairo and thought his face generally unknown. Still, it was the doorman's job to know these things and he might well have spotted him. Owen thought it probably wouldn't matter if he had. He would tell Anton and Anton would worry; but so long as Anton himself was not involved in the plot he would probably keep his worries to himself. Even if he knew what was going on in the cloakroom he would probably stay out of it. He might have received an inducement to turn a blind eye, but a blind eye was what he would turn, especially with the Mamur Zapt there. Owen doubted if he would warn them.

The important thing was that Berthelot shouldn't recognize him. Owen didn't think he would. He thought the disguise and the darkness was proof against that. Anyway, Berthelot was concentrating on the play.

"Faîtes vos jeux, messieurs," the croupier said. *"Faîtes vos jeux."*

Berthelot hesitated, then added to his stake.

"Rien ne va plus."

The croupier spun the wheel. There was a sudden intentness, a catch of the breath. The wheel slowed and came to a halt. Berthelot shrugged and turned away. The croupier began to rake in the chips.

"It's Anton's lucky night tonight," said a Greek standing beside Berthelot.

"It's Anton's lucky night every night," said someone from across the table.

There was a general stirring and one or two people left the table, either to refresh themselves from the jugs of iced lemonade which stood on a shelf behind them or simply to ease their backs.

Berthelot and the Greek turned at the same time.

"Pardon, monsieur."

"Pardon!"

Berthelot made way for the Greek, who went over to the shelf and poured himself a glass of lemonade.

"Monsieur?"

He offered to pour for Berthelot.

"Merci, monsieur."

They stood sipping the lemonade together.

"It's a hot night," said the Greek.

"Is it always as hot as this?"

There were fans working but since the room had no windows they merely moved the hot air round.

"It's been hot all day. Monsieur is new to Cairo?"

"We've been here just over a month."

"Ah. Not long enough to get used to it."

"How long does it take to get used to it?"

The Greek spread his hands. "A lifetime. And then it's no use!"

They went back to the table. The play began again.

The room was long and thin with deep luxurious carpets and heavy wood panelling. A door led off into an inner room, out of which waiters emerged regularly with drinks. They brought the drinks to the players. There was no bar as such. Drink was incidental at Anton's. Besides, most of the players were Moslem.

An arch behind Owen led back into the entrance vestibule. Through it he could see one end of the cloakroom counter. Since Berthelot had arrived one player had left and four more had entered. The one who had left had departed soon after Berthelot had appeared and, Owen thought, had gone straight past the cloakroom. It was a hot evening and very few people had brought coats. A number had brought walking sticks which they deposited.

No one, Owen was pretty sure, left the playing room during the evening to visit the cloakroom. The obvious pretext would have been to use the toilets but they were off the main room next to the door through which the waiters came and went. He had watched the waiters particularly carefully. He was sure that none of them had gone out into the entrance vestibule. There might, of course, be a door from the inner room into the entrance vestibule. If there was, it would be at the far end and he had seen no one walk past the arch from that direction. As the evening wore on, the possibilities narrowed down.

Although he took short breaks from time to time, for most of the evening he had to play. He found himself worrying about the money he was losing. It was Departmental money but he would still be held to account for it. The Ministry's accountants would allow a certain amount of expenditure of this kind in view of the peculiar nature of the Mamur Zapt's operations but the amount was, in Owen's view, ridiculously low. It must have been much easier being Mamur Zapt in the days before Cromer, the previous Consul-General, had introduced a stringent financial regime. In those more relaxed days Anton would probably have been on the payroll. The Mamur Zapt himself might even have taken a cut.

At last Berthelot looked at his watch.

"You're probably right," said his neighbor, the talkative Greek. "The only person who's going to do well tonight is Anton."

He stepped back from the table with Berthelot but only to pour himself some more lemonade. The Frenchman went on out of the room and made for the cloakroom. One of the attendants came forward with his case.

"Can I leave that here?" Berthelot asked. "I've got to go on to another place."

"Of course, Monsieur," said the attendant. "We are open till four. There will be someone here after that but we shall have gone off duty. Perhaps I should give Monsieur a receipt. Then he has but to hand it in and there will be no complication."

"That seems a good idea," said Berthelot.

The attendant produced a receipt, which Berthelot pocketed without looking at it. As he went out of the door Owen moved unhurriedly after him.

"I am just going out for some fresh air," he told the porter.

Berthelot was just stepping into an arabeah. As the carriage moved off into the night another arabeah drew out of a side street and set off after it.

There was a man standing in the shadows.

"OK?" asked Owen.

"OK," said the man.

Owen went back inside. The Greek had taken his place at the table but made room for him.

"There's still time to lose a fortune," he said cheerfully. After a little while, seeing how circumspectly Owen was playing, he added: "Though if you want to do it tonight you'll have to hurry up."

"Why hurry?" asked Owen.

They had been playing for about half an hour when a suffragi came in.

"A letter," he said, "for Mr. Stefanopoulos."

The Greek put up his hand, though without taking his eyes off the play. The bearer stuck the letter in it. The

Greek waited until the croupier began to rake in the chips before he opened the envelope.

"It's from my wife," he said to the croupier. "She says she forgot to tell me before I left this evening that the house is already sold."

The croupier smiled mechanically.

"That being so," said the Greek, "I shall have to earn some more money before making a present of it to Monsieur Anton."

"A bientôt," said the croupier as the Greek left the table.

"Such domestic fidelity is an example to us all," said Owen, and got up too.

Owen and the Greek went down the stairs together. Not until they were outside did the Greek speak. Then he stepped aside into the shadows and said familiarly:

"Which way did he use?"

"The side door."

"As expected. Good. Who's following him?"

"Abou and Sadiq. Sadiq is here."

A man came out of the shadows.

"You are Sadiq?"

"Yes, effendi."

"Where is he?"

"He is at the Mosque of El Hakim. Waiting."

"Take us there," said the Greek, whose name was not Stefanopoulos but Georgiades, and who was one of the Mamur Zapt's most experienced agents, "and we will wait too."

4

At the end of the street was a large, ruined mosque. It was solid and fortresslike, possessing the grandeur but lacking the grace of the other great Cairo mosques. Everything about it was square and formidable. Even its minarets were not true minarets but mabkharas, structures like the pylons of the ancient Egyptian temples. It grew out of Saladin's old city walls, sharing with them secret rooms and hidden defensive passages. It was the mosque of El Hakim, the fourth oldest of all the mosques of Cairo, one of the few remaining from the former city of El Kahira.

Although it was ruined it was not deserted. The ordinary poor had come to live in it, and now wherever there was an arch intact or a few bricks to give a patch of shade an assembly of cooking utensils and a fire announced the hearth of a household.

There were even, among the ruins, workshops and small factories. Space was scarce in Cairo and enterprising entrepreneurs took it where they could find it.

The Egyptologists, thought Owen, spoke of Egypt's

traditional preoccupation with death and pointed to the Pyramids. But the Pyramids had been built by workmen from the villages roundabout and from those villages also had come generations of grave robbers who had not been afraid to pillage the tombs. The Egyptologists spoke of the Pyramids and not of the grave robbers; but it was the grave robbers with their need and their greed, with their anarchic rejection of the dead hand of authority and with their obstinate instinct for life, who were in the end characteristic of Egyptian society.

It was typical of Egyptians to take over something dead and make it a place for living. The mosque might have been an empty shell; instead, it hummed with life. Even now at night there were pinpricks of light beneath its arches.

Sadiq led them toward one of these, threading his way through a grove of still intact pillars, some of them still supporting arches. They were going through the liwan, the deep central space or room which served as the sanctuary. In the old days, when El Hakim was still functioning as a mosque, the faithful would have gathered round the pillars in the shade of the arches to hear the Holy Word expounded. At the far end of the pillars there was a light.

Sadiq stopped. A second figure appeared beside him. The two figures merged together for a moment and then the second figure detached itself and came across to Owen.

"He is still there, effendi," a voice whispered in his ear. "No one has come. He sits with the watchman. He has a case with him."

He put his hand on Owen's arm and guided him forward. Ahead of him was a deeper darkness, something screening off the light, a wall perhaps.

Abou brought him up to the wall and then stopped.

There was a gap through which Owen could see. In front of him two Arabs were sitting on the ground with an oil lamp between them. One of them was an old man in a torn, dirty galabeah, the night watchman presumably. The other was a suffragi in a spruce gown. Owen thought he recognized one of the attendants from the cloakroom. On the ground beside him was Berthelot's case.

Owen shifted his position and something flashed in his eyes, dazzling him. Involuntarily he jerked his head back and was dazzled again. For a moment he could not work out what was happening. Then he realized. There was some glass opposite him which was catching the light from the oil lamp. Several bits of glass, because as he moved there were different flashes.

He looked more closely. At first he could not make out what it was. Then he saw and could not believe his eyes. The space in front of him was piled deep with lanterns. That was what the "wall" consisted of: lanterns, hundreds of them. They stood in heaps and piles all around this part of the liwan, bright, colored lanterns with gaudy paper and flashy dangling beads.

Then he remembered. The mosque was used to store the lanterns used on feast days to decorate the city's streets and squares.

The two Arabs went on talking quietly. From time to time the watchman looked at the case. The other man did not stir.

At one point the watchman got to his feet and shuffled off into the night. Owen tensed expectantly but the suffragi did not move nor did anyone come. Eventually the watchman shuffled back, this time with a dirty black can. He produced two small enamel cups from the folds of his galabeah, set them on the ground and filled them from the can. The suffragi drank with appropriately polite smacking of lips.

They resumed their conversation. Owen could follow it only in parts. It was purely trivial in nature. They were just passing the time. Owen felt sure the suffragi was waiting for somebody.

Georgiades had slipped away. Owen knew what he was doing. He was making his way 'round to the other side to cut off possible escape routes.

If the man was coming, though, it would have to be soon. The sky was beginning to lighten.

The watchman produced some bread and an onion and offered to share it with the suffragi. The suffragi refused politely.

Owen was beginning to get bothered now. It was getting light so quickly that a man coming through the liwan would be able to see the watchers. He signalled to Abou, who was standing beside him and they moved in front of two pillars to be less visible from behind.

Still no one came.

In the strange gray light that came before the dawn in Egypt things stood out as clearly as if it were day but with a gentle softness which lacked the harsh clarity of the sun. Owen always woke early. He would be awaking now if this were an ordinary day.

Any moment now the sun would come over the horizon. The watchman leaned forward and extinguished the lamp.

The suffragi rose from his squat and picked up the case. He bade the watchman the usual extended, ceremonious, Arab farewell and then walked off down the colonnaded arcade.

Abou looked at Owen questioningly.

Owen nodded and the tracker slipped off through the pillars. Owen followed a long way behind. Tracking by daylight, when it was so much easier to be seen, was far harder than tracking by night. It was best left to those who knew how to do it.

He could not see Sadiq. Georgiades, he knew, would be doing the same as he was.

They followed the line of the old city wall. The houses in this poor quarter were made of mud. Every year when the heavy rain came it washed away some of the mud and left the houses slightly shapeless, their corners blurred. Then the sun came and dried the mud until it cracked. Little by little it would crumble and then be washed away when the rain came again. Many of the houses were little better than ruins.

The suffragi went into one of the most ruined of these. There was not even a proper door, just a gap in the wall.

The trackers waited at a discreet distance. Georgiades and Owen came up with them. Georgiades looked at Owen and made a face.

"Nothing else for it!" Owen said resignedly. He waved the trackers in.

They were holding the suffragi when Owen stepped into the room. The suffragi was putting up no resistance; indeed, there was a smile on his face.

Owen went across to the case and snapped it open.

It was empty.

● ● ●

"It was a decoy," said Owen bitterly, "just a decoy."

"And you fell for it," said Garvin, with a certain grim satisfaction.

"You've got the man, though," said McPhee, loyal to the last.

"Yes, but I can't hold him. What's he done?"

"He has deceived us," said McPhee stiffly.

"The way you're conducting this investigation, that'll be

true of half the population by the time you've finished," said Garvin.

"Anyway, that doesn't constitute a crime."

"Stolen a case."

"He's not stolen a case," said Owen. "It's his case."

"Not Berthelot's?"

"No. Like Berthelot's. Exactly like."

"What absolute nonsense! What is a suffragi doing with a case like that?"

"He says he uses it to take his supper to the club. Anton won't give him any food, so he has to take his own. He used to take it wrapped in a newspaper but Anton didn't like that. He said it lowered the tone. So now he takes it in a posh case."

"Just like Berthelot's?"

"Just like Berthelot's. Pure coincidence."

"Coincidence!" McPhee fumed.

"And meanwhile the real case went somewhere else, I suppose," said Garvin.

"No. It's still in the cloakroom, where Berthelot left it. The attendant says he can't give it to us unless we produce a receipt."

"Oh really!"

Garvin laughed. "I take it the money is no longer in it?" he said.

"There never was any money in it. According to Berthelot."

"Just a case, which he properly left in the cloakroom?"

"And the cloakroom has properly looked after it."

"Well," said Garvin, "they're certainly running rings around you."

"They're just laughing at us," said Owen. "Everyone's laughing at us. The donkey-boys are laughing, the bazaar's laughing, even you're laughing."

"I'm not laughing," said Garvin, "not any more. The French—"

"Ah yes," said Owen uncomfortably.

"—are not laughing either. They're hopping mad. They say it's all our fault. If we'd not messed things up the exchange would have gone ahead as planned and Moulin would now be a free man."

"It's hardly fair—"

"Isn't it?" Garvin cut in. "You were at Anton's, weren't you? Well..."

He tossed a piece of paper on the table in front of them. Owen read:

> Because you've broken your side of the agreement and told the Mamur Zapt, we are breaking our side of the agreement."

"When they got to the address Berthelot was given," said Garvin, "they found the house empty. There was just this note left on a table."

"No Moulin?"

"No Moulin," said Garvin.

•　•　•

Owen poured out his troubles to Mahmoud, who listened sympathetically and then took him out for a coffee to restore him. They chose a café in one of the small streets opposite Shepheard's: the Wagh el Birket, in fact. It was just after midday, however, and the ladies of the night were still sleeping off the effects of their labors. The shuttered doors on the balconies were closed, the cheap bands in the arcade opposite stilled. Only a few of the cafés were open and these were the traditional Arab ones which catered for the humble local clientele. They picked a table outside one of these and sat down in the shade.

Mahmoud had problems too. He had only just finished questioning all potential witnesses. The list had been a long one, including as it did the staff of the hotel, guests who had been on the terrace, and an assortment of donkey-boys, arabeah-drivers, street-vendors, and general bystanders, of whom, as was usual in Cairo, there were a lot. These latter were especially eager to contribute their impressions and it was only after much patient sifting that Mahmoud was able to establish whether they had actually been present on the day or not.

An additional difficulty was the fact that the incident had been the main topic of conversation in the neighborhood ever since Monsieur Moulin had been reported missing. Whatever may have been the original perceptions, by the time they were reported they had long been confused by a mass of eager embroidering, ill-informed conjecture and plain fantasy. By the end Mahmoud was in despair.

"I've got to find a way of going back to the beginning," he said. "This is hopeless."

Owen commiserated.

"How about a reconstruction?" he suggested.

Mahmoud at once brightened. The Parquet, French-trained and French in style, adhered to French methods of investigation, of which the "reconstruction" of the crime was usually part.

"That's a good idea!" he said enthusiastically. "I might try that."

Owen, whose own training was limited to a brief exposure to English police methods while serving under Garvin at Alexandria, was less convinced in general of the value of "reconstructing." How could one re-enact an event as fluid as Moulin's disappearance, with so many holes and loopholes? He could, however, see a case for it on this occasion. Seeing even a crude dramatization of the incident might jog the memories of people as inclined to the dramatic as most Egyptians were.

Mahmoud, happy now, could turn back to Owen's problems. He sipped the iced water which came with the coffee and thought hard.

"Anton's," he said after a while. "Why did it happen there?"

"No special reason. That's just where it happened to happen."

"It's a surprising place for it to happen to happen."

"Why?"

"If they've Senussi connections, as Nikos thought. That sort of Islamic fundamentalist wouldn't go near a gambling salon. He wouldn't even have *heard* of Anton's."

"There's no real evidence that they have Senussi connections. It was just the name that suggested it to Nikos—'Zawia.'"

"'Zawia' can mean a lot of things."

"I thought it might be Nationalist. You know, 'turning-point,' that sort of thing."

Mahmoud, who was himself a member of the Nationalist Party, laughed.

"You see Nationalist influence in all sorts of funny places," he said drily.

"I know. There's nothing much to suggest it in this case. Except that it was aimed at foreigners."

"They kidnapped a foreigner," said Mahmoud, "on this particular occasion. That doesn't mean their target is foreigners in general. Next time it could be an Egyptian."

"Even if it was an Egyptian, there could still be a Nationalist group behind it. Most of the kidnapping in Cairo is done to raise money for political purposes."

"So they say."

Owen sensed he had better move off the topic. Mahmoud and he got on very well together but there were some issues it was best to steer clear of. The Egyptian Nationalist movement was one.

"I agree with you," he said. "If they're Senussi, Anton's is a funny place to use."

"If they're fundamentalist at all it's a funny place to use. It's not just they'd avoid it, it's that they wouldn't know enough about it to be able to use it."

"Maybe it's not a fundamentalist group."

"There's another thing. You said that in their note they didn't tell Berthelot how to get to Anton's. They knew he already knew. How did they know that?"

"Seen him go there."

"What strikes me," said Mahmoud, "is how remarkably well informed they are on the habits of guests at Shepheard's."

"It must be an inside job, you mean?"

"Or else they've got a very good contact there. Now if you put the two together, Shepheard's *and* Anton's, you get a picture of a group with a background of knowledge very different from that of the usual group. It could hardly be a fundamentalist group. It's most unlikely, I would have thought, to be one of the student groups at El Azhar. They wouldn't have the money for a start and it's all a bit sophisticated for them. Too Western. It's even a bit Western for the Nationalists."

"I've seen Nationalists at Shepheard's," Owen could not forbear saying.

"And I've seen Nationalists at places like Anton's. But on the whole they're not the sort of places where you would expect to find them. The Nationalists you do find there are—"

Mahmoud stopped.

"Successful politicians?" suggested Owen.

Mahmoud was reluctant to say anything which might yield a later opportunity for criticism of the Nationalist Party.

"They are not always very good Nationalists," he said unwillingly. "They are a bit too fond of Western ways."

He closed his lips firmly. You knew he would rather bite off his tongue than say any more.

"Not the sort of people to go in for kidnapping," said Owen helpfully.

"Not the sort of people at all."

●　　●　　●

Mahmoud arranged his reconstruction for the following afternoon. When Owen got there he was having trouble: the usual trouble. It was not that, Europeans apart, people were unwilling to cooperate. On the contrary: they were only too willing; indeed, could not be dissuaded from cooperating. Every waiter in the hotel, whether he had been there on the day or not, stood beaming on the terrace. The waiter who had actually served Monsieur Moulin, distinguishable from the others by the fact that a certain apprehensiveness was mixed with his bursting pride, had only to take a step with a tray for a dozen other waiters to rush forward to help him. Much the same thing went for all the other participants.

On the terrace, apart from the waiters, things were not too bad. Generally speaking, when guests came out of the doors of the hotel and saw what was going on, they recoiled in horror and went to the other end of the terrace. A number of those who had been near the table on the day in question were prevailed upon to stay and sit, stiff and awkward, at neighboring tables. Their general sentiments were expressed most clearly by Mr. Colthorpe Hartley, held back lurking in the hotel on instructions from Mahmoud. "God, how embarrassing!" he kept saying. His wife, doing her duty, was out on the terrace, accompanied by Lucy, the only one who actually appeared to be enjoying herself. She caught sight of Owen in the throng below and gave him a delighted wave. A difficult cast to direct, reflected Owen, but on the whole they were playing their parts.

The real trouble was down below. At the bottom of the steps things were threatening to get out of hand. The vendors who normally lined the front of the terrace had gathered that something special was going on, a wedding, perhaps, or the arrival of a new boatload of tourists, and flocked to that end of the terrace. The space in front of the hotel steps, normally under pressure anyway from encroaching beggars, performers, artists and street sellers, and kept free only by the extreme vigilance of two policemen posted there for that purpose, was now completely taken over by the crowd. So great was the pressure that more sellers were forced up the steps, a situation they immediately turned to commercial advantage, and soon no one could move at all, either up or down.

Assisted by McPhee, who rather enjoyed this sort of thing—it was, after all, very like a football scrum—Mahmoud formed his constables into a wedge and drove straight down the steps, pushing everyone off them and forcing the crowd to give ground. In an instant the constables opened out into a ring, creating a small space at the foot of the steps in which the play was to be played.

The snake charmer, unhappy, and the snake, disdainful, took up their positions. Mahmoud mounted the steps to get a better look, nodded with satisfaction and gave the signal to begin. A small figure, hobbling with gusto, came out of the hotel entrance and began to make his way painfully across the terrace. A posse of waiters descended upon him at once, one taking one arm, another the other, despite the small figure's vigorous attempts to shake them off. Two waiters ran in front of him, pulling back chairs to clear a passage. Another was so carried away that he crouched down in front of the pretend Monsieur Moulin and tried to flick specks of dust from his shoes as he stumbled forward.

"For goodness' sake!" said McPhee.

Mahmoud shrugged and carried on.

"Monsieur Moulin" was escorted to his table and allowed, eventually, to sit down. The waiters gave vigorous final polishings to the table, chair, and anything else that came within reach and then stood proudly by. Mahmoud waved them away. At first they affected not to notice; then, hurt, they reluctantly withdrew. Mahmoud's sigh of relief was audible even where Owen was standing.

Lucy Colthorpe Hartley jumped up.

"This isn't right!" she said.

"Why not?" asked Mahmoud.

"He was already out here when we came out. Come on, Mummy!"

Mrs. Colthorpe Hartley rose reluctantly from her chair and went back with Lucy to the hotel entrance.

"God, how embarrassing!" said Mr. Colthorpe Hartley.

Lucy and her mother came briskly back across the terrace, hesitated for a moment, and then sat down at the table they had previously occupied.

Lucy leaned across to the pretend Monsieur Moulin, a Greek clerk borrowed for the occasion by Mahmoud from the Parquet offices.

"Go on!" she said. "Look around! As if you were expecting someone."

Entering into his part with spirit, Monsieur Moulin did so, craning backwards over his chair the better to see the length of the terrace.

"Waiter!" shouted Mahmoud.

Five sprang forward.

"One of you!" shouted Mahmoud. "Abdul!"

Four fell back wounded. Abdul advanced on the table with flourishes.

"Voulez-vous prendre du thé, Monsieur?"

Like most of the terrace waiters, Abdul spoke some French. The clerk didn't and looked puzzled; then guessed and nodded his head. Abdul gave a deep bow and walked slowly off the terrace; very slowly, dragging out his part, greatly to the envy of all the other waiters.

Mr. Colthorpe Hartley emerged from the hotel and walked determinedly across to join his wife and daughter. As he passed Monsieur Moulin he nodded very deliberately. Monsieur Moulin gave a start and then nodded back. Mr. Colthorpe Hartley sat down, stretched his legs and said loudly: "I'd like some tea, my dear." He took the cup and settled back. "Hot, this afternoon," he said.

"Golly, Daddy, you *are* good," Lucy whispered.

Mr. Colthorpe Hartley meditated over his tea for some time, then looked again very deliberately at Monsieur Moulin. He looked away and then looked back. Something was troubling him. He leaned across, put his hand in front of his mouth, and whispered confidentially: "Fidget!" The Greek looked at him uncomprehendingly. "Come on!" said Mr. Colthorpe Hartley urgently: "You know." He demonstrated with a violent twitch of his body. The Greek looked even more baffled. Mr. Colthorpe Hartley repeated his demonstration. The Greek caught on and responded with a violent jerk. Mr. Colthorpe Hartley gave him an encouraging nod. The Greek, evidently concluding that Monsieur Moulin had suffered a fit of some kind, racked his body with violent spasms. "That'll do, old boy," said Mr. Colthorpe Hartley. "Mustn't overdo it, you know." The waiters watched spellbound.

Mr. Colthorpe Hartley went back to his tea. Another actor stepped on to the stage. This was one of the hotel dragomans dressed for the occasion in a splendid robe and great curving red slippers. He bent impressively over Monsieur Moulin for a few seconds and then stalked across to the terrace railings and looked imperiously down into the crowd. The vendors lining the railings fell back uneasily. Spotting his chance, another vendor rushed forward and thrust a bunch of flowers up at the dragoman. Indignantly the other vendors pushed him out of the way. The dragoman watched the mêlée impassively. Then he turned and stalked back to Monsieur Moulin. He bowed down so that his long, drooping moustaches were dangling almost in Monsieur Moulin's face, muttered something to him and then strode majestically into the hotel.

The little Greek clerk seemed rather overcome by his encounter and huddled deeper into his chair. Mr. Colthorpe Hartley glanced up, glanced away again and sipped his tea. A moment later he looked again. This time he frowned. Again the confidential whisper: "I say, old chap, it's time you went. Imshi!" The Greek shot out of his chair, then stopped and looked to Mahmoud for instructions. Mahmoud came up the steps.

•   •   •

So far, so—moderately—good. It was what came next that was tricky, for now Mahmoud had nothing definite to guide him and was dealing only in possibilities. He had worked out three alternative scenarios. In the first one Monsieur Moulin was to rise from his table and simply walk back indoors. The second envisaged him walking down the terrace steps; and the third saw him being forcibly taken down the steps.

The first one was soon played and was indeed a bit of an anticlimax. The Greek stand-in got up suddenly and walked off and that was that. The spectators clearly wanted more. Mahmoud asked the residents on the terrace whether they had seen anything like this and they said no. He tried the waiters. They were divided. Some claimed to have seen him and described what they had seen in great and implausible detail. Others, equally definite, had seen nothing. The hotel reception was just inside the doors and if Monsieur Moulin had re-entered the hotel he would have passed in front of their counter. They were fairly sure they hadn't seen him. On the day in question McPhee had checked with them virtually as soon as Moulin had been reported missing and they had said the same thing. One of the receptionists was Nikos's informant and Nikos had said he could be trusted.

The second option had envisaged Moulin walking down the steps. Everyone acknowledged that this was a possibility but no one had actually seen him do it. But if Moulin had done that, what had he done when he reached the bottom? The arabeah-drivers and the donkey-boys were adamant that he had not approached them; they were even more confident that no one else would have picked him up—they guarded their rights too jealously for that. Of course, he could simply have walked off into the crowd. But walking was anything but simple for Monsieur Moulin and although it could have been easy for him to disappear into the crowd, he would have found it hard going to make his way through the crush and reach some harbor on the far side. No witness had seen him doing that. Mahmoud tried the tumblers and vendors, some of whom were sharp, observant men, but they had no recollection of an elderly man trying to push his way past them. The snake charmer was so bemused that he could hardly be brought to say a word.

By now Mahmoud's arrangements were coming under severe strain. The crowd had grown still more and now stretched right across the street, blocking it in both directions. A few stranded arabeahs stood out above the sea of curious faces. Some way up the street a wedding procession had come to a complete halt. It was evidently a rich man's wedding for there were musicians mounted on camels as well as the palanquin for the bride. There were probably jesters and mirror-bearers but they were lost in the crowd; although, as Owen watched, he caught the occasional flash of glass sparkling in the sun. This bride, thought Owen, was one who was definitely going to be late for her wedding.

The defensive ring of constables had already given way once or twice under the pressure of the crowd but each time, under the instructions of McPhee, had managed to reassert itself. It had lost ground each time, however, and one more cave-in would see the space at the foot of the steps disappear altogether.

Mahmoud evidently thought the same thing, for he hurried on with the third scenario. This envisaged Monsieur Moulin somehow being compelled down the steps. This sounded unlikely and proved so in practice. The pretending Monsieur Moulin had been allowed a little resistance and in fact he struggled so vigorously that his would-be kidnappers couldn't get hold of him at all until one of them, a constable carried away by his role, tapped him on the head with his truncheon. The little clerk collapsed into immobility. Even so, the kidnapping party found it hard to carry him off down the steps without causing so much commotion that even those people at the far end of the terrace who were not in on the plot looked up to see what was going on. Mahmoud had initially tried two kidnappers only but as the difficulties multiplied had

been obliged to add a third. Eventually they got the
"body" down the steps; but what then?

Mahmoud had had several possibilities in mind. First,
he tried to get an arabeah to the foot of the steps. This
proved quite impossible, given the crowd. Indeed, for
some time no arabeah had been able to leave its rank at
all and the arabeah-drivers were complaining loudly. Then
he had envisaged the kidnapped Moulin being smuggled
away through the crowd somehow bundled up in a cloak.
The little clerk recovered at this point and struck out
feebly with his arms, which made wrapping him up
difficult. The constable produced his truncheon again but
was restrained by McPhee, to the detriment, however, of
the realism of the scenario. Eventually the protesting
form was concealed but then another problem presented
itself. So tightly packed was the crowd that the kidnappers were wedged in, quite unable to move. After a few
abortive efforts they stood there looking blankly at
Mahmoud.

Mahmoud came down the steps and tried to force open
a path for them. As fast as two people were prised apart,
however, someone else stepped into the breach. The
kidnappers left Monsieur Moulin standing and joined
their efforts to Mahmoud's. Unsupported and unable to
see, Monsieur Moulin slowly toppled over. One of the
kidnappers made a despairing effort to save him and was
pulled over on top of him as he fell.

"Don't remember this bit at all," said the donkey-boys,
straightfaced.

One of the constables abandoned his part in the defensive ring and came to help. Immediately, the ring caved
in. The people who had been leaning against it fell into
the space too on top of the kidnappers. One of the more
public-spirited of them, finding himself up against one of
the kidnappers and believing the whole incident to be

real, not simulated, grappled with him in an attempt to prevent his escaping. Fighting broke out.

In the middle of all this the outrunners of the wedding, who had been patiently forcing their way through the crowd, arrived at the foot of the steps.

"Make way for the wedding!" the donkey-boys called ironically to the mass of people struggling on the ground in front of the steps. The leading camel of the palanquin broke through the crowd and sniffed, astonished, at the recumbent forms. The little Greek clerk, who had all this time been struggling to free himself from the wrappings which enveloped him, at last succeeded. As his head emerged he found himself gazing straight into the eyes of the camel. He gave a scream and burrowed back beneath the wrappings. The camel, startled, retreated with a loud jingle of bells.

"By God!" said the snake charmer. "That's it!"

The palanquin threatened to capsize and the bride joined her screams to the general uproar.

Owen suddenly became aware that Lucy's captive subaltern, Gerald Naylor, was standing beside him. He was watching with fascinated disgust.

"What a shambles!" he said. "What a shambles!"

5

Madame Chévènement?" said Zeinab. "But I've met her!"

"You have?" said Owen, astonished.

"She dresses at Jacques Griffe's. That's the one, isn't it?"

"I don't know. All I know is that she's Moulin's protégée."

"I don't know about Moulin," said Zeinab, "but she's certainly the sort of woman who would be someone's protégée."

"How did you come to meet her?"

"She was at Samira's. She's been there several times in the past month."

"Samira's!"

"What's wrong with Samira's?" inquired Zeinab, taking umbrage. "She may be fashionable but she is still—" Zeinab hesitated, searching for the word, and then used the French version—"*intellectuelle.*"

"No, no. It's not that. It's just that it's a bit, well, high. Higher than I expected. Socially, I mean."

The Princess Samira was a cousin of the Khedive's. She had been married off at the age of twelve to an eminent

official at the Ottoman court and had lived for many
years in Constantinople. When her husband died the
independent-minded Samira seized the opportunity to
marry how she wished. Her choice fell on an elderly Bey
living in Algiers. He continued to live in Algiers after
their marriage; but one of the conditions of the marriage
settlement was that for most of the year Samira could
maintain a separate establishment in Cairo. She thus
achieved both status and independence, two things difficult for a woman to achieve in an Islamic society, and was
able to live her life pretty much as she pleased.

Zeinab, who wanted the same things, was impressed
and instructed her father, whenever he raised the issues
of marriage, to find her an elderly Bey permanently
resident in Tunis; but not yet.

Nuri Pasha, one of the old, near-feudal landowners of
Egypt, moved in the same society as the Princess Samira
and, although Zeinab was an illegitimate daughter not
even by someone in her harem but by a famous courtesan, this conferred on her something of the same standing. Samira welcomed her at her soirées, and Zeinab was
glad of the opportunity to meet men, especially the
intelligent, sophisticated men whose society Samira enjoyed.

Samira's house had much the same role in Cairo society
as a Parisian salon. At her soirées or afternoon teas one
would meet people from the major Embassies, up-and-
coming politicians, senior civil servants and interesting
foreign visitors. One even, on occasion, met the Consul-
General; certainly one met his bright young men. One
also met members of the Khedive's own family and
entourage.

Although the criteria for being asked a second time to
Samira's were personal rather than social—Samira couldn't
stand dullness—there was a certain exclusiveness about

her guests; and so Owen was a little surprised to find Madame Chévènement achieve so easy an entrée.

Zeinab considered the matter.

"She is agreeable," she said, "but not original. I don't think Samira would have invited her for her own sake. She must be doing someone a favor."

"I didn't think Samira needed to do anyone a favor."

"She doesn't. But sometimes it is politic to do one."

"When the person who asks is important?"

"If they are important enough."

"You mean...?"

"I don't mean anything," said Zeinab. "I'm just guessing."

"Could you try and find out?"

"Why don't you try and find out? I'll be there this afternoon. You could come too."

•   •   •

Owen walked in past the two eunuchs, named according to custom after precious stones or flowers, across a crunching gravel courtyard where cats dozed in the shade of the palms and in through a heavy wooden outer door. When he came to the inner door which led directly into Samira's apartment he stopped and called out *"Ya Satir*—O Discoverer"—(one of the ninety-nine names of God), the conventional warning to ladies that a man is coming and they must veil. He heard scrambling inside and as he opened the door saw a female slave disappearing up the stairs to "warn" the Princess. He realized he must be the first male guest to arrive.

By the time he reached the drawing-room the ladies were already veiled. He saw Zeinab's eyes sparkling at him from the other side of the room.

"I came early," he explained to the Princess, "so that I

could interrupt your merciless dissection of your male guests."

"Why should you think that would interrupt it?" asked Samira. "However, I'm glad you came early. I haven't seen you for such a long time and I want to talk to you. Come and sit beside me and make Zeinab jealous."

The Mamur Zapt's liaison with Zeinab was well known. In a place like Samira's they could be a couple. When it came to entertaining within the British community, however, he was usually invited alone; which was one reason why he seldom went.

He did not remain the sole male guest for very long. First, a tall, thin, mournful-looking Egyptian arrived, the editor of the Palace "organ" and a fount of useful information which Owen meant to tap later; then two expensively dressed, rather languid Turks, who were, Samira told him, close to the Khedive. Next came a stiff young man from the French Embassy, new to these gatherings, who bent low over Samira's hand. Samira, mischievously, introduced Owen as a great friend of France; then, as the young man began to express his very great pleasure, added: *"Le Mamur Zapt."*

The young man's words froze in mid-flow. Samira burst out laughing and then, repenting, eased his retreat.

"But, really, my friend, it is not so funny at all," she said, *"le pauvre Moulin!* Why do you have to be so hard? Cannot you just let him go?"

"I'm not the one who's holding him," said Owen.

"Ah yes, but without you they would soon reach an accommodation."

"I would be most happy for them to reach an accommodation."

"You would? Then why..." She stopped to look in his face. *"Tu es sérieux, chéri?"*

"Absolument."

"Well, then, perhaps it will all work out. But you know, my dear, you do have an inhibitory effect on things. Perhaps you should go away for a few days. Take Zeinab. Go to Luxor and see the temples. Haidar has a house there. I would ask him to let you borrow it. It's a very nice house. There are orange trees and lemon tress. You would enjoy it."

"I am sure I would."

"No, think about it!" She linked her arm through his and patted his hand. "Seriously!"

He promised he would. She looked at him sceptically.

"You won't, though, will you? Why so determined, my friend? Moulin is nothing to you."

"I would be only too glad to see him restored to the bosom of his family. Or to the bosom of Madame Chévènement, which, I understand, is more appealing."

The Princess laughed.

"La Chévènement!" she said with a grimace.

"I understood she was a friend of yours."

"The friend of a friend, let us say."

"May I ask the identity of the friend?"

The Princess withdrew her arm.

"No," she said, "you may not."

•　　•　　•

It was the middle of the afternoon and the Street of the Camel was unusually quiet. Most of the residents of the hotel were taking their siestas and Shepheard's famous terrace was empty. The normally importunate street-vendors had retreated into the shade. Even the donkey-boys had been driven reluctantly back along the terrace into the shadow cast by a slender potted palm.

On the other side of the steps the arabeah-drivers dozed in the shade of their vehicles or lay stretched out on the ground beneath them. Their horses drooped in the heat. Owen and Georgiades walked along the rank to where three men were sitting together idly casting dice in the dust. They looked up as Owen and Georgiades approached.

"Hello!" they said. "We've been expecting you."

Georgiades dropped into a squat beside them.

"My friend," he said, indicating Owen.

"We know you," they said to Owen. "You're the Mamur Zapt, aren't you?"

"That's right."

"We're surprised you haven't been along to see us before. Everyone else has."

"Because everyone else has," said Owen, "I have not."

"Are you getting anywhere?" they asked. "You don't seem to be."

"I know some things now that I didn't know before."

"We do too. And one of them is how much a thing like this mucks up business."

"You're not going to run it all through again, are you?" asked one of the drivers. "The way you did it the other day? I can tell you that really did set us back. We were blocked in for hours. Couldn't go, couldn't get back. It cost us real money, that did."

"Sorry!"

"It wasn't us," said Georgiades. "It was the Parquet."

"That young chap in the smart suit? He came along and talked to us. He's quite sharp."

"He must make a lot of money," said another of the men. "Look at that suit."

"They all do. Mind you, he works hard. No siestas for him!"

"That's the difference between him and us. I like a siesta."

"It's not the only difference," the other driver insisted stubbornly.

"He's cleverer than we are."

"He's got pull," the stubborn one said. "They all have. That's how they get these jobs in the first place."

"Ah well, the British are different."

"Not very."

They all laughed.

"Ah well, it's the way of the world."

"That old man, the one that's disappeared, he must have pull," said one of the drivers.

"Why?"

"The Parquet's here, you're here. The Bimbashi was here the other day."

"I don't know how much pull he's got," said Owen. "That's one of the things I'm trying to find out."

"And so you come to us."

"So I come to you."

"Well, we can't help you much. We've hardly had anything to do with him. He's never used us much. He doesn't get around."

"It's his friends we're interested in."

"Yes." The driver looked at Georgiades. "That's what your friend said this morning."

"Tell my friend what you told me."

"About that young one? The one with the bulging eyes? Very well, if you want. He's a bit of a sly one, that one. You'd think he never did anything. But he slips out from time to time, at night especially. And comes back late."

"You'd think he was after the ladies of the night," said another of the drivers. "But he's not like that, really."

"He prefers the houses."

"We know about Anton's," said Georgiades. "Which other houses does he go to?"

The men mentioned several.

"But Anton's is his favorite. He goes there regularly. Not just when they're playing, either."

"Not just when they're playing? Are you sure?"

"That's right," another of the drivers confirmed. "I took him there once myself. That was in the afternoon, about this sort of time, and they certainly weren't playing then."

"Did he go to see someone?"

The man shrugged his shoulders. "He just went inside."

"Did anyone come out with him?"

"I didn't see. Anton, perhaps."

"How often does he go? When they're not playing, I mean?"

The drivers consulted.

"Not often. Two, three times perhaps."

"What about the woman?" asked Georgiades.

The arabeah-drivers immediately sat up.

"Ah, now you're talking!"

"She gets around?"

"She certainly does! Andalaft's, Cohen's, Haroun's: she's got money and knows how to use it!"

"Apart from shopping, though?"

"She's got friends. The Princess Samira, the Prince Haidar—"

"She's got bigger friends than that, though."

"Oh? Who?"

"That would be telling."

"We don't really know," said another of the drivers.

"We don't know," said the third, "because when she goes to visit them she doesn't use us."

"Then how—"

"They send a carriage. Especially for her."

"To the hotel?"

"Yes. We don't like it, of course, but we know when to keep our mouths shut."

"And did this carriage often pick her up?"

"Two or three times a week."

"And return her?"

"Yes. A couple of hours later. Long enough."

"If you hurry," said another of the drivers.

"Perhaps she's eager."

The drivers fell about laughing.

"Anyway, maybe it's not that," said the first driver.

"What else would it be?"

They burst into laughter.

"I'll tell you what, though," one of the drivers said to Owen. "Once or twice he went with her."

"Who went with her?"

"That young chap. The one you were asking about. The one with the eyes. Though what contribution he was going to make I can't think."

"You'd better ask Abbas. Abbas!"

Some way along the row of arabeahs one of the other drivers lifted his head.

"What?"

"Suppose a man is with a woman and then another man comes along. What does the other man do?"

A guffaw ran along the line of recumbent arabeah-drivers. The one who had lifted his head sprang to his feet. "I will kill you, Abdullah!" he said, and reached toward his belt. "Be careful!" one of the other drivers warned him: "The Mamur Zapt is along there!" Abbas stopped in his tracks and stood for a moment undecided. "You wait, Abdullah!" he called eventually. "I will come to you later." Abdullah seemed unconcerned.

• • •

Paul rang from the Consul-General's office.

"Hello!" he said. "Are you all right?"

"Yes, thanks. Why shouldn't I be?"

"Everyone's been saying how peaky you look and how you obviously need a rest."

"It's this damned heat," Owen complained. Then it sank in. "Everyone?"

"Everyone who's rung me this morning."

"Samira?"

"Samira, for instance. The other one would surprise you."

"Go on; surprise me."

"The Khedive."

"The *Khedive?*"

"I knew it would surprise you. It surprised me. He's never taken an interest in your health before. Nor in the health of anyone else in the Administration. I congratulate you."

"What's going on?"

"Something, obviously. That's why I rang to let you know."

"Samira was on to me yesterday. She told me to lay off Moulin."

"And now His Highness is telling you the same thing. Isn't that interesting? You must be getting warm."

"Why should he be bothered about Moulin?"

"Why indeed. Perhaps he's not."

"What do you mean?"

"Perhaps he's bothered about something else."

Owen thought about it.

"Paul," he said then, "are you trying to warn me off? Is this something I should clear politically?"

"Who would you clear it with?"

"Garvin, I suppose."

"What would he know about it?"

"The Consul-General, then?"

"Look," said Paul, "the Consul-General doesn't have ideas of his own. He only has the ideas I put in his head."

"And what ideas are you putting in his head at the moment?"

"I don't think you look peaky at all," said Paul. "Quite the reverse, in fact."

•   •   •

"I need your help," said Owen.

Zeinab, lying on the bed, at first seemed deaf to this plea. Then she turned her head slightly.

"What is it?"

"I didn't get anywhere with Samira."

"You were talking to her for a long time."

"Yes, but she didn't tell me anything. Not much anyway. She was more concerned with warning me off Moulin. She suggested I take a holiday. Go away for a few days. Take you."

"That seems a good idea," said Zeinab, sitting up.

"No, it's not. It's just intended to get me out of the way."

"Well, why not get out of the way? Let them get on with paying for that poor man. You're not doing anything to help him. You're just stopping him from being freed."

"I'm not stopping them from paying."

"Yes, but they think you are. They think you're up there like a hawk, hovering, just picking the moment. They don't know you," said Zeinab, "like I know you."

"I don't care tuppence about Moulin."

"Then why don't we go away?"

"Because I think there's something else going on and I want to find out what it is."

Zeinab reached for a cushion and stuffed it behind her back.

"All right," she said resignedly, "I'll help you." She suddenly brightened. "No, I won't," she said.

"Bloody hell!"

"Not unless you promise to take me away for a holiday when this is all over."

"I promise. Samira said she'd get Haidar to lend us his villa at Luxor."

"Luxor! I'm not going there! It's just temples!"

"I'd quite like to go to Luxor."

"It's got to be some place I'd like to go to."

"Oh, very well."

"Promise?"

"Promise."

"Right!" said Zeinab, snuggling back into the cushion. "How can I help you?"

"It's Madame Chévènement."

"Her again?"

"This is definitely work."

"Like that other woman?"

Owen ignored this.

"I asked Samira how Madame Chévènement came to be at her soirées and she said she was a friend of a friend. I take that friend to be the Khedive."

"Right."

"What I want to find out is how she came to be a friend of his. What's the connection? How did they meet? Samira will probably know but she'll be on her guard. Is there someone else in that circle who would know?"

"I know," said Zeinab.

"You know?"

"Yes. Everyone does. He met her at Cannes."

"When was this?" said Owen, astonished.

"Last year. When he was on holiday. He went to Monte Carlo, if you remember."

Owen remembered. The Khedive had needed extra

resourcing in view of his passion for gambling. The funds had been made available but only after a protracted political tug-of-war in which Owen himself had been engaged.

"What else do you know?" he asked.

"About Chévènement? Nothing much. She's very dull, really. Just right for him."

"Did he invite her over here?"

"She invited herself, I think. He was glad to renew acquaintance."

"He's kept it pretty quiet."

"You think so?" Zeinab laughed. "Just because you haven't heard about it, darling, that doesn't mean it's been kept quiet. Still, I agree. It's been kept quieter than she would like. He's seen her only a few times and never in public."

"Still, I ought to have known about it."

She reached out a hand, caught his, and pulled him down.

"You'll just have to come to Samira's more often, darling."

• • •

"It's not just that, though," said Georgiades. "Remember, she took him with her."

"Berthelot?"

'Yes. On at least two occasions, according to the arabeah-drivers. If she was just having an affair with the Khedive, why did she do that?"

"I think we can safely disregard the more ribald suggestions of the arabeah-drivers," said Owen.

"And it's hardly likely to be just a social call. There's an etiquette for those things and the Khedive makes a big issue of it. Which leaves business—or politics."

"It's not going to be politics. The French are not going to have any amateurs coming in on their patch."

"That leaves business. What sort of business is the Khedive likely to be interested in?"

"Any business that makes money. For him."

"Aren't we all?"

"There's a bit of a problem, though, isn't there?" said Owen. "He never engages in these things directly. It's always through the Ministries. If you wanted anything you'd have to go through them."

"His influence might be a help. Maybe that's what they were after."

"Not much of a help. You'd still have to go through the Ministries."

"He might be able to get a personal favor done."

"Chévènement? Then why was Berthelot there? Anyway, he'd be able to get one done only if it was a small one. Anything big would have to go through the Ministries. That's the system. The whole point is to keep his hands off the money. He can't spend a penny without the Consul-General okaying it."

"Maybe he wants to bypass the system."

"He'll have a job!" said Owen, speaking from painful personal experience.

Georgiades sat for a while brooding. Owen suspected it was because he didn't want to go out into the heat again too quickly.

"Look at it another way," said Georgiades, settling himself comfortably: "What sort of business are Berthelot and Chévènement likely to be interested in?"

"Whatever business Moulin is interested in. And we've got a pretty good idea of that. Construction, building—"

"Contracts?"

"Yes."

"The dam contracts?"

"They've been allocated already. They were allocated before he arrived. Paul says there might be a subcontract going, a big one to construct a masonry apron, which they might let the French have as a sop. He thinks Moulin's interested in that."

"Well, maybe that's it."

"The trouble with that," said Owen, "is that all the action is somewhere else. It's all Diplomatic now. Government to Government. Foreign Office to Foreign Office. Not for small fry like Berthelot and Chévènement."

"Maybe they're just jockeying for position in the tendering?" suggested Georgiades.

"If they are, why not do it in the right place? There's no point in wasting time on the Khedive. He's not going to have any say in it whatsoever."

"I keep coming back to Berthelot," said Georgiades. "What's he doing going to see the Khedive? Chévènement I can understand. Private business and good luck. But Berthelot?"

"They're both in it together, whatever 'it' is. Only I should think they've got different roles. She makes the first contact, he follows it up."

"Has he got enough...? I mean, does he *know* enough to follow it up?"

"I think that they'd have to refer pretty soon to Moulin. And that's a point! When I first spoke to Berthelot I asked him if any of Moulin's business friends had been in contact with him. He promised to check but never did."

"It would be interesting to know who they were. Then we'd get some idea of where particularly his business interests lie. Maybe I'll have a look at that," said Georgiades.

"OK. And while you're doing that, take a look at something else, will you? I'm getting a picture in which Chévènement makes the first contact, then brings Berthelot in. At a very early stage, right at the start, probably, she gets the Khedive's blessing. That maybe is why she takes him to meet the Khedive. Now they're going to have to follow that up, which means him meeting other people. Maybe when he meets the Khedive he gets introduced to these people. Even so, he's going to have to meet them again to get negotiations started. I don't know if it's possible for you to find out who these people are. Other visits Berthelot's been paying. But you might take a look at it."

"Could the Princess Samira come into this?"

"How?"

"Well, suppose they didn't meet the people who were going to follow it up for the Khedive when they went to see him. After all, it would take time, and while I don't go along with the arabeah-drivers altogether, I don't see the Khedive wanting to spend all the time he has with Chévènement on business matters. In that case he might want to find some other way in which she could meet them. You said he asked the Princess to invite her. Maybe that's where she made her first follow-up contact. After that there would be another one, this time with Berthelot."

"I'll ask Zeinab if she can give me the names of people who've been at Samira's soirées recently. She's not going to like it, though."

"I'm going to have to try to get out of the arabeah-drivers a list of all the people Berthelot's been to see. All the places, too, because the drivers are going to know places, not people. To get the people I'm going to have to follow it up. It'll take hours. In this heat, too! Do you think I like that?"

"Yes, but you're paid to like it and Zeinab's not."

"From what you told me earlier," said Georgiades, "I think the Lady Zeinab is going to insist on payment too."

• • •

Madame Moulin was waiting for him in the grand central hall of the hotel, under the glass dome. She was having coffee with the French Chargé and Mahmoud. There was no sign of Berthelot.

She was in her early or mid-seventies and was wearing a long black gown which even Owen could see belonged to the last century. Her hair was gray and tied up behind in a severe bun. She had been traveling continuously since she had received news of her husband's disappearance and had arrived only that afternoon; but the eyes which registered Owen's entrance were bright and alert.

"Cap-tain Owen. Le Mamur Zapt," the Chargé introduced him.

Owen took her hand.

"Enchanté de faire votre connaissance, Madame. I am only sorry that it should be in such circumstances."

The old lady inclined her head graciously. Then the head came up and the sharp eyes regarded him appraisingly.

"Vous êtes capitaine, Monsieur?"

"Oui, Madame."

"Du militaire?"

"Oui, Madame. I was in the Indian Army before coming to Egypt."

"Vous avez tué?"

Owen was taken aback. Had he killed? Well, yes, he had, but it was not something he liked to be asked quite so definitely.

"Oui, Madame. Je le regrette."

"We all regret it," replied the old lady, "but sometimes it is necessary."

She completed her inspection.

"C'est un brave homme!" she announced to the Chargé.

"Of course!" said the Chargé enthusiastically.

"He has been tried in action," said Madame Moulin.

"That is what makes a man. Not sitting about in offices."

"Of course!" agreed the Chargé, slightly less enthusiastically this time.

"It is something I am always telling Monsieur le Président. My cousin's husband, you know. 'Gaston,' I say: 'what has happened to our young men? All they think about is drinking wine and chasing women and sitting about in offices.'"

"And what does Monsieur le Président reply?" asked Owen.

"'Monique,' he says: 'young men have always drunk wine and chased women.' 'But not sat about in offices!' I say. We are becoming," said Madame Moulin triumphantly, "a race of degenerates."

"*Oh là là!*" said the Chargé, and clicked his tongue reprovingly.

"A nation of degenerates," Madame Moulin repeated with emphasis, looking fiercely in his direction.

Owen, who got along well with the Chargé, despite present difficulties, tried to rescue him.

"But, Madame," he said, "we serve our country in different ways. The skills the diplomat needs are not those of the soldier."

"I am not talking of skills," said the old lady dismissively. "I am talking of character."

There was a little silence after that. It was Madame Moulin herself who broke it.

"And what, precisely, are the skills which you yourself bring to this sad affair, Monsieur le Capitaine? Those of a soldier?"

"Certainly not. Those days are long behind me."

"Then...?"

It was the sort of question which the French—and the Egyptians—were always asking and one which Owen found it very difficult to answer. Both countries had a tradition of professionalism which made it hard for them to see the obvious advantages of English amateurism. Owen decided to shift the question slightly.

"I am assisting Mr. El Zaki," he said. Seeing from Madame Moulin's expression that this needed amplifying, he added, "I look after the political side."

"Ah? So this has a political side?"

"No, no. Not necessarily. It's just that it may have. It could possibly have. It is just a precaution. My role is very minor. Mr. El Zaki—"

Madame Moulin took no notice.

"Moulin dabbles too much in politics," she said darkly. "These big contracts! I have told him time and again that one day he would burn his fingers. Perhaps this is the day."

"We have no reason to think—"

"Moulin is a fool. An old fool, too, and there's none worse. How many times have I told him to stop gadding around and to stay at home and look after his own business! That could do with some attention, I can tell you! He's let it go while he's been chasing around at the beck and call of all those big firms. On yes, they give him a commission, and a big one too, but is it worth it? That's what I ask him. Gadding around like this all over the world, that's the short way to finding yourself in a wooden box, I tell him. At his age! And with his heart!"

"That is something that concerns us, Madame," said Mahmoud. "As far as we know, he is being well treated, but of course, he won't be taking his medication."

"He doesn't anyway," said the old lady. "He's too pig-headed to take his pills. He says he forgets them but I know differently. He forgets them deliberately. Those Provençal people are all the same. They don't trust anyone, not even their own doctors. They won't poison you, I tell him. I'm the one you've got to worry about. And I will, too, one of these days, if I catch you playing around with any more of those fancy women. Did you hear that?" she asked Mahmoud.

"No," said Mahmoud.

She laughed heartily.

"That's the right answer," she said. "You could have been one of our policemen at home. They know what to hear and what not to hear."

She suddenly changed tack.

"So it's just a question of money, is it?"

"Yes," said the Chargé.

"Well, we've got plenty of that. Mind you, I don't believe in giving in to them, not as a general rule, but it's a bit different when it's your own, isn't it? I don't expect you agree with me, though, do you?" she said, looking at Mahmoud.

"No."

She sighed. "Well, you're right, I suppose. We could do with more men like you. All the same—"

She seemed to be thinking.

"I don't suppose you're getting anywhere, are you?" she asked Mahmoud. "No? Well, you wouldn't be, and at least you're man enough to say so. If you were, you see, I might be willing to wait, though it'd be hard on poor Moulin. At his age, too—"

"And in the heat," said the Chargé.

"Yes, in the heat." She shook her head regretfully. "No, it won't do. I'll have to pay. As I said, we've got money enough."

She suddenly looked sharply at Mahmoud.

"How did they know we've got money? What made them pick on poor Moulin?"

"Anyone who stays at Shepheard's—" began Mahmoud.

She brushed his words aside impatiently.

"Someone must have told them," she said. "Otherwise

they wouldn't have known. He doesn't show his money around, he's too much of an old peasant for that. Someone must have told them. And I know who. Yes," she said, her lips tightening, "I know who."

"Who, Madame?"

"That nephew of his. That degenerate."

"But—"

"Berthelot," she said.

6

A new party of tourists had arrived at the hotel; and as Mahmoud and Owen came down the steps a small group of them were being introduced by their dragoman to the donkey-boys.

"This Daouad, this Ali," said the dragoman, selecting two of them not quite at random since Ali was the biggest of the donkey-boys and Daouad the richest.

"Fine donkeys," said Daouad. "You want ride?"

They were fine donkeys. There were little white ones with gay blue and silver necklaces and saddles of red brocade. These were for women and children. And there were big Assiut donkeys for the men. These stood tall as ponies, with their forefeet on the pavement, brushing away the flies with independent motions of their enormous ears, their tails bright with henna. A triangular silver charm containing a verse form the Koran hung below their throats and somewhere about them (as on all the cab-horses) was a blue bead to keep off the evil eye. Those for hire bore a number plate in English and Arabic—"Donkey No. 153"—on their saddle pommel.

The dragoman performed one of his party tricks. He borrowed a cigar from one of the tourists and puffed cigar smoke up the nostrils of one of the donkeys. The creature closed its eyes and laid its head back in voluptuous ecstasy.

"Shame on you, Osman!" said another dragoman who was passing at that moment.

"And shame on you, Abdul Hafiz!" Osman retorted spiritedly.

Only the strictest Moslems objected to smoking and dragomans were not usually among the strictest Moslems. The donkey-boys, who had developed the trick in the first place, stood smiling broadly.

The tourists giggled. Osman, encouraged, or possibly provoked by Abdul Hafiz, went a step further. He stuck the cigar in the donkey's mouth.

"Why, Mum, it's just like Daddy!" said a small boy and dodged the clip on the ear his father gave him.

The dragoman offered the cigar back to its owner. The offer spurned, as he had hoped, he put out the cigar and stuffed it into the folds of his gown. The party moved off.

The donkey-boys looked up at Owen and Mahmoud as they passed.

"We've fallen out of favor," they said. "You don't come to see us these days."

Owen and Mahmoud didn't even need to look at each other. With one accord they dropped on to their haunches beside the donkey-boys.

"It's being so busy," said Mahmoud.

"Yes," said the donkey-boys, "we've watched you."

They passed them two small enamel cups and one of the boys refilled the pot.

"Let it stand for a bit," said Daouad, who seemed to be their natural leader, if any group so anarchic could be said to have a leader.

"You're not getting very far, are you?" one of the other donkey-boys said to Mahmoud.

Mahmoud did not reply, just smiled.

"These things take a long time," said Ali, who as well as being big was rather indolent.

"Are they going to pay?" asked Daouad.

"They might," said Mahmoud, "but that wouldn't mean the end of it for us."

"You'd go on, would you? What's the point? It would all be over and done with."

"Until the next one."

"Yes," said Daouad, "there's always that."

"They'll have made a nice bit of money," said another of the donkey-boys. "One hundred thousand piastres! That's not to be sneezed at!"

As always, the donkey-boys' information was accurate. In Cairo it was never possible to keep anything secret for long.

"Yes," said Daouad thoughtfully. "Do that once or twice and it would set you up for life."

"Get caught," said Mahmoud, "and you'd be set up for life all right."

They all laughed.

"Don't worry," they said. "The Mamur Zapt has got us frightened."

Owen knew he was being mocked; but laughed with them. Almost shamefacedly they poured him some tea. He was a guest and under the strong law of hospitality, while a little teasing was allowable, offence should not be given.

"You haven't found him yet, then."

"No," said Mahmoud, "although I've been all along the Wagh el Birket. Slowly."

They roared with laughter.

"I'll bet you saw some other interesting things, though."

"But not him. Anyway," said Mahmoud, "for all you say, that's not the sort of place where one would be likely to find him. He's too old."

"You'd be surprised."

"He wasn't as old as that to start with. He just got like that through going there."

"It takes some people that way. Look at Daouad!"

"I don't go to the Wagh el Birket!" said Daouad indignantly.

"Not now he's married."

"I'm not married!" protested Daouad.

"Oh? I thought you'd been to a wedding recently?"

The donkey-boys doubled up with laughter. It was obviously some inside joke. They wouldn't leave it alone and Daouad became angrier and angrier. Eventually Mahmoud was able to steer the conversation on to another subject. Another group of tourists came down the steps and Owen and Mahmoud, after the traditionally profuse Arabic thanks, left the donkey-boys to get on with their business.

It was still very hot and really too early to go on expeditions but the tourists were newcomers and had not yet discovered this and the dragomans, having once secured their customers, were certainly not going to tell them.

"They might suggest it later," Mahmoud said, "when they've become their regular dragoman and make definite appointments. Even then, though, they're not allowed into the hotel unless they're a properly accredited hotel dragoman. That's where the hotel dragomans have an advantage. Mind you, they're not allowed to pester the guests. There's a corridor behind Reception—it leads out into a little backyard behind the kitchens—and they have to stay in that. When their party arrives, if they've made an appointment, or if somebody comes along who looks as if they might want a dragoman, the staff on Reception give the dragomans a signal. If it's not an appointment they have to take it turns. The first in the line comes forward."

Mahmoud had been doing some research on the hotel dragomans. There were seven of them, all properly licensed by the police. "I thought we might go along afterwards," he said, "and look at their files."

On the day that Moulin disappeared there were only five of them on the premises, the other two having gone with parties to the Pyramids. Of the five, two who had appointments for later had spent the afternoon asleep in the backyard (confirmed by various members of the kitchen staff who had also gone out there to sleep where it was cooler), one had gone on an errand, and only two had been in the corridor at about the time in question. They had stayed in the corridor, according to their own account and confirmed, though not confidently, by Reception, until about half past four, when the first of them, Osman, the smoke-puffing one, had been summoned to take a party off to the bazaars. The second, Selim, had been called for about ten minutes later.

"But by then we're not really interested," said Mahmoud. "It's really from about four o'clock to twenty past four that we're concerned with."

"Presumably you've asked those two in the corridor and they've denied ever having gone out on to the terrace?"

"Oh yes. May God strike them dead, etc. They'd have to deny it because the hotel is very strict on the point. They've got to stay in the corridor."

"Is it possible to get from the corridor to the terrace?"

"Oh yes. It's only a few steps and if the Reception staff were busy...Still, there would be a risk."

"But one of them couldn't have gone out without the other knowing."

"That's right."

"So they'd both have to be in it together."

"The trouble with the whole affair," said Mahmoud, "is that everyone is in it all together."

Mahmoud being Mahmoud, he had not taken anything for granted but had checked stories whenever he could. The dragoman who said he'd gone on an errand, Abdul Hafiz, had indeed gone on an errand. He had gone to collect a parcel for one of the guests from one of the shops in the bazaar, had definitely done so and had handed it in to Reception soon after four-thirty. No doubt on that point at least, for Abdul Hafiz had wanted to give it directly into the hands of the guests (because of the bakhsheesh) and had been very reluctant merely to deposit it at Reception. It was something that all participants remembered and had clearly made an impression on all of them.

Likewise the two dragomans who had been with parties to the Pyramids had definitely been there and for the whole day too. It would have been impossible for them to have slipped back to the hotel at any point.

And the two dragomans sleeping in the backyard appeared genuinely to have been sleeping.

"Though, of course," said Mahmoud, "there is no real precision about times."

"And the yard is just at the other end of the corridor," Owen pointed out. "They could have slipped along it easily enough."

"Yes. Though there would have been a risk. They could easily have been seen."

"That applies to them all."

"Yes."

It applied particularly on the terrace where if a dragoman had appeared, as Colthorpe Hartley reported, he must have been seen—indeed, was seen—by Colthorpe

Hartley. Mahmoud had tried repeatedly to see if Colthorpe Hartley could identify the dragoman. That, in fact,
had been part of the point of the ill-fated reconstruction.
However, that attempt, like the others, had failed. Faced
with the hotel dragomans, Colthorpe Hartley was barely
able to tell them apart. His mind, he assured Mahmoud—
and this Mahmoud could readily accept—went blank,
"absolutely blank, old boy." He was, however, quite posi-
tive that he had seen "one of those fellows" and Mahmoud
was inclined to believe him.

"It fits in with what the snake charmer told us," he said.
"Someone from above the steps."

"That could apply to a waiter."

"But Colthorpe Hartley saw a dragoman."

Naturally enough Mahmoud had tried to find corroboration for Colthorpe Hartley's account. That, too, had
been part of the point of the reconstruction. He had
wanted to see if any of the street-vendors remembered
the dragoman. His intention had been thwarted by the
general rush of all the vendors to that end of the terrace
on the day of the reconstruction, which had resulted in a
complete mix-up of regulars and general sightseers. He
had tried again on the following day when conditions
were normal but had not achieved quite the clarification
he had desired.

"No one saw a dragoman?"

"Oh yes, everyone saw a dragoman. But they all saw
different dragomans!"

Most of the vendors had testified in detail as to the
appearance of the dragoman. The flower-seller had described with considerable accuracy one of the dragomans
who had been incontrovertibly at the Pyramids on the day
in question. The sweetmeat-seller had given a vivid picture of one of the dragomans asleep in the backyard.
Four witnesses described with lurid detail the dragoman

who had acted the part in Mahmoud's reconstruction. And the filthy-postcard-seller described a sinister figure with a hunched back and a wall eye and the Fang of the Wolf and—until Mahmoud shut him up.

Mahmoud, ever-hopeful, was still hopeful, though. That was part of the purpose of their stroll across the street. He wanted to reconstruct the image of Moulin's disappearance again in his own mind, to note the vendors actually present, to see if there was anyone he had missed out. He had, moreover, not given up hope of assisting Colthorpe Hartley's mind to some merciful clarity of vision and meant to try him again.

He and Owen stood in the shade and watched the events across the street. It was nearly four o'clock and people were coming out on to the terrace for tea. Lucy Colthorpe Hartley appeared with her mother and a little later, regular as clockwork, Colthorpe Hartley himself appeared. Waiters came and went, Mahmoud checked them off against a list.

A dragoman came out of the hotel. Owen tensed for a moment but he was with a party. The party was straggly and ill-disciplined—hence the gap—and the dragoman had to rush around making sure they were all there. This particular dragoman—Owen did not recognize him but thought he might be Abdul Hafiz—looked extremely harassed, too preoccupied with his charges to be mindful of other things.

"All the same," said Mahmoud, "there is considerable freedom of movement. If you saw a dragoman on the terrace you'd probably assume he was just chasing up stragglers."

"Porters," said Owen. "Wouldn't there be porters?"

"Yes. But not at this time of day. Guests arrive earlier or later."

"Suppose a guest has been buying things in the bazaar?"

"The dragoman would help carry. If it was heavy Reception would get porters."

"Reception," said Owen. "Do they ever come out on the terrace themselves?"

"Never. Once you've made it to Reception you don't do things like that. That's for underlings."

It had to be the waiters or the dragomans. Mahmoud had been through the waiters with a fine-tooth comb. Certainly they would have helped Moulin down the steps, if he had gone down the steps. But on the terrace it was busy and you couldn't afford to be absent from your post for too long. Being a waiter at Shepheard's was a plum job and not one you would want to throw away too easily. Of course, it wouldn't have to take long. It would take only a moment to help Moulin down the steps. Someone must know. The snake charmer. The donkey-boys.

Near to where Owen and Mahmoud were standing was another donkey-vous. It was on the opposite side of the street from the hotel donkey-vous and as far removed from it in self-esteem as it was possible to be. The donkeys here were shadows of the splendid beasts on the other side of the road. Their trappings were tawdrier, the saddles more worn, the henna less dazzling. The donkeys themselves were older, smaller, flyier, more careworn, more beaten down. They were also cheaper and this was the only thing that kept the donkey-vous going. Few tourists came their way—the hotel donkey-boys would consider themselves disgraced if they let a tourist through who then went across the street and chose a donkey from a rival donkey-vous. The clientele was local and Arab and on the whole from the poorer streets by the Wagh el Birket.

The donkey-boys, too, seemed a beaten-down lot, sitting subdued in the shade, hardly daring to pluck up enough courage to address Owen and Mahmoud. Or perhaps not courage but hope. They seemed a hopeless bunch, listless and faint-hearted.

One of them, however, after a while summoned up enough assertiveness to ask Owen if he wanted a donkey. He seemed quite relieved when Owen said he didn't. The ice thus broken, however, he seemed emboldened enough to want to chat.

"You're often over there, aren't you?" he said.

"We have been lately," said Owen.

"Ever since that old man went from the terrace. That was a smart move! No one knows who did it or even how it was done. Smart work!"

"I'll bet they'll make a lot of money," said one of the other boys enviously.

"A hundred thousand piastres!"

They shook their heads almost in disbelief.

"I wouldn't mind that," said one.

"They'll have to share it."

"Still..."

It was obviously the main topic of conversation in the neighborhood.

"What I'd do with it—!" said a boy dreamily.

"You wouldn't have it long. The police would get you."

"Not before I'd spent it. It would be worth it."

"Anyway," one of the other boys put in, "the police haven't found out yet and maybe they never will!"

"If you could get away with it—!"

"One hundred thousand piastres!"

The incident was fueling pipe-dreams all along the Street of the Camel, thought Owen. That was another reason why, even if Moulin were released, it could not be allowed to rest.

"You were talking to Daouad," said the first donkey-boy diffidently.

"Was I?"

"Yes. Over there!"

He pointed across the street to the other donkey-vous.

"I know Daouad," he said with pride. "He's going to marry my sister!"

"Ah. I think I heard them speak of it."

"It won't happen," said another boy spitefully. "Your family can't pay a dowry big enough for someone like Daouad."

"My sister's beautiful."

"That may be. But someone like Daouad isn't looking for beauty, not when he marries, that is. He'll want money."

"My uncle may help us."

"Your uncle!"

"He's doing well. He's just bought a new horse for his arabeah."

"To go with his old one. One new horse, one old horse, that isn't a fortune!"

"Your uncle drives an arabeah, does he?" asked Owen. Arabeah-drivers were generally one up from donkey-boys, though this would have been hotly disputed by the donkey-boys across the road.

"Yes," said the first boy proudly.

"One of those over there?"

"No. He is in the Ataba el Khadra. Sometimes he brings people to the hotel."

"Does he ever take people from the hotel?"

"They wouldn't let him! Not those drivers over there!"

"He took someone last week."

"Ah, but that was different."

"Why was it different?" asked Owen.

"Because he was only picking someone up from the hotel. There was someone in the arabeah already."

"Does that often happen—other carriages come?"

"No. Not often."

"It happened the other day, though, didn't it?" said one of the other donkey-boys with a grin.

They all laughed.

"It was for that woman, the one your uncle picked up. We know whose carriage it was, too!"

"A posh one," suggested Mahmoud.

"Very posh. A bit different from your uncle's," they said to Daouad's friend, who appeared to be something of a butt; though perhaps they were merely envious.

"All the same, your uncle did pick her up," said Owen consolingly.

"That was on another day. She's popular, that one."

"Did he pick up anyone with her?"

"A man."

"I didn't know your uncle's arabeah would take three people, Ali," said one of the donkey-boys.

"It can do."

"If they sit on each other's knees."

"That new horse of your uncle's would have to work hard."

"Because the old one doesn't."

"A two-man arabeah will take three people," Ali insisted.

"But not your uncle's."

The conversation seemed to be setting into a groove. Owen and Mahmoud walked slowly back across the street. They would pick up the question of Ali's uncle and his passengers later.

They took an arabeah themselves to the police headquarters at the Bab el Khalk. That was where Owen's own office was but they weren't going there. Instead, they went down to the basement and got a clerk to bring them the files of the hotel dragomans.

There was little in them: application forms for a dragoman's license (all the dragomans could write); health certificates (in case of contagious diseases) and testimonials. There were quite a lot of these, copied out in the ornate script of the bazaar letter-writer. Many were from former guests at hotels, some implausibly effusive, others deliberately ambiguous. Most were politely appreciative, one or two genuinely perceptive. Of Osman someone had commented: "You can trust this man absolutely provided you pay him more than anyone else does." The testimonial was written in English and transcribed faithfully by the letter-writer. Of Abdul Hafiz someone had written, again in English: "Can be relied on for confidential commissions." Owen wondered what they were.

Mahmoud went through all the files, including the ones of those dragomans who had been at the Pyramids on the day Moulin had disappeared. He concentrated particularly, though, on the two who had been in the corridor. One of these was Osman.

Osman had been at Shepheard's longer than any other dragoman, a tribute to his dexterity if not necessarily to his integrity. He was better educated than the other dragomans, having been not only to the madrisseh, the secondary school, but also, for a time, to the University of El Azhar. The university admitted students at an early age and Osman had gone there when he was thirteen and left when he was fifteen, without completing his studies. At El Azhar these were mainly of a religious character. It could well be that Osman's bent was more for the secular, since he had started by serving in a hotel and worked gradually toward the status of dragoman.

The other dragoman who had been in the corridor, Selim, was more of a shadowy figure. He had worked for some time at Luxor before coming to Cairo and had developed there a vivid but not necessarily accurate knowledge of antiquities which stood him in good stead when he took parties to visit the Pyramids.

The only thing of interest about Abdul Hafiz was that

he was a Wahhabi. It was something Owen might almost have guessed from Abdul's reaction to Osman's tricks with the cigar smoke, for the Wahhabis were a strict sect with severe standards; so severe, indeed, that it was a little surprising to find Abdul in the post of a dragoman, which would necessarily bring him into contact with the more indulgent standards of the West. Life, and poverty, however, forced compromise on even the strictest and no doubt Abdul, like many Cairenes, was glad of the money. Certainly he had performed his duties, according to the testimonials, in exemplary fashion.

●　　●　　●

Owen had heard nothing for a while from either Berthelot or from Madame Moulin and suspected he was being deliberately kept ignorant of developments. That there were developments became clear when he received a phone call from his friend Paul at the Consulate-General.

"Keep off Moulin for a bit," he said.

"Is that an order or a diplomatic request?"

"It's a Diplomatic Request to us, it's an order to you."

"From the French?"

"Who else."

"It means they're going to pay."

"Very likely," Paul agreed.

"They're going to meet the kidnappers' demands."

"That's right. And they don't want you mucking it up this time."

"Is it really a Diplomatic Request?"

"Yes."

"And the Old Man has agreed?"

"Why not? It doesn't cost us anything. And it's about time we did something to oblige the French."

"It's the principle," Owen complained.

"There are several principles involved. One is not to give in to kidnappers. The other is to oblige the French when it doesn't matter. The second principle has higher priority at the moment."

"It hasn't usually."

"That's why it has now. They're getting restive, not just over the contracts, and we need to give them a sop."

"It's OK from the point of view of Moulin himself, poor sod," said Owen.

"Quite right. A touch of compassion. We have a heart too. I told the French that only this morning."

"It's just that it might encourage other people to do the same."

"Kidnap Frenchmen? Well, as long as it's Frenchmen..."

"It could be anybody."

"I know. I'm not suggesting you drop the case. I'm just suggesting you take a break."

"Go to Luxor?"

"Well..."

"I thought you were saying the other day I didn't need a break?"

"You don't. But what you do need for a couple of days is a change of activity. Preferably one which would take you out of Cairo."

"OK," said Owen resignedly. "Two days, is it?"

"Make it three. I'll let you know if you can come back earlier."

Zeinab's father, Nuri Pasha, had offered to lend Owen a house in the country, so Owen took him up on the offer. It was a small estate about forty miles out of Cairo with cotton fields and orange trees. Owen found it interesting to ride around the estate and see the work that went on: the picking of the cotton, the threshing of the corn with buffaloes, the milking of the buffaloes and the watering of the oranges. Zeinab did not and sulked most of their stay. Owen had hoped this might count as the holiday he had promised her. Zeinab, comfortable only in Cairo and Paris, made it clear it did not.

No message came from Paul, so they took the full three days. When they got back to the station one of Paul's bearers was waiting for them. He handed Owen an envelope. Owen opened it. Within was a single sheet of paper on which was written simply (!)—an exclamation mark. There was nothing else.

Later Owen found out that the proposed exchange had fallen through. The kidnappers, at the last moment, had insisted on more money. "If we give in they'll merely up it again," Madame Moulin had said, and declined to deal.

• • •

It didn't take Georgiades very long to find out who Ali's uncle was, nor to find out that on one occasion he had indeed picked up Madame Chévènement and Berthelot from the hotel. And it was the work of the time it takes to drink a cup of tea to find out where he had taken them. It took, however, rather longer to persuade Ali's uncle to take Georgiades and Owen to the spot himself, but this was because Ali's uncle, seeing the chance of a bargain, had stuck out for an inordinately large sum of money. In the end, though, he was persuaded to take them there for not much more than the price of an ordinary fare.

The arabeah was waiting for them in the Ataba el Khadra, the busy square from which nearly all the tramways of Cairo started. Georgiades had considered, since it was such a hot day, asking Ali's uncle to pick them up from the Bab el Khalk but had decided that so close a proximity to the police headquarters would alarm him unnecessarily.

He was alarmed enough as it was, staring fearfully at

them from his perch at the front of the cab. The cab itself was old but roomy, with torn, shabby seating leather and a distinct smell of sweat. The two white horses were twitching at the flies with their hennaed tails and Owen was able to impress Georgiades by referring familiarly to the obvious newness of one of them.

New or not, it shared its senior's obvious reluctance to raise its pace above a steady amble. The place they were going to was on the outskirts of the city and Owen soon realized that it was going to take them a long time to get there.

He used the time to bring Georgiades up to date on recent developments: such as the collapse of the arrangements to ransom Moulin.

"They're getting cocky, aren't they?" said Georgiades. "One hundred thousand piastres is a lot of money. You'd think they'd take it and run."

"They think they can make more. That's the trouble about giving in too quickly. It gets taken as a sign of weakness."

"You've got to start dealing at some point. It's hard to get it right."

"If you have to start dealing."

"If you don't, you get what that poor bastard Tsakatellis got."

The arabeah turned toward the river and began to go across the bridge. They got the first puff of the river breeze.

"Incidentally," said Georgiades, "about Tsakatellis; you talked to his mother. Did you talk to anyone else in the family?"

"Only the Copt who ran the shop."

"It might be interesting to talk to someone else. In the family."

"She rather gave me the impression she was in charge."

"Greek mothers are like that," said Georgiades, sighing.

"She handled the whole kidnapping thing herself."

"That's why I'd like to talk to someone else about it. Do you mind if I do?"

"Go ahead," said Owen. "You're the expert on things Greek."

Crossing the bridge, revived by the breeze, the horses had positively—well, at least strolled. Now they seemed to have stopped altogether.

"What's going on?" said Georgiades.

"Nothing is going on," said Ali's uncle.

"I know. That's why I'm asking. Why have the horses stopped?"

"They have not stopped," said Ali's uncle, hurt. "They have merely slackened their pace."

"Why?"

"There is a camel in front."

"Then overtake it."

"I cannot."

"Why not?"

"Because in front of the camel there is a cart."

"Cannot you pass both of them?"

"No."

"Why not?"

"Because coming in the opposite direction is a donkey with a load."

Georgiades leaned out to inspect.

"The donkey is still far away. Even *your* horses could pass. Where is your spirit, man? Are you not an arabeah-driver?"

Thus goaded, Ali's uncle attempted to overtake, but so half-heartedly that in the end he was obliged to cut in on the cart, which earned him a torrent of abuse from the carter. Instead of instantly responding in kind, as most arabeah-drivers would have done, delighted at the chance to display their own rhetorical skills, he cracked his whip over his horses and scuttled away fearfully. He seemed as low-spirited as his nephew.

"How did Izkat Bey come to choose him?" asked Owen, astonished.

Izkat Bey was the man who had been in the arabeah when it had picked up Madame Chévènement and Berthelot from Shepheard's.

"Accident. He came out into the street looking for an arabeah and to his misfortune he found this one."

Ali's uncle, who did not usually attract such splendid custom, had been only too ready to reveal the identity of so distinguished a person to Georgiades.

"Why didn't he use his own arabeah?" asked Owen.

"Didn't want to be recognized, I suppose."

Izkat Bey was one of the Khedive's senior Court Officials. His function at Court was obscure but of his power there was no doubt. He was close to the Khedive and, like most of those close to the Khedive, a Turk. He shared the ruling circle's arrogance toward the Egyptians and antipathy to the British and seemed particularly to relish those commissions of the Khedive which gave him opportunities to display both those qualities. His name was one of those that appeared on Zeinab's list.

When Owen had asked Abdul for a list of Samira's guests she had at first refused. "I do not spy on my friends," she said haughtily. Then, characteristically changing her mind, she had furnished him with a list. "It is not complete, however," she had warned him. "I have left off all my friends."

The inference was that Izkat Bey was not one of Zeinab's friends. This was quite likely as the Bey had a traditional view of the role of women. He came to Samira's because she was royal and because he was bidden; and Owen guessed that he saw the occasion as one for the transaction of business rather than for the pleasures of social intercourse.

The arabeah threaded its way along beside the river bank until it had left most of the built-up area behind it. They came to an area of market gardens, cultivated fields and fields of maize. They came suddenly upon a great pile of pumpkins which marked the spot where a small secondary track, barely a yard wide, ran off to the left down to the river. All around were patches of peas, beans, tomatoes, onions, cauliflowers, mangoes, guavas, figs and watermelons. There was no one in sight except for over to the left where a small boy on a buffalo was working a sakiya, one of the traditional, heavy wooden water-wheels.

It was here that Ali's uncle stopped.

7

This is where you brought them?" asked Owen.

"Yes, effendi," said Ali's uncle humbly.

"If you are playing tricks with me—"

"I am not, effendi. I swear it!" Ali's uncle protested vigorously.

"You brought them here? To this very spot?"

"Yes, effendi."

Owen climbed out of the arabeah and looked around him. In the distance he could hear the regular, rhythmic creaking of the water-wheel and then, far away across the cauliflower and maize, the faint singing of peasants at work in the fields.

"Did they come here to meet someone?"

"I do not think so, effendi," said Abdul's uncle diffidently.

"You saw no one?"

"No, effendi."

"They just came here and looked around?"

"They talked, effendi."

"What did they talk about?"

"I do not know, effendi. I did not hear."

"They just sat and talked?"

"They stood and talked. They descended from the arabeah."

"And then they went home again?"

"Yes, effendi."

Owen looked around, completely baffled. There seemed nothing here but garden crops and in the distance fields of berseem, the green fodder which the camels brought in every day across the bridge for the use of the donkey-boys and the arabeah-drivers.

Owen's heart began to sink.

"Have they tricked us again?" he said to Georgiades, who had come across and was standing beside him.

"They can't have! They couldn't have known."

"They might have done it as a precaution."

"Just on the off-chance that someone would be trying to check on the journeys they had made?"

"It sounds ridiculous."

"It is ridiculous. No," said Georgiades, shaking his head. "It's not that."

"Then what is it?"

Georgiades walked over to inspect the cauliflowers. They were planted in rows and there were little channels running between them. The channels were hard-caked and smooth. As he watched, a little trickle of water began to run along them.

"The dam," said Georgiades. "Is it something to do with the dam?"

"Not up here," Owen objected. "It can't be, surely."

The water was coming from the sakiya. It was just reaching the field of cauliflowers. More and more trickles appeared in the channels and in some of them it was now flowing freely.

"Did they walk anywhere?" Georgiades asked Ali's uncle.

"No, effendi."

Ali's uncle seemed daunted by it all. Perhaps it was leaving the city for the great open spaces. But then, Ali's uncle was easily dauntable.

"I heard them talk of the river," he volunteered, though, hopefully.

"What did they say?"

"One could travel by river."

"Who could?"

"I do not know, effendi. I did not hear."

He had caught the mention of travel by river, though from where and where to and for what reason had passed him by, as did most things in life, Owen uncharitably felt.

He and Georgiades walked down to the water-wheel. A raised, banked-up main channel ran back alongside the path in the general direction of the river. At intervals subsidiary channels took the water off and distributed it through the fields. They could see the water running down the furrows between the plants and suddenly turning the parched soil into soft, fertile mud.

As they neared the river they saw that the water came from the water-wheel. It was a traditional native wooden one, consisting of a heavy horizontal wheel, turned by a buffalo working 'round it, and connected through cogs to a large vertical wheel at the river's edge. There were buckets set all 'round the vertical wheel which scooped up the river water as the wheel turned and emptied it into a steep gutter from which it flowed into the distributing channels.

On the top of the buffalo was a small boy.

"That is a big buffalo," said Georgiades, "for a small boy."

"It is my father's buffalo," the boy said proudly.

"Oh? Then you are not a boy hired for the day but work on the buffalo as your father's son?"

"That is true," the boy agreed.

"That is a heavy responsibility for one so young."

"I am nine," the boy said.

"Are you?" said Georgiades, affecting surprise. "I would have said thirteen."

"I am big for my age."

"That is fine, but it means you get taken for a man when there is work about."

"I could do a man's job," said the boy, "but my father won't let me. He keeps me on the buffalo."

"Well, that is important. And hard! I expect you work all day?"

"All day and every day."

"And all alone, too. You don't see many people here."

"Only the people in the fields."

"And the occasional stranger."

"Not many of them."

"Are there any?"

"There were some the other day. They came like you in an arabeah."

"And did they come down and talk to you?"

"No. They stayed with the arabeah."

"It was too hot for them, I expect."

"It was the afternoon. Still, there was a Sitt with them."

"A lady? Then she would not want to walk far. I expect she just wanted to see the fields."

"They are good fields," said the boy with an air of experience.

"Indeed they are. Lucky the man who owns them. Not your father?"

"No. They belong to Sidky."

"Does he live in the village?"

"No, no. He's a rich man. He lives in the city."

"And doesn't come down here very often, I expect."

"He was down here the other day. He came with another man and showed him the fields."

"They are good fields."

"Yes. I think the man liked them, because he came again."

"By himself?"

"No, no. With the others."

"Others?"

"The man I told you about. There was the Sitt and another man."

They stood talking with the boy while the buffalo wound 'round and 'round and the sakiya squeaked and the water plopped out from the buckets into the gutter. As the sun began to set, the opal of the sky was reflected in the changing colors of the river, blue then green then yellow then red, and finally white. A man began to come across the fields toward them.

"That is my father," said the boy.

The man came up, unhitched the buffalo and lifted the boy down. They stood exchanging greetings for a while and then man, boy and buffalo set off back across the fields while Owen and Georgiades went back to the arabeah.

"It is all very beautiful," said Georgiades, "but I find it hard to believe that Madame Chévènement and Berthelot are interested in taking up market gardening."

• • •

It was only half past three and the terrace was still deserted, but already the keenest vendors were creeping back to take up strategic positions in front of the railings. The choicest positions were those nearest the steps and the vendors here guarded their privileges jealously. Despite the heat, they had already reassumed their pitches but since there were as yet no customers above they had squatted down in the dust and were engaged in desultory conversation.

It was a good moment to catch them. Mahmoud had talked to them all separately, but for that it had been necessary to abstract them from their normal setting and converse in privacy. The artificiality had made them uneasy and he felt they might talk more freely in more natural surroundings. Besides, there were some advantages in them hearing what their neighbors said, as soon became apparent.

Mahmoud was still trying patiently to identify the dragoman who had been on the terrace and soon after he and Owen had joined the squatting circle he brought the topic up. Which of them had the dragoman actually spoken to?

"Farkas," said the strawberry-seller definitely.

The filthy-postcard-seller at once denied it.

"It wasn't me," he said.

"Yes, it was," the strawberry-seller insisted. "I was hoping his party wanted some strawberries and he was coming to me but he walked right past me. *Mush kider*—is that not so?" he appealed to the flower-seller beside him.

"No," said the flower-seller. "He wasn't coming to you, he was coming to me. I thought perhaps the Sitt wanted some flowers."

"She wouldn't have wanted flowers, not if they were going out. She would have had to carry them. On the way in, perhaps."

"She certainly wouldn't have wanted strawberries. It would have made her hands too messy and then she would have had to have gone back to her room to wash them."

"She could have just popped them into her mouth," said the strawberry-seller.

This kind of batty, circumlocutory conversation ensued whenever you questioned Arab witnesses. When Owen had first come to Egypt it had regularly driven him to fury. It was Garvin, curiously, who had once taken the trouble to explain to him that that was how an Arab conversation worked. On arriving in Egypt and before taking up his duties as Mamur Zapt, Owen had been posted to Alexandria for a spell under Garvin to learn his trade. His duties had involved going round with Garvin to some of the little rural villages along the coast and hearing lawsuits brought by the villagers. Proceedings were always protracted and on one occasion Owen had boiled over.

Afterward Garvin had taken him aside.

"Look," Garvin had said, "for Arabs, truth is not something you know privately and then describe. It is something you work out together."

"But, Christ!" said Owen. "If they're a witness—"

"It's the same thing. What you saw is ingredients for a picture and it's not until the ingredients have been put together, and that has to be done socially, that you know what the picture *is*."

The apparently circumlocutory nature of the discussion was necessary because it was a way of making sure you had all the pieces of the picture that you wanted to fit together. It also allowed each piece to be weighed and tested against a variety of perspectives so that in the end you got something which everyone could agree was a more or less faithful representation of the facts.

"But it could take hours!"

"Well, yes," Garvin had admitted. "It does."

In the villages that was OK. In the cities it sometimes caused problems. Owen had learned the mode and developed patience: but sometimes that patience was put under strain. As now.

He looked at Mahmoud. Mahmoud so far had not turned a hair.

"Great, then," he said calmly, "was the misfortune for both of you when you found that he went not to you but to Farkas."

"That was another day," said the filthy-postcard-seller. "He did not come to me that day."

"It *was* that day," insisted the strawberry-seller. "Don't you remember? You were showing someone your cards when you dropped them."

"I didn't drop them. Somebody jogged my elbow."

"They fell in the dust and the turkey ate them."

"It did not eat them. It slightly chewed one of them."

"It was a bit more than a slight chew, though, wasn't it?" said the flower-seller. "Don't you remember? It was that card where she—"

"And this was when the dragoman came over to see you, was it?" Mahmoud intervened.

"No, before then," said the flower-seller.

"He had just picked them up," said the strawberry-seller.

"That was another day," insisted the filthy-postcard-seller.

"No, it wasn't!" said the strawberry-seller and the flower-seller firmly, both turning on him.

Farkas was slightly taken aback.

"I didn't mean that wasn't the day when the cards fell in the dust," he protested. "I meant that the day the cards fell in the dust wasn't the day the dragoman came over and spoke to me."

"What?" said the strawberry-seller, bewildered.

The flower-seller seemed bemused.

"What day did he come and speak to you?" asked Mahmoud.

"I forget now."

"And what did he want to speak to you about?"

"I forget."

The strawberry-seller and the flower-seller both laughed.

"He doesn't want to say."

"It's a business secret."

"Oh?" said Mahmoud.

The flower-seller took it on himself to explain.

"Sometimes," he said, "the customers don't like to speak to him directly."

"So they send a dragoman."

"That's right. Or the dragoman suggests it. They get a cut, you know."

"Is that what happened this day?"

"I expect so."

Even Mahmoud could not forbear a sigh.

"Did you actually *hear* him?" he asked, with only the faintest hint of exasperation in his voice.

"They couldn't have," said the filthy-postcard-seller, "because it was another day."

"Whichever day it was," said Mahmoud patiently, "did you hear him?"

The strawberry-seller took one of his strawberries, put it in his mouth and then restored it to the pile glistening with moisture. It looked fresher and more tempting that way.

"I can't remember," he said. He turned to the flower-seller. "Can you remember?"

"Yes," said the flower-seller unexpectedly. "But he didn't really say anything. He just made a sign."

"What sign was this?"

"It was to ward off the evil eye, I expect," said the strawberry-seller.

"It wasn't that sort of sign."

"Abdul Hafiz always makes the sign of the evil eye when he sees Farkas."

"So does Osman. You wouldn't think that, would you?"

"Which of them was it?"

"Abdul?" said the flower-seller.

"Osman?" said the strawberry-seller.

"It was another day," said the filthy-postcard-seller.

"I remember now," said the strawberry-seller, popping another strawberry into his mouth for a few seconds.

"Yes?"

"It wasn't the sign of the evil eye. It was another sort of sign."

"What sort of sign was it?" asked Mahmoud wearily. "Show me!"

The flower-seller made an unlikely motion with his hand.

"And then Farkas went away," he said.

"Went away?"

"It was another day," said Farkas faintly, as if he had given up hope of convincing anyone. "My supplier had come. He was just pointing him out."

"There was no message from the old man on the terrace?"

"What old man?" asked the strawberry-seller and the flower-seller, turning to Mahmoud with surprise.

"Jesus," said Owen under his breath.

People were coming out on to the terrace above. The vendors gathered their wares.

"Why!" said Lucy Colthorpe Hartley's voice suddenly from above. "There's Captain Owen sitting in the crowd! You do look comfortable, Captain Owen. Can I come down and join you?"

"For Christ's sake, no!" said Owen, scrambling hastily to his feet.

"Then come on up and join us! Please do. Mummy is desperate for someone to talk to. Daddy isn't saying much today and Gerald is having a fit of the sulks."

The vendors had all resumed their places by the railings. There was no point in going on talking to them now. Business was business.

Owen had got half way up the steps when he remembered

Mahmoud and looked around for him. Mahmoud was walking off in the opposite direction.

"And you, too, Mr. El Zaki!" Lucy hailed him.

Mahmoud stopped. He half turned and then saw Naylor and Mrs. Colthorpe Hartley.

"No, thank you," he said and continued walking.

"Damn cheek," said Naylor.

"Do be quiet, Gerald!" said Lucy Colthorpe Hartley. "He just didn't want to talk to you, and I can understand anyone who feels like that."

"Will you have some tea, Captain Owen?" asked her mother. She poured a cup for him. "And how are your investigations getting on?" she inquired.

The tea had the distinctive, insipid taste of tea drunk the English way with milk.

"Slowly, I'm afraid."

"It seems bewildering," said Mrs. Colthorpe Hartley. "You would have thought—"

"They're all in it," said Naylor. "That's the trouble."

Mrs. Colthorpe Hartley raised eyebrows at him. He took it not as a sign of reproof but as a request for expansion.

"That's why it's hard to get anywhere. They're all lying through their teeth."

"All?"

"All. Or pretty damned nearly all. Work it out for yourself. That French chap was out here on the terrace, right? Now if he went back into the hotel the staff on Reception would have seen him. If he went down the steps the drivers would have seen him. And if he stayed where he was but someone came and took him the waiters would have seen it. Whichever way it happened, someone would have seen. But no one saw. That can't be right. So," Naylor concluded triumphantly, "they must be lying."

"All of them?"

"Yes," said Naylor seriously. "You see, whichever way it happened there was always the risk that someone else would see, someone who wasn't supposed to, who wasn't in it. They wouldn't have risked that. So they must all be in it."

"Yes, but—"

"Oh, not to the same extent, I grant you. I expect a lot of them were just bribed to keep their mouths shut. But they must all have known about it."

"I find it hard to believe—"

"That's because you don't know these people, Mrs. Colthorpe Hartley. You haven't had the advantage of being in this country for—"

"Six months," said Owen.

"Over a year. Oh, you think they're charming and friendly and polite and so they are: to your face. But behind your back they're very different. Very different indeed, Mrs. Colthorpe Hartley. They resent us being here—"

"So they should," said Lucy.

"Oh no. That's—well, I was going to say it's liberal talk, but it's just that you haven't been here for very long. They ought not to resent us, they ought to be well and truly grateful that we are here, for before we came they'd got themselves into a most frightful mess. They had to invite us in to get them out of the mess! Don't forget that, don't ever forget that: we're here by invitation."

"Yes, but how exactly does that bear upon the present case, Mr. Naylor, the disappearance of this poor Frenchman?"

"Well, it's just that you can't trust them. They resent us, you see, they all resent us. You can see it in their faces. Even that Zaki fellow. They'd have us out of Egypt in an instant if they could. Of course they can't. We're too strong for them. They don't have the guts to face us directly. But behind our backs—well, as I was saying, behind our backs it's a very different matter. Still, as long as they keep it behind our backs I don't mind. It's when they do it to our faces that I object. We call it dumb insolence, you know, in the army, Mrs. Colthorpe Hartley. And we ought to treat it in the same way. If I catch any of my fellows giving me or any of the sergeants a bit of dumb insolence, I give him what-for, I can tell you. And we ought to do the same with these fellows. We're letting them get out of hand, that's the trouble. We ought to put them down and keep them down! That's what I always say."

"Always?"

"In the Mess."

"Very rousing, I am sure," said Mrs. Colthorpe Hartley, who sounded occasionally very like her daughter. "But how exactly would you apply it to poor Monsieur Moulin?"

"Arrest the lot of them," said Naylor confidently.

"But how exactly would that—"

"They're all lying, Mrs. Colthorpe Hartley, so we've got to get the truth out of them. Well, get them in our barracks for a day or two, Mrs. Colthorpe Hartley, and I can guarantee we'll soon have it out of them."

"But Captain Owen has been working hard, I am sure, and he—"

"It's the difference between a civil administration and a military administration, Mrs. Colthorpe Hartley. The civilians are too soft. There! I've said it! It's not what some of those at home would like to hear when you're out on the Frontier—"

"Egypt? The Frontier?" said Owen.

"The trouble with civilians," said Naylor, nettled and thinking he was being offensive by using the term, "is that they forget the realities of power."

"Gracious!" said Lucy, resting her elbows on the table. "And what are they?"

"Britain governs Egypt because of her army."

"So?"

"We ought to be allowed to get on with it."

It was a staple theme of the Messes, echoed not just by subalterns but by those higher up. The Sudan, to the south, had a purely military administration. There were those who felt that Egypt should have one too.

Not just in the army.

"You should talk to Madame Moulin," Owen said to Naylor. "She had ideas which are not dissimilar."

"Madame Moulin?" Lucy looked surprised. "I thought she had—"

"You're thinking of Madame Chévènement. This is Monsieur Moulin's wife. An elderly lady, dressed in black. She has only recently arrived. You may not have seen her."

"Poor woman!"

Mrs. Colthorpe Hartley looked thoughtful. "Lucy, I think perhaps we should leave our cards."

"We should certainly do something. But how exactly does one leave cards in a hotel? Push them under the door?"

"We will leave them at Reception," said Mrs. Colthorpe Hartley with dignity. "And we will do it now," she said, getting up from her chair.

Everyone rose to their feet. Lucy went with her mother. Naylor, after a moment's hesitation, followed them. Owen was about to depart when Mr. Colthorpe Hartley laid a hand on his sleeve.

"Hold on," he said. "Want to talk to you."

They sat down again. Having announced his intention, Mr. Colthorpe Hartley seemed a little at a loss how to proceed.

"It's this damned dragoman business," he said at last.
"Yes?"

"Bad," he said. "Can't remember."

"Which one it was?"

Mr. Colthorpe Hartley nodded. "All look alike to me."

"Perhaps it will come."

"Been trying. Know it's important."

Owen tried some of the usual cues.

"Any distinguishing features? Face? Hands? Marks? Scars, for instance? Personal jewelry? Rings? Clothes?"

"These fellows all dress the same."

"You saw him walking. Think of him walking."

Mr. Colthorpe Hartley thought. After a while he shook his head.

"Not that," he said.

If not that, then something. Owen hardly dared to breathe.

"Nearly got it," said Mr. Colthorpe Hartley after a while.

He thought on.

"Gone again," he said.

"Would it help if you saw them? Would you like me to arrange a parade?"

Colthorpe Hartley shook his head vigorously, possibly remembering Mahmoud's reconstruction.

"Good God, no!" he said.

"Hello, Daddy," said Lucy Colthorpe Hartley. "Are you helping Captain Owen?"

"Trying to."

"Good!" said Lucy, sinking into a chair. "I've delivered my card. What a sweat! I've lost all mine but Mummy had some of mine spare."

"Not going to get it," said Mr. Colthorpe Hartley. "Will come tomorrow."

"If it does, let me know," said Owen.

"Will do."

He levered himself out of his chair and went off shaking his head.

"Poor Daddy!" said Lucy, looking after him. "He doesn't remember so well these days, not since—"

"I'm sorry."

"Oh, he's much better. He's getting better all the time. And he usually does remember things in the end."

"We'll keep hoping."

The vendors jostled for Lucy's attention. This time the strawberry-seller won. Lucy stretched out a hand toward the strawberries.

"I wouldn't do that if I were you," said Owen hastily, remembering.

• • •

The meeting had already gone on for some time. It was being chaired by Saunders, a Scot from the Ministry of Public Works, who was proceeding painfully slowly through the business, referring meticulously at every stage to a vast sheaf of papers assembled for him by the Coptic clerk to the committee, consulting at every turn the maps and diagrams spread out on the table in front of them. There was also Martin, another Scot, representing, however, the main contractors, Aird and Co., two civil servants from the Ministry, both Copts, Paul from the Consulate-General (what he was doing there Owen could not figure out) and Owen himself.

What *he* was doing there Paul alone knew. He had rung up Owen the day before saying there was a meeting he would like Owen to attend.

"But I don't know anything about that sort of thing," he had said.

"You don't have to. All you have to do is come in on cue."

"But I—"

"I'll tell you when. It will be pretty clear anyway."

"But what am I supposed to be saying?"

"You're supporting me. You're supposed to be the voice of political wisdom."

"I thought you were?"

"I am. But there are times when it is as well to have an independent voice saying the same thing. I'll meet you half an hour before the meeting and explain it to you."

But in the event Paul had been held up at the Consulate-General and there had been no time for him to give the briefing. He had slipped into his chair only the minute before the meeting started (much to Owen's relief) and had just had time to mutter to Owen "You support me," before the Chairman opened the meeting.

The subject of the meeting was the issuing of the remaining contracts for the next phase of construction at the Aswan Dam. The main ones had already been issued, mostly going to Aird and Co., but there were some subcontracts still to be placed for ancillary works. The most substantial of these was for the construction of a masonry apron downstream of the dam sluices.

"Of course we could do this at the same time as we're doing the others," said the man from Aird and Co.

"Haven't you got enough on your plate as it is?" asked the Chairman.

"There are advantages in doing the two together. There would be men and equipment already there."

"Would there be economies, then?" asked one of the civil servants.

"Oh, certainly."

"Would they be reflected in the tender price?"

"Up to a point, yes."

"That's funny," said Paul, "because the price Aird and Co. are tendering at is quite a bit higher than some of the other tenders we have received."

"You can always be undercut," said the man from Aird and Co., "by fly-by-night outfits. If you'll take my advice you'll have nothing to do with any of them."

"Dassin, Laporte et Lebrun are hardly a fly-by-night outfit," said Paul.

The man from Aird and Co. made a dismissive gesture.

"They've not been doing too well lately on some of their contracts in Turkey. Anyway, for a job like this it's experience in Egypt that counts. The Nile can be a tricky river."

"They're quite a lot cheaper," said one of the civil servants.

"Yes, but when you think of price you've got to think of quality too."

"We ought to be able to specify quality."

"Yes, but if you're underfunded you might not be able to deliver the quality in the time available. This is an important part of the works. We can't afford to have a delay in completion."

"I thought we were already running behind time on the main work?" said Paul.

"Oh, surely not," said the man from Aird and Co. "Not by much, anyway."

"Can we check?" asked Paul. "We've got the schedules there."

"I don't think we need bother," said the Chairman.

"I think if you give it to Aird and Co. you'll be pretty satisfied."

"We've certainly been satisfied up to now," said the Chairman.

"Yes," said Paul, "but there are other considerations."

"Really?"

"Political ones."

"I think you'll find," said the man from Aird and Co., "that there's a lot of support for Aird and Co. back home."

"I'm sure there is. But we have to take an international view."

"Do you? I'm not sure a lot of people at home would think that. Wasn't I reading in *The Times* just before I came out here that some questions have been asked in the House about the Foreign Office failing to support British industry abroad?"

"I hardly think Aird and Co. are in a position to complain of lack of support when they have landed the lion's share of the contracts."

"Ah, well," said the man from Aird and Co. with a broad smile, "quality will tell."

Paul smiled too.

"I think it does tell," he said, "and will go on doing so. All the same, it would be unfortunate if because of its very success Aird and Co. began to suffer through being too—exposed."

The man from Aird and Co. looked thoughtful.

"You think so?"

"A question of proportion—that is all."

"But such a small contract—comparatively—"

"Because it is small," said Paul, "that makes it all the better."

"Well, yes, that's certainly true, if you see it that way."

"You wouldn't have to give up much. And Aird and Co. might get quite a lot of benefit."

"You think so?"

"Yes."

"Well, we would wish to take a responsible view—"

"I'm sure you would. And it's because of that that I've brought Captain Owen along this morning. The Mamur

Zapt, I should explain, is responsible for law and order in the city. He will be able to tell us about some of the present tensions in Cairo, the political scene, Nationalist pressure—"

He paused invitingly.

Owen responded to his cue and talked briefly about the current political scene in Egypt: the growing strength of nationalism, the rise of the Nationalist Party, increasing resentment of foreigners ("Why, only recently they went so far as to kidnap a foreign businessman: a Frenchman, fortunately"), mounting hostility to wealth passing out of the country, as the Egyptians saw it, in the form of lucrative contracts awarded abroad. In this situation it was only too easy for unscrupulous interests, too often, regrettably, easily identifiable with foreign powers ("Shocking!" said Paul, "shocking!"), to stir up trouble.

"And the trouble with that," said Paul, coming in smoothly, "is that it could so easily have repercussions on agreed programs of development, which would be in no one's interest."

"Quite so," said the man from Aird and Co.

In the circumstances, Paul went on, it was only prudent to head off trouble, not to spoil the ship for a ha'porth of tar, to cast a little bread upon the waters, etc., etc. Paul, who despised clichés, was a master of them when he chose and felt the opposition deserved.

"Give the dogs a bone or two to fight over," said the man from Aird and Co.

"Exactly," said Paul.

The upshot was that the contract for constructing the masonry apron went to the French firm and another, smaller, contract to an Italian firm.

"Three countries involved, I don't think anyone can complain about that," said the Chairman.

"But not Egypt," said one of the civil servants.

"They're hardly ready yet," said the man from Aird and Co. "Give them a year or two, or perhaps a little longer, and they'll be among the tenderers."

"There may be an Egyptian tenderer sooner than you think," said the other civil servant.

"Oh?" The man from Aird and Co. was interested.

"If what I've heard is true."

"What have you heard?"

"There's a big deal in the offing. Egyptian interests only."

"I've not heard of a big deal," said the man from Aird and Co. "Are you sure?"

"It may be only talk."

"It would have to be a private development."

"I think it is."

"Public works is where the money is. Still, it would be interesting to know more."

"If I hear anything I'll tell you."

After the meeting Paul and Owen walked out together.

"Satisfied?" asked Owen.

"Greedy buggers, aren't they?" said Paul. "Yes, I'm satisfied. This will keep the French off our backs for a day or two. Want a drink? I'll buy you one. It will have to be somewhere close because I've got something I'm going on to. Shepheard's?"

•   •   •

In the bar they met the French Chargé. He waved to them in friendly fashion and pointed to his glass. "A drink?"

"My turn," said Owen. "Fortunately, Paul is buying this round."

"You ought to be buying me a drink," Paul said to the Chargé, "after what I've been doing for you this morning."

"I will buy you a drink," said the Chargé. "What have you been doing?"

"Giving Dassin, Laporte et Lebrun a contract, I hope," said Paul, waving the barman down.

The Chargé looked at him curiously. "Really?"

"Yes," said Paul. "What'll you have? The same again?"

"Yes, please. Funny," said the Chargé, "I thought... Well, I thought you were operating against us."

"Me?" said Paul. "I'm a Francophile at heart. And an Egyptophile. I'm every sort of phile except an Anglophile after a morning like this."

"You've obviously had a hard morning. But productive, I would say," said the Chargé, "and I certainly will buy you a drink when you've finished that one."

"How's Madame Moulin?" inquired Owen.

The Chargé pulled a face and drank deep.

"I'm waiting for her now. In fact, I'm waiting for her all the time. She's supposed not to move a step without me. But that means I can't move a step without her. It's terrible! It's killing me!"

He looked at Owen.

"I had hopes..." he said. "Look, you're not hiding Moulin yourself, are you? Because if you are, I beg of you, I plead with you—" he clasped his hands in mock prayer—"let him go, just for my sake, so that she will go away again!"

Paul pulled out his handkerchief and pressed it to his eyes.

"This is a pretty powerful plea," he said to Owen. "*Are* you holding him?"

"I wish I was," said Owen. "Then I could release him and we could *all* go home. I'll tell you what," he offered, "since it's for your sake, I'll try harder."

"Thank you," said the Chargé.

"Anyway," said Paul, "he's more interested in holding Zeinab."

"Zeinab!" The Chargé's eyes lit up. He put his hand on Owen's sleeve. "You can help me!"

"What, again?"

"I need a woman, an Egyptian woman."

"Well…"

"No, no. It's for Madame Moulin. She wants to meet some Egyptian women. How about dinner? You can come too. Tonight? Tomorrow? Please! She's driving me crazy."

The Chargé had a French cook. Consequently, an invitation to dinner was not something you lightly turned down. Moreover, it was very rare for Owen and Zeinab to be invited anywhere *à deux*. He was sorely tempted.

"Please!"

Owen made up his mind.

"It would be very nice. Thank you. We would love to come."

"Oh, thank you! Thank you a thousand times!" The Chargé drank his glass at a gulp and ordered another round immediately. "You don't know what this means to me."

Eventually, Paul definitely had to have gone and he and Owen got up together. As they turned to go the maître d'hôtel ran into the room. He made straight for Owen.

"Monsieur! Oh, Monsieur!"

"What is it?"

"Come quickly!"

"What is it, man?"

"Monsieur Cole-torp 'Artley. He has disappeared."

"Disappeared?"

"Like the other. Oh, Monsieur, a second one!"

8

The kidnapping of Colthorpe Hartley was not the same in all respects as the kidnapping of Monsieur Moulin. Like Moulin, Colthorpe Hartley had been on the terrace when it happened, but as it was just before lunch time and still very hot the terrace had been half deserted. Some people liked to take their drinks out there, the heat notwithstanding, but most preferred to retreat indoors into the shuttered shade. Colthorpe Hartley, however, always liked to sit out there while awaiting the return of his wife and daughter from their shopping expeditions.

"Always?"

"Yes," said Lucy Colthorpe Hartley. "We do something every morning and always try to get back just before lunch and Daddy is always waiting for us. He can't come with us himself, you know, he's not up to it. But he likes to sit and wait for us where he'll see us the moment we arrive. I think he misses us, even when it's just for the morning, especially since his stroke."

"It's pretty hot out there."

"He doesn't sit there for long. He knows when to

expect us and goes out about ten minutes before. And," said Lucy, trying to make a joke of it, "he's never once been late!"

"So when you didn't see him there today—"

"I knew something had happened to him. I thought perhaps—well, you know, there's always the risk in his condition. I rushed straight indoors because I thought he might be in his room. Then I ran down and asked one of the suffragis to try the Gents. Then I spoke to Monsieur Vincent in case he had fallen somewhere. Monsieur Vincent immediately got everyone looking and I went back out on to the terrace and told Mummy. We asked people on the terrace but they hadn't seen him. None of the waiters had either, though one of them thought he had definitely seen Daddy go out on to the terrace. We tried the arabeah-drivers, I mean, it's not very likely, but there was just a chance, but none of them had seen him either. And then Monsieur Vincent came out looking very grave and said he thought we should ring the police. And only then did I think—well, it's so unlikely, isn't it? I couldn't believe it. I still can't! Even when it's somebody sitting right beside you, like Monsieur Moulin, it's somehow remote, the sort of thing you read about in the papers but which never happens to you. It's as if you've got a great big wall around you and then suddenly the wall falls down and all sorts of horrible things are happening."

There was this difference, too, from the Moulin case, that the alarm was raised almost immediately. Colthorpe Hartley could have gone out on the terrace no more than a quarter of an hour before Lucy and her mother arrived and it could have been no more than a quarter of an hour later that Monsieur Vincent had rung the police.

And Owen had been on the spot all the time.

"At least you weren't out on the terrace," said Garvin sourly.

Gavin had come across straight away, arriving with McPhee. Owen had had time to get a message to them before they left telling McPhee to bring as many men as he could lay his hands on. As soon as they had arrived he had thrown a cordon around the hotel. It was probably locking the door after the horse had gone but there was a faint chance that Colthorpe Hartley might be hidden somewhere close and every chance had to be followed up.

McPhee, as before, organized the searching. His face was pale and pink and distressed. These things ought not to happen in his ordered world.

Garvin was tight-lipped and grim. Like Mahmoud, he had gone straight to the street-sellers. He had been a policeman in Egypt for years and knew not only the language but also how to talk to people.

Mahmoud himself arrived shortly after. When he was really concentrating he allowed himself little of the Arab expansiveness of gesture and talk which were characteristic of him normally. He was concentrating now. He listened to the manager's account of what had happened, nodded and went out to the terrace where he stood for some moments thinking. He saw that Garvin was questioning the vendors nearest the terrace and ignored them. After a moment he crossed the street and began to talk to people on the other side.

Owen had already questioned the hotel staff. The staff on Reception thought they had seen Colthorpe Hartley pass them on his way out to the terrace at about his usual time. He had collected a drink at the bar, the other end of the bar from where Owen had been talking with the Chargé, and then taken it outside. The bartender remembered this. The waiters had a half-impression of his being at a table but since he had made no demand on them had not really bothered to register his presence. There had been only a few guests out on the terrace and

they had seen or remembered nothing. When Owen
questioned them, though, their response was different
from what it had been when Moulin had disappeared.
This time there was a distinct uneasiness and a kind of
sudden shrinking. Owen knew what it was: fear.

Mrs. Colthorpe Hartley and Lucy had gone inside and
Mrs. Colthorpe Hartley was lying down. Lucy came down
to see them and tell him as much as she could, but then
she went back to be with her mother.

Word spread quickly. As guests came out of the dining-
room and sat down in the lounge areas to take their coffee
those already in the know brought them up to date.
Guests returning late from the bazaars were drawn aside
into the little groups that stood talking in the foyer or in
the bar. On the previous occasion the management of the
hotel had played everything down. There was no point in
doing that now. The managers themselves were searching
with their staff.

Owen checked the dragomans. They had all been out
that morning with various parties. As each party had
returned, in time for lunch, the dragoman had shepherded
its members up the steps and across the terrace and into
the hotel, where he had parted with them after effusive
farewells and pocketing his piastres. Then he had gone
down the corridor behind Reception and out into the
yard by the kitchens.

Owen went to the yard to check. It was a small area
hemmed in by the backs of buildings and reeked of
kitchen refuse. Nevertheless, it was highly regarded by
the hotel staff. This was because with high buildings all
around it there was permanent shade. At any time of the
day people could be found lying there. In the afternoon,
after lunch had been cleared away and the world was at
siesta, it was hard to find a space. By lunch time the
sleepers were gathering and the yard would normally have

been well occupied. All the local staff had been summoned, however, to help search the hotel. The dragomans, not strictly speaking staff members, would nevertheless have helped but Owen pulled them aside for the moment. They crowded around him, anxious and concerned.

"Another one? That will be bad for the hotel."

"It will be bad for us," said Osman. He had obviously been recumbent when the summons had come, for he had taken off his fez and skullcap. His hair was clipped and gray and stubbly, which gave him an oddly undressed look. Owen felt almost embarrassed and looked away. Osman felt the embarrassment too and covertly put on the small embroidered skullcap. "It will be bad for us, by God."

Abdul Hafiz, beside him, winced ever so slightly at his taking the name in vain.

"It is a bad thing to do," he said, "and bad men must have done it."

"I know the English ladies," one of the dragomans volunteered. "They were in my party. I like them. Especially the young one. She talks to me as if I were a person."

"What is your name?"

"Ismail."

"And were they in your party this morning, Ismail?"

"As always. I am their dragoman."

"They came back with you, then?"

"Yes. The young one ran on up the steps to speak with her father. She respects her father, even though he is strange."

"I like to see that," said Osman, who, Owen realized, now that he had seen his hair, was older than he looked.

"It is a good thing in children," asserted Abdul Hafiz. "Who does not respect his father respects no one."

"This English lady respects her father," said Ismail, "and so I am sad to see him taken."

"The English lady ran on ahead?"

"Yes. She usually does."

"How far ahead?"

"Not far. I saw her going into the hotel as I came to the foot of the steps."

"You followed her in with the rest of the party?"

"Yes. And then she came running down the stairs and spoke to her mother and her mother went pale and I thought: This is a bad business, surely. I thought perhaps the father had been taken ill and when the mother did not at once fly up the stairs to their room to tend him, I wondered. But then one said to me what the matter was and I understood."

"So what did you do then?"

"I thought the mother was going to be overcome so I helped her to a chair. I stood by for a little—I had not been paid—and then I thought: In distress one wants those near to one and not a stranger. So I left the ladies and came to the yard and told the others."

"Were you all here?" Owen asked the dragomans.

"I wasn't," said one of them. "We were late today. They wanted to spend more time in the House of Tsakatellis."

"You came after?" said Owen, noting the man.

"Yes. When I came Zaki Effendi was standing on the steps looking stern. I said to myself, there is trouble. But I thought perhaps they had found the body."

"The body?"

"Of the Frenchman. The one who was taken previously."

"The Frenchman is dead, then?" said Osman, aghast.

"I expect so."

"But you have not heard so?"

"Not yet."

"The rest of you," said Owen, trying to recover the thread, "were all here, then?"

"That is right."

"How long had you been here? Who was the last of you to arrive?"

"I was," said Ismail.

"No, not you. Before you."

"I was, I think," said Abdul Hafiz, doubtfully.

"No, I was," another dragoman corrected him. "Your party was still in the hall when I arrived, so I kept mine back."

"They came very nearly together."

"And when was this? How long before Ismail?"

The dragomans consulted.

"It was before Mohammed arrived, because we were all given bread."

"Except me," said Ismail.

"Well, yes," said Abdul Hafiz. "I was keeping your bread for you."

"We were early this morning," said Osman. "We usually have to keep the bread for two or three."

"We were early," the others agreed.

Owen would check the time of Mohammed's arrival independently. He would have been bringing them bread from the kitchens. The dragomans received no wages from the hotel, relying on what they made from their clients for income. The hotel, however, extended hospitality to them in the form of bread (and usually quite a lot of other things) in recognition of their being, as it were, part of its family and not part of another.

"And did none of you leave?"

They knew what he meant.

"None of us left," said Osman soberly. The others confirmed that with nods. If there had been doubt it would have been indicated.

"None of us had a hand in this," said Osman.

•   •   •

McPhee's meticulous searching failed to uncover any more sign of Colthorpe Hartley than it had of Moulin. Nor did Garvin's and Mahmoud's questioning produce anything.

"I find it incredible," said Garvin, "that a man could be kidnapped from the terrace of Shepheard's in full view of about a hundred people not twenty yards away without someone seeing something."

But no one apparently had. Colthorpe Hartley had disappeared from the face of the earth as completely as Moulin had.

More completely, for whereas on the first occasion Colthorpe Hartley himself had been able to report something, the presence of the unaccounted-for dragoman, on the occasion of his own disappearance no one had seen anything.

"And maybe there's a connection," said Garvin, frowning. "Maybe Colthorpe Hartley was taken just because he saw something. You said he was on the point of telling you, didn't you?"

"I wouldn't put it as strongly as that," said Owen. "He might have been on the point of remembering something. Something about the dragoman."

"How can you be on the point of remembering?" asked Garvin crossly. "You either remember or you don't."

"Not in Colthorpe Hartley's case. He's had an illness or something. It's left him a bit impaired. It's as if there are things at the back of his mind which don't quite reach the front."

"Jesus!"

"I can understand that," said McPhee seriously. "I'm like it sometimes. There's something at the back of my mind, I can't just put my finger on it, it's almost on the tip of my tongue but it just won't come. And then next day, perhaps, out it pops."

"You're bloody impaired too," said Garvin disgustedly.

"That's how it was with Colthorpe Hartley. He thought there was a chance of it popping out the next day."

"Did anyone else apart from you hear him say that?"

Owen thought.

"It was out on the terrace," he said.

"That's where you conduct your inquiries, is it? Out on the terrace where every bugger can hear?"

"He asked me to join him. I didn't know what he was going to say."

"But others could hear?"

"Yes," said Owen, remembering. "We were close to the railings. The vendors could have heard."

"Could have seen, too. *Should* have seen. Probably *did* see. We're back to them again."

"And to the dragoman, too, if that's what he was taken for."

But here Owen's inquiries, too, had shown a blank. He had checked Mohammed's delivery of the bread and had been able to establish the time precisely since the maître d'hôtel had intercepted him on his way. Mohammed had confirmed that all the dragomans, bar Ismail, had been in the yard. There was multiple independent confirmation of this, too.

"One of them could have slipped out," said Garvin.

Owen had done his best to check this too. Those in the yard were adamant that this hadn't happened. They had been having a particularly lively conversation and others besides the dragomans had been involved. If it was so lively, was the possibility not even greater that someone could have slipped out unnoticed? No, because they were all sitting up in a ring of about a dozen people and if anyone had got up the others would have seen. Besides, no one *did* get up because they were all too engrossed in what was being said. Owen could believe this at any rate since several of the participants, dragomans and nondragomans alike, had repeated large parts of the conversation word for word for his benefit.

In the end one couldn't be absolutely sure that no one had slid away unobserved, but Owen felt inclined to believe them. The dragomans, behind the parade they put on for the benefit of tourists, were serious, intelligent men. They understood exactly what effect this second kidnapping might have on the hotel's trade and indirectly on them. Besides, several of them were plainly shocked. They were involved with their clients and were upset that such a thing should happen to them. Their cooperation, he felt, was considered and genuine.

"If anyone had slipped away," said Osman quietly, "we would have seen them and we would tell."

Which was all very well, but where did it leave the inquiry?

"Right back at the beginning," said Garvin.

Right back at the beginning, very much as it had been on the day that Moulin disappeared. They had found out some things, but they were not things that appeared to lead anywhere. Berthelot was clearly up to something, but whatever he was up to was hardly likely to involve Colthorpe Hartley. The second kidnapping took them back to first facts, which were that Moulin had been kidnapped by a terrorist group called Zawia about which nothing was known beyond their name, and that they had declared themselves.

Not surprisingly, other people noticed the lack of progress; and fingers began to be pointed. They were pointed, obviously, at Owen.

"New in the country," he overhead someone say. "Still wet behind the ears. A good job they've brought Garvin in now."

Too trusting, was the charge. Even more deadly: "Too friendly with the Gyppies."

Increasingly, though, the fingers began to be pointed at Mahmoud. He was, after all, formally in charge of the investigation. "Not really his show," Owen's defenders maintained on behalf of Owen. But it was inescapably Mahmoud's show. He had been conducting the investigation since the hour of Moulin's disappearance and what results had he to offer? You need time for an investigation like this, the Parquet's defenders—and there were few of them in the British community—argued. "Gyppies always need time," was the reply. "The forever *bokra* boys."

Bokra. Tomorrow. Mañana. It was unfair on Mahmoud, who of all people was the most businesslike and undilatory. But then, people weren't thinking in personal terms. It wasn't Moulin and Colthorpe Hartley who had been attacked but foreigners in general, not Colthorpe Hartley as an individual but the British community in Egypt as a whole. Mahmoud was an Egyptian and that was enough.

Meanwhile, they had to get on with their work. Mahmoud went through his questioning as meticulously as before but with the same result. No one had seen anything or heard anything: not even, this time, the old snake charmer, who merely stood shaking his head as if totally confused.

Like Moulin, Colthorpe Hartley had disappeared "into thin air," as McPhee infuriatingly kept putting it.

The ransom note came and Lucy Colthorpe Hartley brought it out to them. It was in much the same terms as before and for the same amount. As before, it was signed "Zawia."

"A hundred thousand piastres," said Owen. "It's a lot of money, Miss Colthorpe Hartley. Can you pay it?"

Lucy hesitated.

"I suppose we can," she said, "if we sell a few things. A lot of things. Daddy isn't as well off as you might think. But ought we to pay it?"

Owen took his time about replying.

"No," said Mahmoud. "No, Miss Colthorpe Hartley, you should not pay it."

Lucy looked at him.

"I know you're right in principle, Mr. El Zaki. Still, when it's your own father..." She turned away and went back into the hotel.

"I wouldn't press her," said Owen.

"You see where you get if you give in," said Mahmoud savagely. "After Moulin, Colthorpe Hartley. Give in over him and there will be another. And another, and another, until people refuse to pay."

"Or until we catch them."

"We haven't made much progress so far." Mahmoud looked weary.

"Let's get out of here," said Owen.

They walked across the street and into the Wagh el Birket, where they found a table outside a restaurant.

"I don't understand it," said Mahmoud, pulling a chair into the shade and sinking down tiredly. "You usually come across a loose end, something you can pull and go on pulling."

"The loose end was the dragoman, wasn't it?"

"In the case of Moulin, yes. But even then, pulling it doesn't seem to have got us very far."

"It doesn't seem even a loose end so far as Colthorpe Hartley goes."

"Except in so far as he might have been about to identify the dragoman who spoke to Moulin."

"True."

The boy brought coffee and two large tumblers of iced water.

"There could be a dragoman in it," said Mahmoud, sipping the water first. "There's obviously someone involved who knows the hotel well. That's true for the latest one, too. Whoever took Colthorpe Hartley knew his habits well enough to be sure that he would be on the terrace at that particular time. So they'd have to be connected in some way with the hotel—"

"With the front of the hotel," said Owen. "That's all the knowledge they'd need. It could be someone on the street."

"A vendor? Yes. Though don't forget they also knew about Berthelot's visits to Anton's, which argues some inside knowledge. That's more likely to be a dragoman than a vendor."

"If it was a dragoman, though, would he be in Zawia?"

"Why shouldn't he be in Zawia?"

"If it's fundamentalist. Or nationalist."

"Look," said Mahmoud, "the only thing that makes you think it could be fundamentalist or nationalist is the name."

"Yes, but the names usually mean something."

"'The Bloody Hand?' 'The Evil Eye?' That means something?"

"'Revenge of Islam.' 'Free Egypt.' 'Sword for the Oppressors.' They mean something."

Mahmoud could not restrain his exasperation.

"The only thing that makes you think it's that sort of group is the name. And that could mean a variety of things. It doesn't just mean a convent or religious center. It means—"

"Turning point. I know."

"Corner."

"You turn the corner and you get to something different. A different way of life. Revolution."

"You still think it's nationalist, don't you?"

"I think it could be. Why else should it be aimed at foreigners?"

"It's *not* aimed at foreigners. Moulin and Colthorpe Hartley have been taken not because they're foreigners but because they're *rich*."

"They're rich and foreign. A good target."

"Tsakatellis—if he's anything to do with it and not someone dragged in by some crazy association of Nikos's—"

"Nikos is perceptive on these matters," said Owen coldly. Too coldly. He hadn't meant it to come out like that. "Anyway, doesn't Tsakatellis support my argument? He's foreign."

"He's not foreign!" Mahmoud made an angry gesture with his hand. Dismissive. Contemptuous.

"To an Islamic fundamentalist he's foreign."

"To a nationalist, too, I suppose?" Mahmoud suddenly boiled over. "Why are you so suspicious?" he shouted. "Why are you always so suspicious?"

"I'm not—"

"You don't trust us! You are like all the British. You don't trust Egyptians. You hate us!"

"For God's sake—"

Mahmoud leaped to his feet and pounded his fist dramatically upon his chest.

"You don't trust *me*! Your friend!"

Faces began to peer out of doorways. There was a succession of bangs as the shutters on the doors of the flats of the ladies of the night above began to be flung open.

"Sit down, for goodness' sake!"

"You are cold! Deep down you are like all the British. Cold!"

"Sit down. Just sit down."

"You drink coffee with me and then you do not trust me! Your friend."

"Of course I trust you, I wasn't talking about you. I was talking about Zaw—"

Mahmoud stormed off.

Owen was left agape. This kind of thing had happened before. It was not, in fact, untypical either of Mahmoud or of Arabs. But it always took him by surprise. Something would happen to upset them and then suddenly out of a clear blue sky you'd have a raging storm. The good thing was that it was likely to blow away as quickly as it had come. Even so...

You expected more sense from Mahmoud. This kind of thing was ridiculous. To fly off the handle over a thing like this! It was only a suggestion, damn it all, and not such a bad one at that. It was all very well for Mahmoud to go on about it just being to do with the name but the names terrorist groups chose for themselves often were significant. OK, some of the student groups chose names straight out of the *Boy's Own Paper*, they were very young after all, fifteen, sixteen, though that didn't stop them kidnapping and garrotting. But the names of the serious groups often really did tell you something about the groups. It was a sort of declaration of their allegiances and purposes. Nikos knew more about this sort of thing than Mahmoud did. It was all very well for Mahmoud to talk so dismissively of Nikos's crazy associations, but Nikos spent all his time dealing with Cairo's uneasy political underworld and knew the way it worked. Mahmoud was just a straight crime man.

Not only that, Mahmoud was hardly a neutral in these matters. He was himself a Nationalist. OK, the Nationalist Party was fairly moderate and committed to legitimate constitutional change, but it was often hard to draw the line between moderate nationalism, and the sort of crazy stuff that Owen often encountered. Mahmoud was a reasonable guy and thought that everyone else was a reasonable guy. Well, they weren't, they certainly weren't. For a start, anyone who kidnapped two elderly men from the terrace at Shepheard's was hardly moderate and committed to legitimate processes.

Why had they gone to the lengths of taking them from the terrace, anyway? It would have been much easier to have done it somewhere else, in the bazaars, perhaps.

OK, then you would have had to kidnap someone else because neither Moulin nor Colthorpe Hartley went to the bazaars, but if you were just after money it wouldn't really matter who you took, there were plenty of rich Europeans, or rich Egyptians, for that matter. They could have kidnapped Nuri, for a start. No, perhaps they'd better not take him, Christ knows how Zeinab would react, but there were plenty of others. It would have been easy. But to do it from the terrace at Shepheard's, in full view of everybody, that wasn't easy, in fact it was going out of your way to make it difficult. Why had they done that?

There could be only one answer. They had done it precisely because it *was* difficult, because it *was* in the public eye. They had wanted to show that it could be done, that all these fine people strutting up there on the terrace were just as vulnerable as anyone else. And why was it important to show that? Because those people up there were those who ruled, those who governed Egypt. OK, nor directly. They were merely representative. But what they represented were Britain and France.

That was it! Why Moulin? Because he was French. Why Colthorpe Hartley? Because he was British. Why Shepheard's? Because everyone could see.

You could strike back at the oppressors. That was the lesson. That was what they wanted to show. And they wanted to show it in the most conspicuous way possible. Shepheard's! The very symbol of foreign privilege! The terrace! The most conspicuous place in Cairo.

And if that wasn't a nationalist lesson Owen was a Dutchman.

Mahmoud was up the creek. For all that fancy French reasoning of his, he was missing the point. He had his blind spots and nationalism was one of them. There were some things he didn't like to face. The fact that there was a continuum between legitimate nationalist activity and illegitimate nationalist activity was something he could not accept.

Well, you could understand that. But it was a blind spot all the same. It meant there were some things you could work with Mahmoud on and some things you couldn't. That was the plain fact of it. He had gone on about trusting, made a big thing of it. Well, Owen did trust him, in that he believed him to be completely sincere and honest. He would stake his life on that. But that didn't mean accepting that he had no blind spots. Nationalism was one of them and on anything to do with nationalism, well, no, at the end of the day you couldn't trust him. That wasn't because he was disloyal or dishonest, it was just that, well, he couldn't be relied on. His judgment wasn't as good on that as it was on other things. He was too emotionally involved.

That was another thing. Mahmoud was too emotional. Underneath that cool, French, Parquet-style logic Mahmoud was still very much an Arab, emotional, intuitive, hypersensitive. Owen often thought he could understand Mahmoud, and perhaps Arabs in general, better than most Englishmen because he himself was not really an Englishman but a Welshman and Welshmen were supposed to be a bit like that themselves. Usually he got along well with Mahmoud but there were times...

He sighed and sipped his coffee. On the opposite side of the street little boys were putting out tables for the evening. The cafés on that side of the street filled up in the evenings because the tables gave a good view of the ladies of the night in the rooms above Owen. They bent over the balconies in their filmy gowns, giving observers opposite a great deal more pleasure, Owen suspected, than they actually obtained when they plucked up enough courage to cross the street and go inside.

Why had Mahmoud chosen this moment of all moments to fly off the handle, just when it was particularly necessary to keep a clear head? OK, he had been working hard and it was damned hot and he was probably a bit on edge anyway. Maybe he'd heard some of the criticism. Well, Christ, Owen had heard some of the criticism too. You had to put up with these things. It was no good being thin-skinned.

Of course, it wasn't so easy for an Egyptian, there were other things in it as well for them, the fact that the British were their bosses and foreigners, for instance. It wasn't easy to take—he didn't find it easy himself, that bit about Garvin coming in over him for a start—but you hadn't got to let it rattle you. You just had to get on with the job. God knows, they weren't doing too well in that line just at the moment.

The thought came to him that maybe that was why Mahmoud was so rattled. It wasn't like him, though.

Then another thought struck him. Perhaps the reason why Mahmoud had blown his top was that he had not wanted to admit, not even to himself, that there might be truth in what Owen had said, that there was, indeed, a nationalist connection.

The thought occurred to other people, too. Along with the earlier whispers about Mahmoud came a new one. If Mahmoud was so good, why hadn't he found out more? Because he wasn't trying to, came the answer.

9

Owen's relations with the Army were not universally unfriendly. He sometimes played tennis with one of the Commander-in-Chief's aides-de-camp and had been doing so that afternoon. Afterward they had gone to the bar. This was not purely a matter of conviviality. Playing in that heat meant that the body lost water heavily and it was necessary to replenish it. They were, in fact, drinking pints of lemonade, which was certainly not the case with all the other people in the bar at the Sporting Club.

Among these was a group of young Army officers. They included Naylor. He and Owen nodded to each other politely and Naylor looked curiously at John, whom he knew to be a pukka Army officer and therefore, in his view, surprising company for the Mamur Zapt. One of the other subalterns actually knew John and it was not long before they were drawn into a common conversation.

"Bad show, this kidnapping business," one of the group remarked to Owen, on learning from John who his companion was. "How are you getting on?"

"Slowly."

"Not easy," said the other sympathetically, "not with all these Egyptians having a finger in the pie."

Owen muttered something noncommittal.

"Is it true that the Senussi are involved?" another officer asked.

"The Senussi?" said Naylor.

"So I've heard. I'm sure you're in a better position to answer that, though, than I am, sir."

He turned politely to Owen. The Mamur Zapt, he vaguely knew, was something to do with Intelligence. Besides, Owen was senior.

"There have been rumors, yes."

"I thought the Senussi were desert people," said someone.

"They are. That's why the rumors are unlikely to be true."

"They have contacts in the main cities, though, don't they?" said the subaltern who had first asked about the Senussi. "I've been reading about them in the latest batch of newspapers from London. There's a new book just come out. Caused quite a stir. It's reviewed in all the papers."

"Which book was that?"

"*The Grand Senussi Conspiracy,* it's called. The chap who wrote it actually spent some time in the Senussi convents at Siwa."

"Convents?" said Owen.

"That's what they call them. Sort of religious centers."

"They've been quiet since the last time we gave them a dusting," said an officer who hadn't previously spoken.

"Yes, but that doesn't mean they've given up," said the eager young subaltern who had read all about it. "According to this chap, they've got tentacles all over the place. Chop one off and they merely stretch out another."

"The French have more to worry about than we have," said John.

"Yes, they're strong in Tunisia and Morocco, of course. But this chap says they've got ambitions all over North Africa. And Egypt, he says, is a special target."

"Suez," said one of the young men knowledgeably.

"India," said another.

"Yes, they could threaten our supply routes, all right." The subalterns looked grave.

"And you think they could be behind these kidnappings, sir?" one of them asked Owen.

"No, no, no. Highly unlikely."

"But I've heard—" said the first young officer doggedly.

"Just a possibility."

"All the same—"

"I don't think Captain Owen wants to say any more just now, Stephens," one of the others, more senior, cut in.

"Oh, I see. Sorry, sir!" said Stephens, abashed.

"I think we all understand, sir," said the more senior one, turning to Owen. "You can count on us."

"Well, it's not quite—"

"The civilians. We understand, sir."

"The civilians. Of course!" said the others.

"Don't want them to get rattled," said someone.

"We won't say a word. You can rely on us. But when you need us—"

"We will be ready," someone finished for him.

"Thank you," said Owen, at a loss.

John led him out, leaving the subalterns gathered in a tight group, heads all together, quiet but buoyant.

"What the bloody hell's all this?" asked John, the moment he got Owen outside.

"I didn't say anything!" Owen protested.

"Yes, but is there anything in it?"

"No!" Owen told him.

"Nothing much to go on," said John. "In fact, bloody

nothing to go on. Hope it doesn't get around, though. The Army twitches whenever it hears the word 'Senussi.'"

•   •   •

The Army twitched. Owen's phone never stopped ringing. He was asked by all and sundry for "appraisals" of the Senussi threat. Losing his patience—Mahmoud wasn't the only one who was volatile—he took to referring them to Army Intelligence as this was an Army matter. Ah yes, said some of the inquirers, but what about the civilian threat? What civilian threat? said Owen, and banged the phone down.

Curiously, the whole business redounded to Owen's credit. The Mamur Zapt, it was well known, was a deep one. If he denied something you could be sure he had his reasons for doing so. Of course he wouldn't let on. You couldn't expect him to. He kept a cool front, went to the opera, went to the Club as usual, played tennis. But behind the scenes he was very active.

He was, for instance, in close touch with the Sirdar. Not directly, of course, he was too wily for that, but he had been seen playing tennis with one of the Sirdar's aides. You could make of that what you would! The Army, certainly, was making preparations.

Owen knew what he was doing, there was no doubt about that. But he had his problems. Those damned Gyppies! Could they be relied upon? Take those kidnappings: there was talk that the Senussi were involved, and certainly the Mamur Zapt was taking quite an interest in them. But the Parquet's investigation hadn't got very far, and why was that? It was because when you got down to it those damned Gyppies weren't sure whose side they were on. How hard were they trying? Did they want to clear things up? Or were they content not to press things too hard, not wanting to rock the boat so far as the Senussi were concerned in case there might come a time when it would be politic to have been friends with Senussi agents.

The word "Senussi" was on everyone's lips. How it came there Owen could not be sure. But wherever he went he couldn't escape it.

When he went to Shepheard's, for example, to check with Mahmoud how things were going (Mahmoud wasn't there), he saw Lucy Colthorpe Hartley on the terrace and went out to have a word with her. She was talking to Naylor and Owen overheard part of their conversation.

"It's the Senussi, you see," he heard Naylor say as he approached.

"The Senussi?"

"They're a sect, a great Mohammedan sect, based out in the Sahara. In fact, to all intents and purposes, they control it. They French have no end of trouble with them. Tunisia, Morocco, Libya—they're strong in all of them. And they've got their eyes on Egypt. Well, they'll find us a harder nut to crack than the French, I can assure you. We'll be ready for them! Just let them come our way and we'll give them what-for!"

"Yes, but how exactly—I mean, poor Daddy—"

"Oh, they're behind it."

"But why should they pick on poor Daddy?"

"Money. They need money to buy arms. And to finance their filthy propaganda."

"And so they kidnap Daddy?" Lucy glanced up. "Oh, hallo, Captain Owen. Do come and join us. Gerald was telling me about the Senussi."

"Yes, that's right," muttered Naylor, a little embarrassed.

"I'm sure you know all about the Senussi, Captain Owen."

Owen had no intention of entering into competition.

"A little. But there's no real evidence that they have any

connection with your father's disappearance, Miss Colthorpe Hartley."

"Just a possibility," muttered Naylor, backing off shamefacedly.

"I've heard of the Senussi," said Lucy unexpectedly. "Aren't they very fanatical?"

"They're very strict in their behavior. They are not allowed to smoke or drink or even take coffee, which is quite a hardship for an Arab, Miss Colthorpe Hartley. They have to give up all things of the flesh—"

"Oh dear!" said Lucy.

"—and that includes such things as dancing—"

"I don't think I'd like that."

"—and conjuring."

"Gracious!"

"All levity. That would be a blow for you, Miss Colthorpe Hartley!"

"Thank you."

"They are forbidden to have any dealings with Christians. That includes doing business with them, buying things from Christian-owned shops, even talking to Christians."

"That is puzzling," said Lucy, wrinkling up her nose. "I thought you and Mr. El Zaki were sure that it was someone working at the hotel. If they were doing that, how could they be Senussi?"

"They needn't be Senussi themselves," Naylor broke in. "They could just be an accomplice. And it's not just one. They're all in it, you know, the whole pack of them."

"Yes," said Lucy. "I remember you saying that before. Do you think they have an accomplice in the hotel, Captain Owen?"

"They could have. But actually it wouldn't be necessary to go outside the Senussi orders for that. A certain category of Senussi is permitted dealings with Christians.

For business purposes only, of course. They're called Wekils."

"And you think there could be a—a Wekil on the hotel staff?"

"I don't think we have to assume that there's necessarily any Senussi connection at all, Miss Colthorpe Hartley."

"Quite," said Naylor, remembering that he was not supposed to be alarming the civilians. "Quite so. You mustn't be alarmed, Lucy. The Army is here to protect you."

"If the Army is all like you, Gerald, dear," said Lucy, "I am sure I feel greatly encouraged."

•   •   •

There were fourteen for dinner at the Chargé's. There were two couples from the French consulate, another couple from the Italian, Owen and Zeinab, Madame Moulin and the Chargé, a Syrian businessman and his wife, who hardly said anything the whole evening, and a visiting American lady who spoke a great deal, which served Paul right, who was supposed to be looking after her.

Madame Moulin had taken a fancy to Zeinab and after dinner motioned to her to come and sit down on the chaise longue beside her. The Chargé had gone Arab to the extent of having dispensed with chairs and the guests sat around on cushions. In deference to senior visitors, however, which would shortly include his mother, who was, he informed Owen, very demanding, he had acquired a low chaise longue. Zeinab swept elegantly across the room and soon she and Madame Moulin were chatting happily away.

French was, actually, the language Zeinab naturally spoke. The Egyptian upper class was thoroughly French in style. The children grew up speaking French and went to French schools; the women took their fashions direct from Paris; the men used French rather than Arabic in their normal intercourse at work. It was customary for wealthy Egyptian families to spend some part of each year in France, either on the Riviera or, more often, since Egyptians were unimpressed by mere sunshine, in Paris. They read French newspapers, went to the French theater, enjoyed French music (not Arabic) and Italian opera, collected French paintings.

They also brought back to Cairo a taste for French-style conversation and the level of intellectual discussion was much higher among educated Cairenes than it was in the expatriate communities. The bright young men around the Consul-General and the Sirdar were much more at home in these French-speaking native Egyptian circles than they were among the stolid English. Paul was often in despair after another dour evening with the British élite and greatly preferred the company he met at Samira's. The only drawback was that even at the most elevated levels you were unlikely to meet women on equal terms. The Ministers all preserved their harems. Even a person as free-thinking as Nuri Pasha, Zeinab's father, would never think of inviting his wife or wives to a gathering such as the present one. It was only in circles where there was a combination of wealthy, relative youth, and a slight Bohemian flavor that women would be present who were at all emancipated.

Zeinab, who was as strong-willed as her father and as independent as her mother, a famous courtesan who had rejected Nuri's itself emancipated proposition of a formal place in the harem, found only a few circles in which she was acceptable, so she rather enjoyed social occasions like the present one.

Madame Moulin, whose shoulders bore, though at a

certain remove, some of the burden of the French Presidential mantle, was glad of the opportunity to talk to one of the daughters of France's dominion abroad. She still considered Egypt part of that dominion, believing the present to be merely a temporary hiccup in the natural process of historical continuity. As with many French people, her imperialism took a cultural form and she was delighted to find so striking an example of exported French culture as Zeinab. Indeed, she was a little daunted, for Zeinab was more Parisian than she was. Her clothes rather exposed the provincial character of Madame Moulin's own dress and they were worn with an elegance which, Madame Moulin assured her, could be found only in Paris.

Zeinab appeared to lap this up, though that could well have been just politeness, for Zeinab took all this pretty much for granted. She was, however, intrigued by Madame Moulin's description of domestic Provençal life, which seemed to her as exotic and, it must be confessed, unsophisticated as that of the Shilluk tribes in the furthermost reaches of the Sudan.

After a while Madame Moulin beckoned Owen over.

"You have a beautiful fiancée," she informed him.

Taken by surprise at this sudden formalization of their relationship, he found himself falling back on the Chargé's "Naturally. Naturally." He stole a glance at Zeinab's face. It was expressionless.

"I certainly think so," he said.

The French made much less fuss about the nature of relationships, whether formal or informal, than the English did. It was part of their general belief that whoever shared the French culture was French. It was quite all right, therefore, for a white to marry a black, or, in this case, a brown a brown.

"What is important," declared Madame Moulin, "is character."

Zeinab, puzzled, was half inclined to take this as a personal reflection.

The Chargé, overhearing, thought that Madame Moulin was getting at him again.

She was, however, thinking about the unfortunate Berthelot.

"He should have been in the Army," she said, looking at Owen. "It would have made a man of him."

Now it was Owen's turn to feel uncomfortable.

"*Comment?*" said Zeinab, at a loss.

"Berthelot!" said Madame Moulin firmly. "This gambling of his. It is weakness of character. It runs in the family. On Moulin's side. How many times have I told Moulin not to encourage him! But he took no notice. I told him again last year when Berthelot came. 'To go is to encourage him,' I said. But go he would."

"To Cairo?" Owen hazarded.

"No, no!" said Madame Moulin impatiently. "To Cannes. Last year. When Berthelot came. He wanted Moulin to go back with him. 'At your age!' I told Moulin. 'You ought to know better.'"

"Monsieur Moulin was going there to play?"

"What else does one go to Cannes for?" asked Madame Moulin scornfully.

• • •

Nikos knocked on the door discreetly and stuck his head in.

"He's here now," he said.

"OK, show him in."

A stocky, gray-haired figure in a white galabeah but

without either turban or fez came into the room. He was carrying a skullcap, which he fingered uneasily.

"Greetings, Sidky," said Owen.

The man looked uneasy at this familiarity with his name but responded with the usual courtesies. Nikos took up position against the wall, from where he could see the man's face. It was Nikos who had found out the details.

Owen motioned Sidky to a chair, on which he perched uncertainly, as if the object and situation were new to him.

"You have good fields, Sidky. What crops! Peas, beans, cauliflowers, pumpkins, mangoes, figs! And the watermelons! I have never seen such big ones."

"The earth is good," said Sidky modestly.

"It is good because it is well-watered."

"Mother Nile has been kind to us."

"Such a plot must be highly sought after. Was it always in your family?"

"Since my great-grandfather's time. The plots were small then. There was not much on that side of the river then—just the fields along the river and around the villages."

"The other water that builds a plot is the sweat of the men that work it. For many years now it has been your family's sweat that has watered the fields."

"True," assented Sidky.

"Then why do you wish to sell your land now, Sidky? It is good land and you are not a poor man."

Sidky seemed troubled. He stared at the ground and fumbled with his skullcap. After a while he raised his head and looked at Owen.

"It *is* good land," he said, "and my family's land. I had not thought of selling it. But one came to me and said, 'That is good land and I will pay you well for it, Sidky.' 'That may be,' said I, 'but you will not pay me what the

land is worth to me.' 'I wouldn't be so sure, Sidky,' the
man said; and he named a figure which took my breath
away."

"Who was that man, Sidky?"

"You know the man," said Sidky, glancing at Nikos.
"Otherwise I should not have told you. Izkat Bey."

"Did he tell you what he wanted the land for?"

"He wanted to build there."

"Building is fine," said Owen, "but it seems a waste of
such good land."

"That is what I told him. 'If you want to build,' I said,
'there is plenty of land for that. Try Rhoda Island.' I know
about the island," Sidky explained, "because my camels
carry rubble for the building works there. That is why I
am rich. It is not the farming. Farming is an honest trade
and my fields yield well, but there is no money in it. With
the money I made from farming I bought camels and
with the camels I carry rubble. That is how to make
money."

"And you have made enough money to be able to move
away from your village and into the city."

"I sometimes think that was a mistake. My wife tells me
it was. She preferred the village. She would still like to go
back there. And perhaps we will one day."

"It will not be the same. Especially if Izkat Bey builds
on your land."

Sidky shrugged. "I am getting old now," he said. "My
days of working are past. We have not been blessed with
sons, so there is no one to work the land after I am gone.
It would have to be sold anyway. My daughters' husbands
could work the land but they are not that sort." Sidky
stared sadly at his cap. "I have three daughters," he said
to Owen. "Three!"

"Three!" said Owen in commiseration. "And no sons?"

"No sons."

"For a man such as you," said Owen, "the dowries expected would have been considerable."

"They were," Sidky agreed fervently. "And still they expect more! It is my daughters now. 'Our children will need providing for,' they say. 'Sell the land! Then after you have gone you will know that your grandchildren and their children and their children's children will be able to hold up their heads with honor.'"

"Honor is not just how much money you have."

"Try telling them that!" The wrinkled face broke into a smile.

"How many grandchildren have you?" asked Owen, laughing.

"None so far."

Nikos disapproved of this levity.

"Have you any idea what is to be built?" he asked.

Sidky shook his head.

"No," he said.

"Izkat Bey already has a fine house. Surely he does not need another?"

"A man like Izkat Bey needs a grand house in the city. This is too far out."

"Then what does he intend?"

"In this he speaks for others."

"What do they intend? To build and sell?"

"No. I asked him that. They wish to build and keep."

"And you have no idea what they wish to build and keep?"

"I know only that it is good that it is by the river."

"Why is that?" asked Owen. "I could understand if they were going to keep and farm. But to keep and build!"

Sidky hesitated.

"They spoke of coming and going by water. They said it would be more secret that way."

"I do not understand."

"Nor I," said Sidky, "but I do understand the money they have offered."

When Sidky had left, Nikos came back into the room.

"I do not understand," he said. "Are they going to build a brothel? Someone like Izkat Bey? With the Khedive behind him?"

"The Khedive is not interested in brothels," said Owen, as the glimmerings of an idea came to him.

● ● ●

It was still early in the morning and the stonework of the terrace was deliciously cool to touch. In another twenty minutes or so the sun would come creeping over it and then the stone would warm very quickly until by midday it would give your hand quite a burn if you touched it. Just now, though, the sun was on the other side of the Street of the Camel, warming up the inferior donkey-boys opposite.

There was, of course, no one on the terrace but from inside the hotel came wafts of coffee as breakfast was served to the early risers. There were few street-vendors in evidence yet—the snake charmer had arrived but had not yet let the snake out of its basket—and the arabeah-drivers were still asleep in their cabs, but the donkey-boys, the superior ones on this side of the street, were already stirring.

A heavily laden forage camel came along the street and stopped beside them. Two of the donkey-boys helped the driver to release its load and then, as the berseem fell to the ground, took forks and spread it for the donkeys.

One of them looked up at Owen standing on top of the steps.

"I wouldn't stand there if I were you," he said. "You might disappear!"

The donkey-boys fell about laughing.

Lucy Colthorpe Hartley came out of the front door of the hotel.

"Hello," she said. "You do start early!"

"So do you, Miss Colthorpe Hartley."

"I haven't been sleeping too well," she said.

"How is your mother?"

Lucy made a grimace. "She's rather shattered, poor dear. The doctor gave her some pills last night to help her to sleep but they didn't work, not for a long time. She was tossing and turning half the night. I thought she'd never get to sleep. I knew there wasn't much point in me trying to go to sleep so I *did* get up."

The smell of fried onions drifted up to them. It didn't come from the hotel but from further along the terrace where, squatted in a circle down in the street, the donkey-boys were having their breakfast.

Lucy turned and faced him.

"Are you getting anywhere?" she asked.

"No," he answered honestly.

She sighed.

"I'm not blaming you," she said. "I know it's hard. Still it's puzzling. Is there anything in this Senussi business?"

"There may be."

"You wouldn't be holding out on me, would you?"

"No."

"It's the thought of—well, that they may not be amenable to reason."

"I don't think you need assume that."

"If they were terribly fanatical—"

"They may not be Senussi. And even if they were, that doesn't mean they're not amenable to reason."

"It's the way they've played with poor Monsieur Moulin, first agreeing, then not agreeing."

"There could be a lot of reasons for that."

"Yes."

She looked along the terrace. The vendors were beginning to appear. Some of them, noticing her interest, showed their goods half-heartedly in her direction.

"I come out here every morning," she said, "while I'm waiting for Mummy to come down to breakfast. Of course Daddy gets down about an hour later. I like to come out here, though, while it's still fresh and cool. It's one of the nicest times of the day in Egypt. That and the evening. It doesn't feel the same now, though. I keep telling myself that when Daddy gets back it will be the same again, but I don't think it will. I don't think it ever will."

She turned to go back into the hotel. Owen went in with her, looking for Mahmoud. He was anxious to make things up. He didn't feel himself to blame, not in the least, but he knew from experience that he would have to make the first move. It was harder for Mahmoud to unbend, perhaps because his Arab pride was involved, than it was for Owen. He knew he would only have to make a conciliatory sign and Mahmoud would come down at once from his high horse.

Mahmoud, however, was nowhere to be found. It was unlike him. Usually he arrived at the job early and stayed late. Perhaps he was working somewhere else.

Owen needed to talk to him anyway. He had become convinced that a possible key at least to Moulin's disappearance and perhaps to Colthorpe Hartley's, too, lay in the unidentified dragoman. He had felt, especially in the conversation with the strawberry-seller and the flower-seller, that he was on the verge of getting somewhere. There was already a difference between their account of what happened on the terrace and that of the filthy-postcard-seller, and he felt that given a little more time he might be able to expose it and drive the postcard-seller into a corner. However, he didn't want to go in too hard, as that would confuse the strawberry-seller and flower-seller and scare the filthy-postcard-seller; but nor did he want to go in too soft as, judging by the previous conversation, it would be only too easy to get lost in the labyrinthine confusion and vagueness of the vendors' responses. What he needed was some guidance from Mahmoud and Mahmoud was nowhere to be found.

He went back to his office and tried ringing Mahmoud in his. Mahmoud was "out." There was something funny about the reply. Owen hoped that didn't mean the Parquet was getting uptight about the situation.

On the whole the Parquet got on fairly well with the British Administration, but it was more independent than the other Departments and Ministries. Since the law was essentially French and based on the Napoleonic Code there was less opportunity for the British Adviser to exercise influence and the Minister in charge, an Egyptian, had correspondingly more autonomy.

The Minister of Justice was, therefore, a politically sensitive appointment. The Khedive used it to test out the limits to which the British intended to use their power and the more extreme British saw it as an organizational anomaly which needed removing. Something like the kidnapping could easily bring things to a head.

The kidnappings could easily bring a lot of things to a head. The Army, for instance, was eager to challenge the authority of the civil administration. A Senussi threat, with its suggestion of military danger, could provide the pretext for the exchange of a military for a civil administration. Owen didn't think there was a Senussi threat, not on that scale, anyway, but that's not how it would be seen either among the British community in Egypt or in Whitehall. The civil administration would have to show that it was on top of things.

He, the Mamur Zapt, would have to show that he was

on top of things. And he bloody wasn't. He was far from being on top of things. In fact, he couldn't even think how to start so far as these damned kidnappings were concerned. What was it Mahmoud had said? That usually there was some loose thread. You could pull it and out would come all sorts of other things which you could follow up. In the end one of them would lead to a solution.

But where were the loose ends here? That bloody dragoman.

Where the hell was Mahmoud? He needed to talk to him.

The telephone rang.

"What are you doing?" asked Paul. "Stewing?"

"Yes."

"Me, too. We had the Sirdar here the whole of yester-day morning. And then the Khedive rang saying he wanted to give the Old Man an audience that evening! Evening! The Khedive doesn't normally give audiences in the evening. He doesn't do anything in the evening, very sensibly, and nor do we. The Old Man was very cut up about it. Still, he thought he'd better go. It was the same thing. SOMETHING MUST BE DONE."

"Look—"

"I know, I know," said Paul soothingly. "It's a hot day and you've been working bloody hard and the fact that you haven't got anywhere isn't your fault, etc., etc. Anyway, I wasn't talking about that. Well, not directly. The point is, the Army must be fobbed off. Otherwise we'll all be kicked out and that wouldn't do at all. So—you're not going to like this, but it had to be done, and I'm just ringing up to tell you it's being done—we have to offer up a sacrifice."

"Me?"

"No. Well, not yet. Mahmoud."

"It's not his fault."

"Of course it's not. He's an amiable, hard-working soul who does his best for us, which is more than we deserve. We'll make it up to him later. But the Army's got to have blood. Well, you'd expect that of the Army, wouldn't you? Heads must roll. And what better head to roll than that of an Egyptian—the Egyptian in charge of an investigation which is getting nowhere. There would," said Paul, "be a case for putting someone else on it anyway."

"I don't think so."

"I knew you wouldn't like it."

"You're bloody right I wouldn't."

"I," said Paul, "am not exactly happy about it."

"Yes, but it doesn't *matter* so much to you as it does to Mahmoud."

"The important thing," said Paul, "is not to let the Army take over. If they take over the Administration it would be a disaster. Not just for me, although naturally that is a consideration. For Egypt. For, well, rationality, which is, really, the only thing in the end which can keep the world ticking over without blowing itself apart."

"What about Mahmoud?"

"He's got a job. He'll still have a job. He's just being taken off this one case. It will probably do him no end of good in his career. Someone who's been victimized by the British! His bosses will like him, the Minister will smile on him. He will certainly be promoted. He'll do much better than if he goes on working along happily with you. It is the way of the world, my friend. Just thought I'd let you know."

Shortly afterward, Garvin called Owen in.

"Mahmoud's been taken off the case," he said.

"Yes."

"You know?"

"Yes. Who's replacing him?"

"No one from the Parquet. They're out of it. This is no longer an ordinary criminal matter. It's a question of public law and order. *Order*."

"You mean—"

"You're responsible for order in Cairo, aren't you? Then you're responsible for this. Formally, I mean. From now on it's all yours."

• • •

Owen sat in his office, too numb to think. He wasn't bothered about the responsibility, in a way he'd accepted that already. All Garvin was doing was landing him with it formally, making bloody sure that he himself was covered. Well, Owen didn't mind that, it was the kind of thing you expected. Owen didn't like being landed with formal responsibility, he supposed no one did. What he preferred to do was work behind the scenes, take responsibility, yes, but in an indirect, shared kind of way. Yes, that was it, shared. He liked to share it with Mahmoud. Mahmoud took over responsibility for running the case, Owen chipped in where he could. That worked well. It had worked well in the past.

He couldn't evade the thought, though, that what he had just told himself was a cop-out. What he was saying was that Mahmoud was the one who really carried the can. Had carried it this time.

• • •

Georgiades came into the office. He stopped when he saw Owen's face.

"OK?"

Owen nodded.

"What is it?"

"I've done what I said I would," said Georgiades, "had a look at the Tsakatellis business. Talked to the family. Not just to the old woman. My God, she terrifies me. Reminds me of my mother."

"Do all Greek women get like that?"

"Yes. It's what stopped me from getting married."

"I felt sorry for the daughter-in-law."

"Feel sorry for all Greek daughters-in-law. This one particularly."

"Did you talk to her?"

"Yes. And to her daughter. That's quite an experience. Fourteen years old and already shaping up to be like her grandmother. She's the one who's putting stiffening into her mother. Though her mother, in her timid way, is pretty game. Unbeknown to the old lady, they've been negotiating with the gang. All by themselves."

"Negotiating?" said Owen. "What about? What are you saying?"

"Tsakatellis isn't dead."

10

Not dead?"

"That's right. Or so his wife believes."

"Well, yes, but surely—"

"She's deluding herself? She doesn't think so. And I'm not sure I think so either."

"Then how—"

"They got the note, remember? Which the old woman showed to the police. The second note, the one with the demand for paying the ransom, never came. The old woman thought that meant they'd found out, about her going to the police, I mean. She thought she'd killed her son."

"Hadn't she?"

"No. At least, I don't think so. You see, the second note *did* come, only this time it was the wife who intercepted it. Or her daughter, that sharp little Rosa. They didn't show it to the old grandmother. They thought she'd say no. So they decided to handle it themselves."

"You mean they paid?"

"Have been paying. Are paying. They couldn't do it in one go. They haven't the money. It's tied up in the business and the old woman keeps a tight hold on that. So they had to do it a bit at a time. Sell off some of the wife's jewels each week. They're down to the clothes now."

"Christ! What do they do when the money runs out?"

"You don't ask that kind of question. In the end they'll have to go to the old mother. That's what the girl wants to do. The wife can't bring herself to just yet. There's such a lot riding on the outcome that she wants to put off bringing it to a head. She'd rather live in uncertainty than be certain the wrong way. The girl says there's no question about it going the wrong way. She'll kill the old lady herself—yes, Christ, and she means it, too! You don't know these Greek families. What with damping her down and being terrified of the old lady and yet being determined to do what she can for her husband, the wife's falling to bits."

"Bloody hell!"

"I thought you might like to meet them."

"Well, yes, I would."

"OK. I'll set it up."

They met in a public gardens by the river where the Greek girls were practicing their dancing. They were rehearsing for Easter Monday when they would be joined in the traditional national dances by the young men, at present rehearsing elsewhere, and the older young women, who didn't need to practice because they knew the dances so well already.

Georgiades pointed out Rosa to Owen. She was one of the oldest and tallest of the girls, imperious with the littler girls, demanding equality with the adult young women assisting the teacher. There was a slight gawkiness about her which showed up in the dance they were presently performing, which involved them ebbing and flowing in a long line and required a girlish gracefulness. The teacher pulled her out and made her dance the part of the boy, which suited her better, demanding assertion and retreat against the withdrawal and advance of the line of girls.

The pattern of the dance suddenly changed and now the initiative came from the boys. The music became staccato, fiery. Rosa responded at once. Gracefulness was clearly a strain; of fire she had plenty.

When the dance ended she rejoined her mother, who was clapping her hands rhythmically in the shade of a bougainvillaea bright with flowers. Owen could tell at once that she was the girl's mother. Both were tall and thin and had the special fairness of the Greeks. As he came up to them he saw that both had gray eyes. The mother was beautiful, the girl showed promise of it.

Georgiades introduced them. There was a general break for picnic. Mothers and daughters sat down on the grass and opened baskets with lemonade and sweet cakes. The littlest children ran off and played games among the bamboos. The dance had been accompanied by a bass viol and two fiddles played by men in national costume, who sat down under a cabbage tree and thankfully pulled off their boots.

The mother could hardly bring herself to look at Owen. She stared down into the basket and played nervously with the contents. She had long, thin, pale fingers which were never still.

"It is a long time now," said Owen gently.

"Yes."

"During that time, have they ever shown you your husband?"

"No." She knew what he was thinking. "But I know he lives," she said defiantly.

"I wondered if by chance they held him in the place to which you take the money."

"I do not think so," she said softly.

"Could you ask to see him? It is just that if they agreed to bring him, he might be freed."

"No!" she caught her breath. "It's too risky! He might be killed!"

"It is a long time and growing longer."

"They would not bring him," said the daughter definitely.

"You are sure? Have you tried?"

The mother could not manage to speak. Her fingers tightened round one of the bottles and she shook her head determinedly.

"You see," said Owen, as gently as he could, "they go on asking for money until they are stopped."

"What have you done to stop them?" asked the girl.

"Too little. That is why I am trying now."

"It is too risky," said the mother.

"I shall not press you."

Two small boys ran up and plunged into the basket. The mother tried ineffectively to stop them. The girl leaned across swiftly, grabbed both of them and hauled them back.

"One biscuit each!" she said warningly. "Then you must go away!"

The boys, clearly used to sisterly firmness, stood obediently, received their sticky biscuit and ran off shouting happily into the bamboo thicket.

"They are good boys," said Georgiades.

"Yes," said the mother, with automatic pride. "They are growing up so quickly."

"We have not told them," said Rosa. "They think our father is away on business."

"Sometimes they ask," said the mother. "Sometimes they ask when he is coming back."

Rosa laid her hand on her mother's. Although it was smaller, not so long, it was recognizably the same hand.

"Do you take the money yourself?" asked Owen.

"I did at first." The mother's voice was barely audible.

"And now?"

The woman did not reply.

"We have made other arrangements," said Rosa.

"Can you tell me what they are?"

"No." Rosa looked him fiercely in the face.

"I wondered if you had seen them," Owen said to the mother. "I thought perhaps you could tell me what they looked like."

"It was dark," said the mother faintly.

"It is always dark," said the girl.

"And always the same place?"

"It has changed," said the mother, "twice."

"You must have talked with them a little. Is there nothing you can tell me? I ask only to stop them taking others."

"You are not to speak like that," said Rosa. "It is hard enough for her already."

The mother gently waved her daughter down.

"I would tell you if I could. I haven't been there for some time. The first time there was a man. I could not see his face. It was dark and he held a galabeah over it."

"What did he say?"

"Only that if I wished to see my husband again I must pay. I told him," her voice faltered, "I told him all. About our mother. The business. I said, 'I will bring you what I have.' He pressed me but I could say no more. Then he told me to go away and come again the next day. And so I did. When I came again there was another man. He questioned me fiercely but seemed satisfied. 'Very well,' he said, 'bring us money every three weeks. Do not miss a payment or it will go hard with your husband.' I said: 'If I pay you, will you give me back my husband?' 'Yes,' said the man. 'We have no quarrel with your husband, nor with you. Except that when you have finally paid and get back your husband, then you must go. You must leave Cairo and go. Egypt is Arab and is not for you.'"

The woman lifted her head and looked Owen in the eyes for the first time.

"He would not have said that if he had not meant to return my husband. That is why I know he is still alive."

The men had put on their boots and were tuning their instruments. The line of girls in their fine lawn chemisettes was starting to form.

"Go away," said Rosa, "and do not come back!"

There came a squeal from inside the bamboo thicket. The mother hesitated, muttered a goodbye, and then as another squeal came dived after it.

Owen and Georgiades turned to go.

"We don't know he's still alive," said Owen, as they set off along the path. "They may just be conning her."

There was a noise behind him. He looked over his shoulder. Rosa was about three yards behind.

"Don't ever say that again!" she said. "Don't ever say that! Don't you dare even whisper it! She still believes."

They stood abashed and awkward.

Rosa came up to them.

"You keep out of it!" she said to Owen. "You keep right out of it!"

●   ●   ●

Owen called Berthelot in to the Bab el Khalk. This was to be no cozy tête-à-tête in the hotel. He wanted him in his office.

"Monsieur!"

They shook hands.

Nikos went out again, leaving the door open. It was late morning and the shutters of Owen's room had been closed to keep out the sun. That made it airless if the door was closed. Having the door open had another advantage. Nikos could hear.

There was something different about Berthelot. After a moment Owen realized what it was. Berthelot was braced.

He sat down expectantly on the edge of his chair while Owen took his hat and stick and put them in the corner. Owen came back to his desk and sat down.

"I have asked you to come, Monsieur, because I hope you may be able to help us."

Berthelot suddenly looked relieved.

"Thank God!" he said.

"Comment?"

"Your pardon, Monsieur. I was afraid that...I thought that perhaps you were going to tell me...my uncle..."

"Nó, no."

Berthelot's relief seemed genuine.

"Mille pardons. It is just that—"

"Nothing new has come through."

Berthelot visibly relaxed.

"Thank God." He took out his handkerchief and made to mop his face, then wiped his hands instead. Owen switched on the fan. The great blades above began to whirl noisily, making all the papers on the desk flutter.

Berthelot stopped his wiping and looked at Owen.

"It is strange, *n'est-ce pas,* to be thankful for that? But one is grateful for small mercies."

"Not so small."

Berthelot nodded.

"They will deal in the end," said Owen.

"Will they? They do not seem anxious to."

"That is part of the dealing."

"If one could be sure—"

"I think you can be sure."

"But if they should lose their heads—"

"This lot," said Owen, "are unlikely to lose their heads."

Perhaps some bitterness came through, for Berthelot gave him a quick glance.

"Of course!" he said. "You are against us dealing. That is proper of you. But..." He shrugged his shoulders.

"I don't mind if you deal."

"You don't?" Berthelot was surprised. "But I thought ...the first time..."

"I don't mind you dealing. It's just that I'm still going to try to catch them."

"Of course, of course." Berthelot looked at his hands. He was still holding his handkerchief. He put it away. "Our interests are different," he said. "My chief interest is in getting my uncle freed. After that, well, anything I can do to help."

"Tell me about your dealings with Izkat Bey."

Berthelot looked startled.

"That is nothing to do with the—the disappearance of my uncle."

"Tell me about them, nevertheless."

"They are perfectly normal business dealings. Confidential, of course." He stopped. "Are you saying—? Well, I did wonder about it myself. But then I couldn't see why—Well, only in general terms. And, besides, how could they have known about it?"

"Tell me."

"Very well. Only it is in confidence, of course. Normally, I wouldn't—but in the circumstances—"

"Yes," said Owen. "In the circumstances."

"Well—how much do you know?"

"Just tell me."

"Very well. Izkat Bey is helping us to buy some land. I won't say where the land is—"

"On the other side of the river."

"Well—"

"Sidky's land."

"You obviously know all about it."

"Why Izkat Bey?"

"He was our contact."

"With Sidky?"

"Of course."

"Other people would have done for that. Why Izkat Bey?"

"He was also a contact with other people."

"I won't ask you to name them."

"I wouldn't tell you their names."

"Just tell me the nature of their interest."

Berthelot looked puzzled.

"Their interest wouldn't be commercial, would it?"

"Yes."

"I thought the person we were talking about wasn't the sort of person to have commercial interests?"

"Well, call it a financial interest."

"He expected to make some money out of it?"

"Yes. Not out of our side, of course, the building side. But when it was up and running. Privately, of course. Very privately."

"He wouldn't be running it himself?"

"Oh no!" Berthelot was shocked. "He couldn't possibly." He hesitated, and then said, "That was, in fact, where we came in. You see, we could offer not just construction facilities and not just the necessary finance, but also a management team. We provided a complete package."

"What was the nature of the management team?"

"Well, they had to know how to run a business like that. They had to have the Khed—the confidence of the person we are talking about. That wasn't so easy, actually, because he knows a lot of the people in the business and knows them only too well."

"Tell me about the business."

"You know about that."

"Tell me all the same. The scale, for a start."

"Oh, big."

"How big?"

"Well, bigger than Anton's."

"*Anton's?*" Owen tried too late to keep the surprise out of his voice.

There was a little silence.

"You didn't know? We were going to Anton for the management team. His syndicate would be putting up some of the necessary finance. We didn't need them, actually, but we thought it was best to cut them in. Local interests, you know. It always works better that way. It's bad to upset rivals. And then the Khedive knew him and our contact in Cannes knew him."

"Was that where it started—Cannes?"

"Yes. Our contact got to know—well, the person we were talking about—when he went there last year. She saw the nature of his interests and got talking. Whether she suggested it or he suggested it, I don't know. We came in later. She approached us. By then it was a proposition."

"That you should—"

"Build a salon. Acquire the land, construct a building, independent and self-standing, but equipped with all facilities, install a management team. Obviously a company would have to be created to run it but we weren't really part of that, except that we have to have somebody to deal with for contractual purposes."

"Izkat Bey?"

"It had to be secret. No one too close to the Khedive. Anyway, it had to be foreign."

"To take advantage of the Capitulations?"

"That's right. It's a foreign-registered company."

"Where is it registered?"

"Montenegro."

"Montenegro!"

"Yes. It has the advantage that it's claimed by about a dozen countries, all of which would be glad to advance their claims by offering the protection of their nationality to any company registered there and operating internationally."

"Let's get this right. You build it, someone else owns it, and someone else altogether runs it?"

"That's right."

"How does our friend come in, the person we were speaking of?"

"He inspired it in the first place. The idea may not have come from him, it may have come from our contact in Cannes, but he certainly encouraged it."

"What does he get out of it?"

"He would probably play there himself incognito. But the main point is to make money. Apparently he's short of cash—"

"He's always short of cash."

"Well, apparently he can't move a finger financially, it's all tied up by the British. Before Cromer came, the Khedive could do what he liked—"

"He bloody bankrupted the country."

"He can't do that now. In fact he can't do *anything* now, not financially, I mean, and he's sore about it. He wants to find a way of bypassing the controls and the only way he can do that is by some sort of secret operation such as this. He gets a steady income flow, unaccounted for, in return for his influence. He says it's good, anyway, to have some enterprises in the country which are Egyptian—"

"Egyptian? I thought you said it was registered in Montenegro?"

"He thinks of it as Egyptian. Anyway, not British, that's the important thing."

"It's a bit risky. It wouldn't do him any good at all if this came out. The Khedive into gambling! Bloody hell! This is a Moslem country. Gambling clubs are officially banned."

"I know. That's why I thought—when my uncle disappeared. I thought someone had found out and wanted to stop it. I half expected them to say that in the note."

"How would they find out?"

Berthelot shrugged.

"I don't know. Egypt is a funny country. Half the people are doing things in private and all the people are telling everyone else about it."

Owen sat thinking.

"The people who would object most are the Moslem fundamentalists."

"Yes." Berthelot looked at him. "Does that fit?"

Owen did not reply.

He became aware that Berthelot was casting longing glances in the direction of the jug of water which, as in all Egyptian offices, stood in the window to cool. He went across and passed him some water. With the shutters closed there was little draught and the water was tepid.

"Tell me," he said, as he handed the glass to Berthelot, "who told you about Anton?"

"Our contact in Cannes."

"How did you know where to find him?"

Berthelot looked puzzled. *"Comment?"*

"When you got here. The city was new to you. How did you find his address?"

"I took an arabeah," said Berthelot, still puzzled.

"Can you remember which? No? Well, it's not surprising. Did you ever send messages to Anton?"

"Yes. I—but nothing important."

"Who took the messages?"

"I can't remember."

"The hotel messenger?"

"Yes. But that was only—a simple note, suggesting an appointment."

"It would be enough."

Berthelot was silent. Then he said: "I wish to help you. I sent other messages."

"How?"

"By dragoman."

"Which dragoman?"

"I used two. I thought it was better that way."

"Which two?"

"Osman. Abdul Hafiz."

"Why them?"

"They seemed sober and reliable. Discreet."

"Yes," said Owen, "they are that."

• • •

"I need some advice from you," said Lucy Colthorpe Hartley.

"Anything I can do—"

"Do I pay? Do I just pay them and get it over?"

Owen was brought up with a jolt.

"Are you still there?"

"Yes. I was thinking."

"I've been doing some of that," said Lucy. "I've been doing a hell of a lot."

"I don't know that I am the person you should ask."

"But I'm asking you. Hello? Are you still there? These phones are a bit funny."

"I'm still here. I still don't think I'm the person you should ask. Is no one from the Consulate helping you?"

"They're all helping me. That's why I need some independent advice."

"I'm not independent."

"You know what I mean."

"If I were you and not the Mamur Zapt, I'd pay. Let the Mamur Zapt sort out his own problems."

"Thanks, love. I knew you were unreliable."

There was a pause.

"Are you still there?" asked Owen.

"Yes. The trouble is, the Mamur Zapt's problems are not just his own problems. If the French had refused to pay, Daddy might not have been taken. If I pay, someone else might be taken."

"Your father's your problem. Leave the other ones to someone else."

"You don't help at all," said Lucy.

• • •

"Someone ought to be giving her advice," said Owen.

"No, they shouldn't," said Paul. "No one ought to give advice on this sort of thing."

"Christ, she's in a foreign country and she's on her own."

"That's what everyone says and they give her advice. And it doesn't help."

"She asked me for advice and I'm the wrong person."

"Oh, I don't know."

"Will you help her?"

"Look," said Paul, "I may be the wrong person, too. I shall take a broad political view. It's my job. The political view is clear. It would look bad if we gave in."

"Suppose we gave in and people didn't see we'd given in?"

"How do we manage that?"

"How the hell do I know? You're the political expert."

• • •

Owen was having difficulty with Mahmoud. He had been trying to contact him all morning. He had finally caught him over the telephone by pretending to be someone else.

Mahmoud had been most unwilling to meet. Eventually, ungraciously, he had agreed to come out for a cup of coffee.

It was the only way. They had to meet face to face. Arabs found Englishmen distant anyway: over the telephone they were like aliens from another planet.

But now they were sitting face to face. Owen was still having difficulty. The problem was not just that Mahmoud had been wounded and offended. He was used to knocks and could shrug them aside. What counted far more was the mood he was in. And just now he was in a particularly bleak mood. Far from shrugging aside the blow he had received, he had brooded on it. And once he had started that, all sorts of other things came in: the iniquity of the British in Egypt, the depressed position of Arabs in the world generally, the general hostility of mankind. The world was set against him, Mahmoud, personally. It was all too big for him and he was too small and it was all unfair.

When he was like this it was very hard to prise him out of it. He seemed slumped in despair. He seemed hardly to hear what Owen was saying.

Owen decided he *wasn't* hearing what he was saying. How could he break in?

He looked around him and wondered if he could risk it. If anyone had done it to him he would have run a mile, but Arabs were always doing it, it was the way they operated, their style of relation. Their emotions were always so ready to bubble over that they had to find immediate physical ways of expressing them. If you *didn't* express them physically they assumed you didn't have them. The cold English were cold because they kept their emotions locked up inside them, they didn't let them out in all the rich variety of the Arab language of gesture.

Owen made up his mind, leaned forward and placed

his hand gently but familiarly on Mahmoud's own. Mahmoud looked up. His expression did not change, his eyes barely registered Owen's presence, but he did not remove his arm.

"I feel for my brother," said Owen, falling naturally into Arabic. "Let me share my brother's distress."

They used all three languages between them, English, French, and Arabic. Normally, when they were on business, they spoke English, though if they were with French-speakers they would speak French. Between them they used Arabic less, perhaps because it was more intimate. Just at the moment, though, the Arabic phrases came more easily to Owen's tongue.

"How can you?" asked Mahmoud. "You are not my brother."

He replied, however, in Arabic.

Owen moved his chair closer to him. Again, it was not a thing he would have done with Englishmen. But Arabs were always doing it. As a conversation progressed and they became emotionally involved, they would move closer and closer until they were almost touching you.

"I share what you feel. Therefore I am your brother."

"No one knows how I feel."

"A brother can guess."

"They do not trust me."

"They do trust you. I was talking to Paul. They had to do this for political reasons which were nothing to do with you. Paul says when this is all over they want you involved again. He thinks a lot of you. He says they all do."

"Then why do this to me?"

"Politics."

"Politics! Politics ought not to interfere with personal relationships."

"Quite right," said Owen. "I absolutely agree."

"They make too much of politics. They see politics everywhere. *You* see politics everywhere!" he said to Owen accusingly.

"But I don't let it interfere with my friendships."

"No," Mahmoud admitted. "That's true. You don't."

For a moment he seemed about to soften. Then he suddenly fired up.

"That is because you think it is all just a game. For you, politics is just a game. For me, it is not a game. No." He beat his hand on his chest theatrically. "For Egyptians politics can never be a game. The English can afford to let politics be a game because they have won. For the Egyptians—"

Owen sighed inwardly. Mahmoud was starting off again. However, he kept his hand commiseratingly on Mahmoud's arm and stared sympathetically into his eyes.

Mahmoud descended, a little self-consciously, from his high horse.

"It is pride," he said. "It is pride."

"The Arabs are a proud people."

"You forget that!"

"Other people may. I don't."

"The English do. The English—" Owen thought he was starting off again. However, Mahmoud suddenly became conscious of himself. "The English don't understand us," he concluded somewhat lamely.

"I know," said Owen soothingly. "I know."

Mahmoud looked at him. Suddenly he reached forward and took Owen in both arms.

"You understand us!" he said. "You are my friend! My brother!"

He hugged Owen tight. Owen looked surreptitiously up the street. Fortunately no one was watching. At the far end of the street some Arabs were talking animatedly, their arms naturally 'round each other. If anyone did see they wouldn't think anything of it.

"I am your brother," he said to Mahmoud.

"You are my brother," said Mahmoud joyfully.

He released Owen and shouted for more coffee. That was another Arab thing. No friendly exchange, hardly even a conversation, could take place unaccompanied by hospitality. It was what cemented bonds.

"Well," said Mahmoud, now completely happy. "How are you getting on?"

He had forgotten entirely about his woes, could barely even remember that he had been depressed. He was his old, animated self, interested, passionately interested, of course, for Mahmoud never did anything without passion, once again in the case.

Owen brought him up to date on developments.

"The dragoman is the key. And from what Berthelot says, there are two contenders: Osman and Abdul Hafiz."

"Of the two, Osman is the more likely," said Mahmoud.

"He's more of a rogue."

"I was thinking of his background. Do you remember? We looked it up. He was at El Azhar. That could be significant."

The great Islamic university was a hot-bed for nationalist movements, particularly, of course, those with a religious inspiration. Hot-beds, too, Owen frequently thought, produced hot-heads and there were plenty of those at El Azhar. Half the terrorist clubs in the city were based in the university.

"I thought we were going to get an identification," Owen said. "That strawberry-seller. He and the flower-seller between them."

"It's not so much that they know something," said Mahmoud, "it's that they've seen something. It's a question of getting it out."

"That's what I wanted to talk to you about. I want to
have another go at them. It's about all we've got to go on.
But I wanted to consult you before trying myself because
I'm not sure how to set about it. If they're all over the
place like they were last time I'll never get anywhere.
You're better with them than I am. You know how their
minds work."

Mahmoud was pleased.

"I'm not sure they have any," he said. "Still, why don't
we try? Why don't we have another go."

Owen noticed he had said "we."

"Yes!" said Mahmoud, firing up with enthusiasm—this
was the other side of his slump into depression—and
eager to start at once. "Let's go! Let's go now!"

• • •

The street was brimming. As well as the usual hawkers of
stuffed crocodiles, live leopards, Nubian daggers, Abyssinian
war-maces, Smyrna figs, strawberries, meshrebiya tables
and photograph frames, Japanese fans and postage stamps,
sandalwood workboxes and Persian embroideries, hippopotamus-hide whips and tarbooshes, and Sudanese beads
made in Manchester and the little scarabs and images of
men and gods made for the Tombs of Pharaohs but just
three thousand years too late; as well as the sellers of
sweets and pastry and lemonade and tea who habitually
blocked up the thoroughfare; as well as the acrobats and
tumblers, jugglers and performing ape managers; as well
as the despairing arabeah-drivers and the theatrical donkey-
boys and the long line of privileged vendors stretching
the whole length of the terrace—a swarm of Albanians,
Serbs, Montenegrins, Georgians, and Circassians had suddenly arrived in front of the hotel to show off their boots.

They were very proud of their boots and had come

along, in traditional national dress with a few props such as guns, daggers and swords, to exhibit them to the tourists to be photographed.

The Kodaks had for once deserted the little white donkeys with their red saddles and blue brocade and strayed out into the street in pursuit of the boots. This had, naturally, brought all traffic to a stop. Equally naturally the traffic was the last to find this out. People continued pushing and shoving, arabeah-drivers continued to urge their reluctant animals forward, various other animals wandered about in bewildered fashion and the only motion discernible on the Street of the Camel was general swirl.

One consequence of this was that most ordinary trade had come to a halt. The tourists on the terrace were too engrossed by the spectacle in the street to pay any attention to the vendors thrusting their wares through the railings at them. A temporary truce was forced on the vendors; and so when Owen and Mahmoud managed to struggle through the crowd and finally reach the strawberry-seller and flower-seller they found them unoccupied.

"By Allah, it is good to see you!" said the strawberry-seller warmly.

The flower-seller inquired after their fathers. Owen's was dead but he refrained from mentioning the fact as he did not want to encourage a diversion. The diversion came anyway because when Mahmoud in turn inquired after the fathers of the strawberry-seller and the flower-seller he was answered at great length, the scope of the reply extending, so it seemed, to the health of the entire village.

Midway through Owen lost track. The heat, the noise, the press of people and the avalanche of detail sent him into a daze. At some point they all sat down in the dust, the better to consider—surely Owen could not be hearing correctly?—the flower-seller's account of the diseased leg of one of the village camels. Sitting might have been more comfortable had it not been for the fact that the pressure of the crowd was forever making people fall over them. Not that that disturbed anyone.

The recital went on for hours, or so it seemed to Owen. The crowd was still as thick, more tightly jammed if anything. For some time he had been conscious of an approaching wail and thump. The wail ceased to approach and continued to sound at intervals forlornly. A wedding must have got stuck in the crowd. The tourists on the terrace above were still disregarding the vendors and following the Balkan display of boots. The vendors, discouraged, turned to the nearer spectacle and formed a little ring around Owen and Mahmoud and the flower- and strawberry-seller and listened rapt to the tale.

Owen abandoned all hope of getting anywhere.

Mahmoud, however, worked patiently on, bent courteously forward to catch the strawberry-seller's words, offering little suggestions now and then which blocked off a detour or returned after a diversion. And gradually, very gradually, he brought the conversation around.

Owen came to with a jolt when he realized that they were talking now about Moulin.

"His wife is here," said the strawberry-seller.

"Is she?" said the flower-seller. "I thought she had gone."

"Not that one. Another one."

"Has he two wives, then?"

"If he has, this is the senior one. She has gray hair and a straight back."

"I have not seen her."

"She does not come out on the terrace."

"What does she do, then?"

"Sits inside, I suppose. Perhaps she stays in the harem."

"Has he any sons?" someone asked from the outer circle.

"If he has, I have not seen them."

"There is that young one with the bulging eyes."

"Ah yes, but he is not a son."

"He is very like a son."

"I don't think the old man has any sons."

"No sons! Then there will be no one to mourn for him after he is gone."

"Or inherit."

"It is very sad if a man has no sons."

"The one with the bulging eyes," said Mahmoud, coming in quickly to cut off a potential diversion, "was he there that day, the day the old man disappeared?"

"Yes, he was there," said the flower-seller. "He came out on the terrace."

"Ah yes, but that was later. After the old man had disappeared."

"He didn't come out before?" asked Mahmoud.

"No." They were quite sure on the point. "He always comes later. The old man sits there first by himself."

"All alone."

"Yes, all alone."

"He has no sons, you see," offered one of the outer-ring.

Mahmoud, foreseeing another diversion, carried on hastily. "He might not have been lonely. He would have spoken to people."

"Not many," said the strawberry-seller doubtfully.

"He spoke to the dragoman," said Mahmoud.

"Yes, but that was only that day."

"Perhaps he spoke to him at other times, not on the terrace?"

"Perhaps."

"If the dragoman was a friend of his, he will grieve for him."

"That is true," they assented.

"I must speak words of comfort to the dragoman," said Mahmoud. "Which dragoman is it?"

"Abdul Hafiz," said the strawberry-seller.

"No, no," said the flower-seller. "Osman."

"It was definitely Abdul Hafiz. I remember, because I was surprised that he should come and talk to Farkas."

"Why should that be surprising?" asked Mahmoud.

"Because Abdul Hafiz thinks that Farkas is ungodly."

There was a general chorus of assent.

"That's why I think it was Osman," persisted the flower-seller. "He talks to Farkas."

"I know. If it had been him I would not have been surprised. But I was surprised. That was because it was Abdul Hafiz."

"Are you sure that wasn't another day?"

"What wasn't another day?"

"That—"

"Where *is* Farkas?" asked Owen.

They looked around.

"He is not here," they said.

"I know that."

"He hasn't been here for some time."

"Perhaps he's getting some more stock," someone suggested. They all laughed.

"How long has he not been here?" asked Owen. It sounded a flower-sellerish sort of question. Perhaps the disease was catching. They understood, however, without difficulty.

"He hasn't been here for several days."

"Can you remember when he was last here?"

"Was it by any chance," said Mahmoud, "the day that we last spoke with you? Was that the last day he was here?"

They thought before replying, understanding the point of the question. Then they looked at each other.

"Yes," they said together.

•　　•　　•

A flock of turkeys had been infiltrating its way through the crowd. One of them came to the strawberry-seller's basket and sampled his wares. The strawberry-seller leaped up with a shout and belabored the turkey, which turned and scuttled off into the crowd. A series of indignant shouts marked its passage. There was a sudden fierce blare of hautboys as it came up against the wedding. Panicking, it turned and rushed back the way it had just come, pecking everything and everyone in its path.

The crowd broke apart. Somebody fell on to the strawberries. The strawberry-seller started beating him. Another turkey appeared, closely followed by another. Owen jumped for the steps, narrowly missing the snake charmer. Mahmoud leaped up beside him.

Two frightened turkeys ran past the bottom of the steps. Bedlam broke out as they reached the donkeys.

There was a sudden fanfare as the wedding minstrels, profiting by the gap the turkeys had made, reached the steps. Behind them, wavering uncertainly between two giant camels, came the bridal palanquin. There was a loud jingle of bells as the first camel went past.

"By God!" said the blind snake charmer, alarmed. "There it is again!"

Mahmoud turned in a flash and ran down the steps.

"You said that before when I was making them play again the disappearance of the old man with the stick. What do you mean, father? There is *what* again?"

11

The bells," said the snake charmer.

"Yes," said Mahmoud. "I hear them too. Was it like that on the day the old man was taken?"

"Yes," said the snake charmer. "Yes. I think so."

"He came down the steps. With difficulty—one was assisting him."

"Yes."

"And then you heard the bells?"

"Yes. I cried out to the old man to warn him. I thought he might be knocked down. But one told me to be quiet."

"Was it the one who was assisting him, the one from above?"

"I do not know. I cannot remember."

"And then the wedding camel moved on and the old man was no longer there. Is that right?"

"That is right."

From further along the street came a confirming tinkle.

"Another man was taken later," said Mahmoud. "An Englishman."

"I know him," said the snake charmer. "He speaks strangely and is the girl's father."

"That is right."

"She gives me a piastre. Every time she goes in, every time she comes out. She did not give me a piastre that day. I did not mind because I knew she was troubled."

"She grieves because she has lost her father."

"These are evil days," said the snake charmer, shaking his head.

"They are indeed," Mahmoud agreed. "And we must stand out against the evil."

The snake charmer did not reply.

"I remember that day the Englishman was taken," Mahmoud declared. "He too was sitting at the top of the steps. And then he came down them, I think. Do you remember?"

"I think he came down."

"Was one assisting him?"

"No. But he was talking to one."

"They came down the steps together?"

"Yes."

"And then you heard the bells again?"

"Yes."

"And after that, as before, the man was gone?"

"Yes."

"Old man," said Mahmoud gently, "the bells ring many times. The wedding camels go up and down the street, and that is good, for weddings are enjoined in the Book, that Allah might bless with children. Do you not hear the bells many times?"

"I do."

"Then why do you remark on them now?"

"I heard the bells," said the old man after a moment.

"I am sure you heard them."

"They came when I was troubled."

Mahmoud deliberated. "Is it," he added, "that usually when you hear them your heart is happy?"

"That is true. My heart is happy."

"But not when the old man with the stick was taken. Then your heart was not happy."

"I was confused. I did not know what had happened. I could not understand."

"I remember you were confused when I spoke with you."

"I was troubled. I knew that bad things were going on. And then the bells! I was confused."

Mahmoud looked at Owen.

"Imagine an old man," he said softly, in English, "blind. He creates his world and it is orderly. It has to be. And this one day, suddenly, it is not orderly. And he remembers. He remembers especially the discrepant things."

"Are the bells discrepant?"

"They were discrepant with the bad things he knew were happening. And," said Mahmoud, "they are discrepant to me, too, for if Moulin had come down the steps and was standing right by the wedding procession, the kidnappers would hardly have chosen that moment to kidnap him. Not with all those potential witnesses. Not unless the wedding was part of it."

He turned back to the snake charmer.

"And then it happened again," he said.

"Yes."

"The Englishman came down the steps. And again you knew that something bad was happening. And again you heard the bells."

"I was confused," said the old man, "troubled. And then I heard the bells."

• • •

"It would be possible to check," said Owen. "Possible, not easy."

"Perhaps you—I have no standing in this case. Officially."

"OK. I'll check."

"If I were you," said Mahmoud, "I wouldn't check with the donkey-boys."

"No? Why not?"

"Because," said Mahmoud, "if anything happened at the foot of the steps, and it did, they must have seen it."

"Weddings," said Owen, "weddings. Do you remember their jokes about weddings? I thought it was because one of them, Daouad, wasn't it, was getting married?"

"Cheeky!" said Mahmoud. "It would have been cheeky of them. But typical!"

"I'll check," said Owen.

"Don't talk to anyone too closely connected with the front of the terrace!" Mahmoud warned him.

Owen endured, on this occasion, Mahmoud telling his grandmother how to suck eggs.

"We don't want another Farkas," said Mahmoud, rubbing it in.

"I'll look out for the postcard-seller too."

They pushed their way back across the street.

"Even so," said Owen, "it wouldn't have been easy."

"It would have been easy to take him. The problem was always getting him away."

"You reckon they put him in the palanquin?"

"Yes. Surround him when he gets to the foot of the steps, throw a blanket over his head and bundle him into the palanquin. Then you can take your time."

"Might have been seen bundling."

"It would have been very quick. The camels would have blocked out anyone seeing from the street side. Mirrors, banners, people everywhere. A small man in the middle of a lot of big men."

"Possible," Owen conceded.

"Why did they come down the steps? That's still the question."

They parted when they got to the other side of the street.

"I'll get on with that checking," said Owen.

"Palanquins are not that easily come by," said Mahmoud. "You could start there."

• • •

Owen put Nikos to work on the palanquin, Georgiades to work on the weddings. They operated in complementary ways. Georgiades would shamble through the crowd, chatting to all and sundry, young and old, beggar and businessman, inviting confidence with his soulful eyes and sympathetic manner. Nikos shrank from the messy business of individuals and pursued the abstract and organizational. Whereas Georgiades would have set about tracing the palanquin by going first to the user and then deciding where a person like that was likely to go to get his hands on a palanquin, Nikos immediately went through a list of palanquin suppliers.

The Georgiades way would probably have worked better in the present situation but they did not have a known person to start from. Owen hoped that if he picked up the "wedding" the other might follow. Cairo was a personal city. Set any group to walk along the street and at least one of its members was sure to be recognized by at least one of those who witnessed it.

Nikos, confronted with what he regarded as a simple organization problem, was ticking along happily. Once he had taken on a problem, however, his mind refused to let it go and he was still thinking about Zawia and the Senussi.

Midway through the morning, and through his pursuit of the palanquin, he stuck his head in at Owen's door.

"It might not be Senussi," he said.

"Might not be Senussi!" Owen was enraged. "Christ, you tell me now, when the whole place has got itself in an uproar about the Senussi."

"What I was thinking," said Nikos equably, "was that it might not be the Senussi themselves but an associated sect. Other sects have religious centers too which they call by the same name."

"Like what sect?"

"The Wahabbi. There has always been a link between the Wahabbi and the Senussi. They are very similar. Both are extremely fundamentalist. And that brings me," said Nikos, "to another point. I was going through the files of the dragomans yesterday."

"Mahmoud and I went through them."

"Yes," said Nikos, unimpressed. "And what I found was that Abdul Hafiz is a Wahabbi."

"I think we noted that too," said Owen.

"Yes. Well, it fits, doesn't it? The Wahabbis are very fundamentalist, just the sort of people to be infuriated by anything to do with gambling. And all the more so if the gambling is anything to do with foreigners, since, like the Senussi, they object strongly to foreigners. Suppose Berthelot was right, and the reason why they picked Moulin was that they had learned that the Khedive intended to build a gambling salon and wanted to frighten him off? Abdul Hafiz might have been the way they learned."

"Berthelot swears he kept things very quiet."

"OK. Suppose they heard about it another way. Quite possible, because there are Wahabbis close to the Khedive. Abdul Hafiz might have been the man they put in to keep an eye on things. Also to take a hand. Remember what the strawberry-seller said. Either Abdul Hafiz or Osman was on the terrace at the time Moulin disappeared."

"The flower-seller thought it was Osman."

"I think it was Abdul Hafiz. The strawberry-seller remembered it because it surprised him. That rings true to me. He was surprised because Abdul Hafiz was not the sort of man who normally talked to people like the postcard-seller. That was because he was a Wahabbi. Strict people like that object to profane images, all the more if they're the sort of images the postcard-seller was carrying around."

"I don't see how the postcard-seller fits in."

"Nor do I. A minor figure, I should think. Perhaps he was the link with the men who were actually going to do the kidnapping. Perhaps what Abdul Hafiz was doing was telling him to give them the go-ahead."

"If it was Abdul Hafiz. Mahmoud thought it was more likely to be Osman. Osman is more Western, more the sort of man you would expect to be au fait with internal arrangements at Anton's. *And* he's got the religious background, if that's significant. He was at El Azhar."

Nikos was not the only one who could pick things up from files.

"Yes," said Nikos. "I saw that too. But that was a long time ago and there's nothing on the files to suggest either that he's had anything to do with El Azhar since or that he is strongly religious. From what you say he's the other way around, if anything. Westernized and secular. That doesn't fit."

"It fits with what Mahmoud thinks. He thinks it was done just for the money."

"Osman does very nicely out of the tourist trade. He wouldn't want to damage that."

"It was Berthelot who thought there might be a religious or moral explanation."

"I think that's more likely. If it was just a straight money job they'd want to do it the easy way. Why go to the trouble of picking somebody off the terrace at Shepheard's? More risky, much more likely to go wrong. You'd do that only if you *wanted* to be conspicuous, to strike a blow which you wanted everyone to see. That makes the religious explanation more likely."

"Or the nationalist one," said Owen.

•   •   •

Nikos went back to the palanquins. Georgiades now appeared. He, too, had been thinking of other things.

"Are you going to leave it?" he asked.

"Leave what?"

"The Tsakatellis business. Do what the girl said. Keep out of it."

"I haven't made up my mind."

"You see," said Georgiades, settling down comfortably—Owen suspected he just wanted to come in out of the heat—"there are two views. Either we can do as the girl said, stay out of it, on the grounds that we'll only make matters worse. Or else we might feel that matters were coming to a head anyway, that the mother's money will soon run out, that they'll have to bring the old lady in, and that she's likely to put the stopper on the whole business."

"Which do you advise?"

"I don't know."

"Thank you," said Owen. "That's where I was too."

"I don't like leaving it," said Georgiades. "I feel worried about that family being on its own. Perhaps it's because they're Greek. They ought to have a man about the house. That girl is taking on too much."

"What girl is this?"

"Rosa. She's a good girl. I've been talking to her a lot. In between the dancing. She's worried about what will happen to them. Suppose the father doesn't come back? Suppose he's already dead? She's tough enough to have asked herself that. A real Greek girl. She says the old grandmother isn't what she was. And the mother isn't the sort of person to run things. Besides, she's got the boys to bring up. They need a man about the house, Rosa says. Things can't go on the way they are. We've got to do something."

"So?"

"So what I've done—"

"Done?"

"—is to put someone on the house. It would be nice to know about the next payment. There aren't many servants in that house and they'd almost certainly send one of them. It will be one who's closer to the mother than to the grandmother, closer to the girl, too. I'm backing the second houseboy."

"Why?"

"The cook and the first houseboy were with the grandmother before the mother came. The second houseboy used to take Rosa to school. Mind you, from what I've seen of him I wouldn't say he's one who could keep a secret. He's more the sort who blabs it all out. Still, my money is on him."

"Was there anything else you needed to know before making your decisions?" asked Owen tartly.

"Just telling you," said Georgiades, retreating.

●   ●   ●

The following day they came together.

"Yes?" said Owen.

"The weddings," said Georgiades.

"Yes?"

"There *was* one."

"One or two?"

"One definite. At roughly the time Colthorpe Hartley disappeared. One possible, when Moulin went."

"We've got the snake charmer as well."

"I thought you wanted independent corroborations."

"I do, really."

"The trouble is, there are a lot of weddings. Why should one stand out?"

"But you think you got corroboration in the case of Colthorpe Hartley?"

"That seems pretty definite. An arabeah-driver was coming in and had to wait. He was bringing someone back to the hotel. There was someone coming out of the hotel and he thought he might be there to pick them up, kill two birds with one stone. He wasn't. By the time the wedding procession had got out of the way and he'd drawn in, the person had gone off in one of the other arabeahs. That kind of thing tends to stick in an arabeah-driver's mind."

"What about the person who came out of the hotel?"

"Checked with them. They confirm. When they got to the steps, the camels were still there, blocking the thoroughfare, so they walked along to where the arabeahs were standing and took one of them. The driver vaguely remembers something blocking the steps but by the time he had pulled out it had gone."

"The person who came out of the hotel: they saw the camels. Did they see anything else?"

"A little group of people, that's all. No struggle, no one being held or supported. No bundle that they can remember."

"Were they able to identify any of the people?"

"They wore masks. Jesters' masks."

"Did you get the person in the incoming arabeah?"

"Yes. They didn't see anything. The crowd was pretty thick. They think they might have seen a camel. They confirm, though, that the arabeah had to wait."

"What about when Moulin was taken?"

"That's harder to get information on. It's too long ago. Several people thought they might have seen something. But then again, they might not have. There was a strawberry-seller and a flower-seller—"

"Oh God!" said Owen with feeling.

"You know them? I didn't get a great deal out of them—"

"No," said Owen, "you wouldn't."

"—but there was someone else who was a bit more forthcoming."

"Not a filthy-postcard-seller?"

"No," said Georgiades. "What made you think of that?"

"Someone else who's got a pitch there. I'm looking for him."

"This was a Turkish Delight seller. He had a tray which he had put down just for a moment—just for a moment, effendi!—and one of the camels in the wedding procession stepped in it and spilled all his stuff in the dust. It was so bad he had to go to a pump and wash it. That must have been bad. Anyway, when he got back from the pump the place was in turmoil because Moulin was missing. The Turkish Delight seller was really fed up, I can tell you. Not only had his Delight been messed up but he had missed most of the excitement. That's why it stuck in his mind. Or perhaps he's inventing it all to compensate."

"Any corroboration?"

"Oh, lots. He's told his story a lot of times now and everyone in the street can repeat it word for word. What is less clear is whether they're remembering the event or just the story."

"You got nothing, then?"

"By the time you get this far," said Georgiades, "the facts have gone forever and these are just stories."

"Well, OK, you've got something. Did you get anything on the palanquins?" he asked Nikos.

"Thirty-eight palanquins were hired for weddings that day," said Nikos.

"Which day? Which one are we talking about?"

"The day Colthorpe Hartley disappeared. In addition to that, there would of course be private palanquins. I've assumed that it was a hired one, not a private one. I also assumed it would be one of the cheaper ones. That cut the number down. I'll check them all but I thought I would start on the basis of probability."

Nikos liked not only to have a system but to explain the system to those less fortunate, which, in his view, generally included Owen and Georgiades.

"OK, OK," said Owen. "So what did you find?"

"Well, I've got a list of names."

"Some of them would have been hired anonymously, surely?"

"No. Under false names, perhaps, but never anonymously. Not often under false names, either, since you're expected to give a friend's name when you go along. "I'm a friend of Mustapha," or something like that, and Mustapha will be a mutual acquaintance. A palanquin represents a substantial sum of money, especially if it's ordered with camels and the owner is careful about hiring. He generally knows who he's hiring to, even with poorest customers."

"So the names might be real."

"They'd have to be real."

"Couldn't you hire under someone else's name?"

"You'd run the risk of the person being asked, "I'm Mustapha, I'm a friend of Ali." Well, they might ask Ali, and he'd say, 'Which Mustapha?' and that way they'd check. The whole business is very personal."

"Of course, if Ali genuinely was a friend, they might get him to borrow it for them."

"Yes."

"Have you checked for that possibility?"

"Look," said Nikos, exasperated, "it takes time to do all this checking. I'm only bringing you my first findings. There's a lot more work to do. I'm coming to you before I'm really ready because you told me it was urgent and I thought you'd like to know."

"I would. You're quite right. It is urgent," said Owen soothingly: and then, tentatively: "Was there anything particular you thought I'd like to know?"

"One of the names on the list is a name you'll recognize."

"Yes?"

"Daouad."

"Daouad?"

"One of the names on the list is a name you *ought* to recognize," Nikos amended.

"Who the hell is Daouad?"

"One of the donkey-boys," said Nikos. "Remember?"

● ● ●

"Greetings to you, Daouad," said Owen.

"And to you, greetings," the donkey-boy returned politely, making to get up.

Owen motioned him down and dropped into a squat beside him.

"Greetings and congratulations," he said.

"Thank you. But why the congratulations?"

"Are you not now a married man?"

"No," said Daouad, looking surprised.

"Your friends spoke of you as one about to be married. And was it not to be to Ali's sister?"

"And yes, but that hasn't happened yet. In fact, it may never happen."

"The dowry may not be big enough for someone like you, Daouad?"

"That is it," said Daouad modestly, but with a faint touch of pride. "The girl herself is pleasing, but the family, alas, is poor."

"Whereas you are rich, Daouad."

"I wouldn't put it quite like that," said Daouad, flushing, however, with pleasure.

"Or going to be."

"So I hope."

"Soon?"

Daouad looked startled.

"I shouldn't think so," he said.

"What you say surprises me, Daouad," said Owen, settling more comfortably on his heels.

"I am expanding," said Daouad. "I have an extra donkey in mind. But—"

"I was not thinking of that. I was thinking of your wedding. Are you not already a married man?"

"No, no. Fatima will be the first. If I marry her."

"That is odd. I thought you had already married. Was not the wedding last week?"

"No, no. What makes you think that?"

"Did you not order the bridal palanquin?"

Daouad froze.

"That was for my sister."

"I did not know you had a sister."

"She is a distant sister. I mean," said Daouad hastily, "that she lives at a distance. In a village."

"That is strange. For the palanquin was ordered here in the city."

"On second thoughts," said Daouad unhappily, "it was not for a sister. It was for a friend."

"The name of your friend?"

"Alas," said Daouad, "I have sworn to keep it a secret."

"It was a very private wedding, I expect."

"It was indeed," Daouad agreed.

"You went to it yourself, of course?"

"Of course."

"Was it a big wedding?"

"Not very big."

"Just a few friends?"

"That is correct."

"To carry the mirrors and act as jesters? Not many minstrels, I expect."

"No," said Daouad unhappily. "There weren't many minstrels."

"They cost money, don't they? Even for one as rich as yourself, Daouad, they cost money. Fortunately, Daouad, you are a man with friends. I expect that helped, didn't it?"

"It did."

"Just a few friends. Were your friends here among them?"

The other donkey-boys were playing their stick game in a patch of shadow further along the terrace. Owen waved a hand in greeting. They waved back.

"Why!" said Owen. "There are your friends! Shall we go and sit with them?"

The donkey-boys looked up beaming as he approached.

"Hello!" they said. "You haven't been to see us for a long time. We feel neglected!"

"I don't think you'll need to feel that any more. How are you, anyway?"

"Oh, we're fine," they assured him.

"Business prospering?"

"You could say that."

"Time passes and Allah blesses the fortunate. Here is Daouad, for instance, now a married man."

"Married?"

"Weren't you telling me that he was to be married? You made a joke of it."

"Ah yes, but—"

"It is not till later that Daouad gets married."

"Oh, of course. I was forgetting. It was the wedding that confused me."

"Wedding?"

"Well, let us say wedding procession. You must have seen it. It passed right by here. Right by the foot of the steps."

There was a stunned silence.

"I don't remember it," said one of the brighter donkey-boys, pulling himself together.

"Don't you? I thought you carried one of the mirrors?"

The donkey-boy looked shaken.

"No," he said, "that was someone else."

"Ah! You were one of the jesters, perhaps!" Owen turned to Daouad. "What good friends you have, Daouad! I expect they all rallied around to help you. But who did you leave with the donkeys? Oh, of course, I was forgetting. You wouldn't have had to have left them for long. Once the camels were moving again, most of you could have come straight back."

One of the donkey-boys began to get to his feet hurriedly but stopped when he saw the constable behind him.

"Do not be in such a hurry to leave us. It is good to sit here and talk. More pleasant than to sit where you will shortly be sitting."

"It is the end," said one of the donkey-boys bitterly.

Owen nodded.

"Yes," he said, "it is the end. For you."

"How did you find out?"

The donkey-boys looked at Daouad.

"It wasn't me!" he said.

"Nor was it," said Owen. He quite liked Daouad.

The smallest donkey-boy began to whimper.

"He will take us to the caracol," he whispered to the boy next to him. "My father will beat me."

"That will be the least of thy worries."

"There must be punishment," said Owen, "But the punishment need not fall equally on everybody."

"Let him go, then," said Daouad, "for he but followed us."

"I might," said Owen, "for you are big and he is small. But it would depend on several things. First, are those you took still alive?"

"Yes."

"Have they been harmed?"

"The Englishman is well," said one of the boys. "I saw him this morning."

"Good. I would need them to be returned to me. Second, I would need to know the names of all involved."

"We were not many."

"Then it should be easy for you to tell me then."

"You know them."

"But I would like to hear them. In fact," said Owen, "you had better tell me the whole story. Begin at the beginning. With the Englishman on the terrace."

"But that is not the beginning," one of the donkey-boys objected.

"There are several tales you have to tell. The Englishman on the terrace is the beginning of one of them."

Owen was not going to have another strawberry-seller/flower-seller kind of tale.

"Begin with the Englishman on the terrace," he said

firmly. "He was up there and you were down here. And then he came down. Why did he come down?"

"We said we had brought him something from the young Sitt. She had directed us to show it him."

"Why could you not show him it on the terrace?"

"Because it was too big. And because one would not allow us on the terrace."

"And he believed you?"

"Yes."

"And came down?"

"Yes."

"And at the foot of the steps?"

"We were waiting for him."

"We were worried," put in one of the other donkey-boys, "for he did not understand us at first and came down slowly. The procession had to wait. We were afraid that would make people look."

"The palanquin was already at the steps when he came down?"

"Yes. There was an arabeah beyond it wanting to come in."

"The palanquin was waiting and the Englishman came down. What then?"

There was a general shrug.

"Daouad put a cloak over his head."

"I thrust him in."

"With my help," said another boy, not wishing to see his part discounted.

"Yussuf stayed with him."

"I tied him," Yussuf explained. "It was like tying a donkey."

"The camels moved on."

"And we took off our masks and went back to the donkeys."

"I had been minding the donkeys," said the smallest boy, not wishing to be left out.

The others shushed him.

"You see," Daouad pointed out. "He was not even with us."

"Was anyone else with you? Anyone who is not here now?"

"No. For then we would have had to share."

"Are you sure? For the procession would have been small indeed if you were all waiting at the steps."

"We weren't all waiting at the steps."

"Only two of us were waiting at the steps," said Yussuf, "the two who spoke to the Englishman, I and Daouad."

"The rest were with the procession," said Daouad.

"I held the mirror," said one of the boys proudly.

"He held one of the mirrors, I held the other."

"We all put on the jesters' masks," said one of the other boys eagerly. "It was a good wedding."

Owen sighed. They reminded him of children. Indeed, they were children. But then, so were some of the worst terrorist gangs he had had to deal with. Being children did not stop them from garrotting or stabbing. Or kidnapping.

"Most of you were with the camels, then?"

"Yes. When Abdul called to us that the camels were approaching, we left our donkeys and donned our masks and went along the street to meet them."

"Who is Abdul?"

"My brother," said Yussuf.

"He is not here?"

"Oh no!" said Yussuf, shocked. "He is too small to be a donkey-boy!"

"He was with the camels?"

"Yes."

"Who else was with the camels?"

"Hassan."

"Who is Hassan? Is he here?"

"My cousin," said Daouad. "No. He is not here."

"He is a camel-driver," someone else said. "He works for Sidky."

"Sidky?"

"You know Sidky? He is a big contractor. His camels take loads to Rhoda Island."

"I know Sidky."

"It was his camels," Yussuf explained. "Hassan borrowed two of them."

"Did Sidky know?"

"Sidky would not have minded. Hassan is a good driver."

"He would have looked after the camels," they all assured Owen.

"That is not the point."

"No?"

"The camels smelled a bit," said someone.

"That was because they have been carrying night soil."

"The smell doesn't matter," said Daouad. "The important thing is that they are good strong beasts and used to carrying loads. Not too spirited."

"Oh, the camels were all right."

"Anyway, Hassan is a good driver. I remember—"

"No more of Hassan," said Owen. "Were there any others, apart from Hassan and Abdul, who were not donkey-boys?"

"Salah."

"Who is Salah?"

"He was playing the pipes. None of us could play them well enough."

"OK. Apart from Hassan and Abdul and Salah, was there anyone else?"

They looked around.

"No. Just us."

"It was all your own idea?"

"It was my idea chiefly," said Daouad with pride.

"And mine too," said Yussuf.

"Yes, but you couldn't have done it without us," objected the other donkey-boys. No one wanted to be left out.

"It was a bad idea," said Owen. "It was a wicked idea. To harm that old gentleman!"

"We wouldn't have harmed him! We have looked after him well."

"We have cared for him as if he were one of our own donkeys."

"We were going to give him back. After we had got the money."

"We were just borrowing him."

It struck them all as a happy thought.

"We were just borrowing him."

"All we wanted was the money," Daouad explained.

"No doubt. But money is not to be had that way."

"We saw others doing it and it seemed to us a good idea. No one gets hurt. No one gets caught."

"And you make a lot of money."

They looked at Owen almost accusingly.

"It's a good way to earn a living. In one day you can make enough to live on for several years."

"We could have doubled our stock of donkeys."

"Hired men in. Then we could have stopped at home with our wives."

"We could have bought a lot of wives."

"However," said Owen, "it so happens that you have been caught."

The bubble of their euphoria was pricked. They looked at him with suddenly doleful faces.

"Yes," they said, "there is that."

"You are going to the caracol, where you are going to stay for a long time."

"What about our donkeys?"

"You will have to get someone else to look after them. I'll tell you what," said Owen. "You can send that little boy off to fetch someone to take charge of the donkeys. Tell them to come here to collect them."

He didn't want to take the donkeys as well to the prison.

"And while we're waiting for them to come, two of you can come with me and show me where you keep the prisoners. Is it far?"

"No," they said, crestfallen. "It's not far. It's just across the road, in fact. In the Wagh el Birket."

"OK. Daouad and Yussuf, you can come with me."

They seemed the two brightest. He didn't want to leave them with only the constables looking after them.

"We come," said Daouad and Yussuf, scrambling to their feet.

"Are they both there?"

"Both?"

"Or all three," said Owen, remembering Tsakatellis.

"What are you talking about?"

"Your prisoners. Those you have kidnapped."

"We have only kidnapped one," said Daouad, bewildered.

"Only one?"

"The Englishman."

"What about the Frenchman, the old man with the stick?"

"We were nothing to do with that," said Daouad, offended.

12

In fact," said Daouad, "that was what gave us the idea in the first place."

"When we saw how simple it was—" said Yussuf.

"And when as time went by you still did not catch them—"

"And we heard the size of the ransom—"

"And we thought of the donkeys that would buy—"

"We thought that Allah had decided to smile on us by placing the opportunity in our way—"

"Which if we did not seize would be clearly to go against his wishes—"

"Let's get this straight," said Owen. "You saw how the Frenchman was kidnapped—?"

"We did."

"And then as time went by and nothing happened you thought you might as well try it too?"

"That is so."

"Had you no thought of evil?" said Owen sternly.

"We thought only of the money," Yussuf said sadly.

"It may be that we have done wrong," said one of the other donkey-boys.

"You *have* done wrong. However," said Owen, as a thought struck him, "it may be that you can a little undo the evil you have done. Let us return to the kidnapping of the Frenchman. Tell me what you saw. There was the Frenchman on the terrace—"

"We did not see him on the terrace. We were watching the wedding."

"But then suddenly there he was on the bottom of the steps, and we were surprised, for he does not usually come down the steps—"

"And then we were even more surprised, for the jesters gathered round him and one put a cloak over him and two bundled him into the palanquin—"

"And then the camels rose and went away—"

"And we were left marvelling."

"This cannot be true," said Owen. "Are you telling me that all this happened without you knowing that it was going to happen? That no one approached you before-hand and said "Here is money. It will be yours if you do not see what happens when the old Frenchman comes down the steps?"

"One approached us and offered us money. But he said nothing about the Frenchman."

"He merely said, 'Tomorrow when the effendi are at their tea a wedding will come to the steps. When that wedding comes, turn your eyes the other way.'"

"And he gave you money?"

"He showed us money and a cudgel. He said, 'Which of these do you choose?' We said, 'Money.' He said, 'So be it. Here is money now. You will get the rest tomorrow. But if you do not avert your eyes or if you tell anyone about it after, you will feel the cudgel.' And he told us about Hamid."

"Hamid?"

"Hamid was found a week ago. He had been beaten until he was nearly dead. The one who spoke to us said that as it had been with Hamid, so it would be with us if we did not do as we had agreed."

"However, you did not do as you had agreed, for when the wedding came you *did* look."

"It was a good wedding."

"Besides, we wanted to see."

"As long as we did not tell anyone, we knew it would not matter."

"But now you have told someone. You have told me and that is wise, for it may be that I shall put in a word for you when you come before the judge."

"That would be kind of you."

"But that depends on how much you are prepared to help me."

"We will help you all we can," they assured him.

"Good. First, the man who spoke to you: would you know him again?"

"We would."

"And is he known to you already?"

"We have not seen him before."

"You do not know his name, or where he comes from?"

"Alas, no."

"He speaks like a villager," someone said.

"A villager from near at hand? Or far away?"

The donkey-boys consulted.

"We think he comes from the other bank of the river," they said.

"Good."

Owen would have them taken—singly—to the villages across the river at nightfall when the men returned to their houses. It was a long shot but there was always the chance that the man might be identified.

"Next, the men in the procession: were these men known to you?"

"They wore masks."

"What about the driver? Did he wear a mask?"

Again they consulted.

"We do not think he wore a mask. However, we did not really see him."

"We saw the camels, though," one of the boys said.

"And would you remember the camels?" Owen asked, not very hopefully.

"Oh yes." The boy was quite definite. "The front one was a fine camel. Besides, I have seen it before."

"Where did you see it before?"

"I saw it at the Market of the Afternoon. And then I saw it again at the Mosque of El Hakim."

It was quite possible. The donkey-boys took a professional interest in livestock, and camels, like donkeys, were all individuals to them.

"Could you take me to where you saw it?"

"I could."

"Good. Then you will do so. Next, the palanquin: have you seen that before?"

"One palanquin looks very like another," they said doubtfully.

"Was it a hired palanquin or a private one?"

"Oh, a private one."

"You are sure of that?"

"Oh yes, quite sure."

"What makes you sure?"

The donkey-boys put their heads together.

"We do not know what makes us sure but we are sure."

"Perhaps it is the ornament," said one of the boys.

Owen was inclined to take their word. Not that it helped. To track down a private palanquin in the vast city was asking the impossible.

"Very well, then. Here is another question: what made the Frenchman come down the steps? You told me yourselves earlier that he was hardly strong enough to fall down them."

"Ah yes, but when a man has the itch!"

"What itch is this?"

"The one between the legs."

"The old man had an itch between the legs?"

"It never goes," they assured him. "Wait till you are an old man and then you will see."

"My uncle—" began one of the boys.

"Even if the old man had an itch," Owen cut in hastily, "why did that make him come down the steps? Surely he was not going to the Wagh el Birket?"

That struck all the boys as funny and it was some time before they could contain their merriment.

"No, no. He was coming down to see Farkas."

"You know Farkas? The postcard-seller?"

"I know Farkas."

Several things slipped into place.

"Farkas had some cards for him?"

"Farkas always has cards. It was just that the old man wanted to see them."

"The old man sent a message to Farkas. He sent one to speak with him. To tell him to come to the foot of the steps. Did you see who took the message?"

"No."

"A dragoman?"

"I do not know who that would be," said Daouad. "It could have been any of them."

"Osman?"

"Osman, certainly."

"Abdul Hafiz?"

"I do not think it would have been Abdul Hafiz."

"Why not?"

"He is a Wahabbi."

"He is very strict."

"He does not like the cards. He thinks they are the Devil's images."

"He thinks Farkas is a son of Shaitan."

"Where *is* Farkas?" asked Owen.

They looked around.

"He is not here."

"He has not been here for several days," said one of them.

"I know that," said Owen, "and I would like to find him."

Daouad hesitated and looked at the other donkey-boys.

"We know where he might be," he said.

"Find him for me," said Owen, "and I shall not forget it."

•   •   •

But first they had to find Colthorpe Hartley. Daouad and Yussuf took Owen across the street and along the Wagh el Birket. There was a little alleyway between two of the houses. At the far end, in the shadows, was a small door which reached up only to Owen's waist.

Daouad stooped and beat his fist upon it. When there was no response he hammered again. A bolt on the other side of the door was half eased back.

"Who is there?" said a voice.

"Daouad."

Once the bolt was pulled fully back the door opened slightly. Whoever it was took a good look at Daouad and then, reassured, lifted the door open.

Daouad bent down and went through, Owen followed him. He did not like stooping in this way. It placed him at a disadvantage. He was glad when he stood up on the other side and nothing had happened.

Although it was dark inside there was light at the far end of the room or corridor. They went toward it. A door was pushed open. They walked through into a bare room, in one corner of which there was a tattered mattress on which someone had been lying.

The man who had opened the door to them peered up blindly at Owen. His eyes were red and, like many Egyptians, he was obviously suffering from ophthalmia. He was old and short and fat and when he spoke Owen realized that he was a eunuch. "Who is your friend, Daouad? He is not one of us."

Daouad took no notice. He went straight across the room to an alcove, in which there was another door. He pulled back the bolts and beckoned Owen.

Colthorpe Hartley looked up.

"Good God!" he said. "You here?"

•   •   •

Owen sent Georgiades with one of the donkey-boys to see if he could find Farkas. They returned some time later holding the filthy-postcard-seller firmly between them.

"I haven't done anything!" Farkas protested, even before he got through the door.

"I am sure you haven't," said Owen.

"No?" said Farkas, surprised and, probably, disbelieving.

"Nor would you wish to," said Owen, "lest you might find yourself in the caracol or helping the men build the dam."

"That is true!" Farkas assented fervently.

"So I know you will help me."

"I will help all I can," said Farkas cautiously.

"You certainly will. And, first, you will tell me why it

was that the old Frenchman came down the steps from the terrace on the day he disappeared."

"I do not know. Why should I know?"

"Because he came down to see you."

"Why, so he did!" said Farkas, after a moment's reconsideration.

"You showed him the cards."

"He may indeed have looked at them."

"And then he was seized. Who seized him, Farkas?"

"I do not know!"

"You were there. You saw. You must know."

"I was there. But...but I did not see!"

"Come, Farkas, you are not telling the truth."

"I swear it!"

"You are a forswearer, Farkas!" said the donkey-boy, clearly enjoying his role. "Everyone knows that."

"It is the truth!" the postcard-seller protested. "I was there, yes, but I did not see. They pushed me aside. Anyway, they were all wearing masks."

"But they weren't wearing masks when they approached you and asked if you would help them."

"It was one man only and I did not know him. He said he would beat me if I didn't agree to help him. He was a bad man, effendi, and I knew he would keep his word."

"Which is more than you would," said the cooperative donkey-boy.

"Tell me what you were to do."

"I was to go to the foot of the steps when I was told. The old man would come down the steps and then I would show him the cards."

"And then?"

"Then I was to get out of the way. And tell no one."

"You *have* told someone," said the donkey-boy, carried away, "you have told us, Forswearer!"

"I would not have told," protested the postcard-seller.

"I tried not to. I ran away after you came the first time because I knew you would come again."

"Farkas," said Owen, "you said you were to go to the steps when you were told. You *were* told and you went. Who told you?"

Farkas moistened his lips.

"If it makes it any easier," said Owen, "I may already know the answer. He came across the terrace, did he not, and spoke to you?"

"Abdul Hafiz," whispered the postcard-seller.

•   •   •

"I had a feeling it was going to be him," said Owen, "even before Colthorpe Hartley told me. While he was being held in that place in the Wagh el Birket he had a chance to do plenty of remembering and eventually he got there. He didn't know Abdul Hafiz by name, of course. He remembered him as the serious one."

"He saw him go across the terrace?"

"And speak to Farkas, yes."

"Did he go straight to Farkas?" asked Georgiades.

"He went to Moulin first."

"Yes," said Georgiades, "that makes sense. I was wondering—"

"Presumably he told him something like that a new supply of cards had come in and would he like to see them?"

"How did he get on this sort of terms with Moulin in the first place? I mean, if I wanted someone to go on a dirty errand for me, Abdul Hafiz is not the man I would choose."

"Abdul Hafiz dragomaned for Berthelot and Madame Chévènement. Moulin must have met him through them. When you first come to Egypt one dragoman looks pretty like another. Think of Colthorpe Hartley. It's only later that you get to see the difference."

"Abdul Hafiz went to Anton's, of course. Carrying messages for Berthelot."

"My guess is that they knew that the plan to build a big salon on the other side of the river was already beginning to seep out. Zawia might have already been tipped off by one of the Khedive's entourage. When it began to break, Abdul Hafiz was the right man in the right place. And Moulin, the man behind it on the French side, became the obvious man to go for."

"You think they were out to stop the Khedive?"

"And raise money. And hit at the Great Powers. Maybe at tourism, too. If you're a Wahabbi you're dead against all that kind of foreign contamination."

"You reckon they're all Wahabbi?"

"If one of them's Wahabbi, the others are likely to be."

"Not Senussi," said Georgiades, as one reporting a fact.

"Not Senussi. That'll disappoint the Army," said Owen with satisfaction.

"Maybe. But it doesn't make it any easier for us. There are a hell of a lot of Wahabbi in Cairo."

"We're not much further," Owen conceded.

"Especially now that Abdul Hafiz has gone," said Georgiades.

•   •   •

Someone must have been watching, for by the time that Owen had got downstairs again after taking Colthorpe Hartley back to his room, Abdul Hafiz had gone. It confirmed for Owen that someone had overheard Colthorpe Hartley's groping attempts to identify the dragoman he had seen when he had been talking with Owen on the terrace, but this was no consolation.

"Abdul Hafiz was about all we had," he said to Georgiades, "and now we haven't even got that."

He consulted the donkey-boys again but this time they were unable to help. They were more than willing—in fact, they were desperately eager to help—but the Wahabbi milieu was not really something they knew about. They were now locked up in the caracol, racking their brains to remember anything which might provide a clue to the dragoman's present whereabouts.

One of them was not in the caracol. This was the boy who had claimed to recognize the camel. He was still at liberty, though accompanied everywhere he went by one of Owen's agents. In the afternoons, he went to the Market of the Afternoon. The rest of his time he spent at the Mosque el Hakim, the two places where he thought he had previously seen the camel. If he saw the camel again he was to come back at once to Owen.

This was about all Owen could do, and he was worried. For he thought that Abdul Hafiz's sudden flight might be a sign of panic. And when kidnappers panicked they usually killed their prisoners.

●　　●　　●

He was quite relieved when he got a phone call from Paul.

"Another Diplomatic Request," said Paul. "The same as before. Stay away."

"At the moment," said Owen, "I am not aware that I am sufficiently near anything for anyone to think it worth-while asking me to stay away."

"You are too modest. Now that the Mamur Zapt has smashed the Donkey-boy Mob, the Cairo underworld is all a-tremble. So think our Gallic colleagues, anyway.

Besides, you have cocked it up for them before and they don't want it to happen again."

"Is it the same thing as before? They're going to hand over the money?"

"In exchange for Moulin, yes."

"What makes them think it'll work any better this time than it did last time?"

"The fact that this time Zawia seem very keen to deal. They swear it will go ahead this time. Besides, the French are offering more money."

"So what do you want me to do? I mean *really* want me to do?"

"Stay away, of course. Like I told you. It's a Diplomatic Request, isn't it?"

"But—"

"I am sure a sharp fellow like you has got it all worked out," said Paul, and rang off.

•   •   •

"They're preparing to pull out," said Nikos.

"Zawia? Or the French?"

"The French pulled out a long time ago. Zawia."

"When they've got the money."

"Of course."

"Presumably they won't get their hands on the money until they've handed over Moulin. That means he's still alive. Which is a relief."

"*Are* you going to stay away?"

"Yes, I bloody am. If the exchange goes ahead at least Moulin is free and out of the way. If it doesn't go ahead they'll probably kill him."

"I would expect so," said Nikos neutrally. Now that it was not Senussi but just another boring kidnapping, he had lost interest.

Further support for Nikos's supposition that Zawia were pulling out came soon after from Georgiades.

"I've been talking to Madame Tsakatellis," he said.

"Which one? The older or the younger?"

"I steer clear of the older. No, the younger. I happened to hear that she was pawning everything she hadn't got. Including the shop. So, naturally, when I ran into her I asked her about it. She says that Zawia have contacted her again. They made her an offer. Bring everything you've got, they said, and provided it's big enough you can have your husband."

"They didn't name a price?"

"They named an 'at least' sort of price. More than she's got, of course. So she's having to raise it."

"Still without telling the old lady?"

"So far. The point is," said Georgiades, "that Zawia seem anxious to settle."

"They'll settle," said Nikos, "and then get out."

"There seems an urgency about this," said Georgiades.

"As with Moulin," said Owen.

"Moulin?"

Owen told him.

"*Are* you going to stay away?" asked Georgiades.

"Yes. I've had a diplomatic request."

"Besides which, you cocked it up last time."

"*We* cocked it up."

"As I said. Of course," said Georgiades, thinking, "you've not had a diplomatic request in the case of the Tsakatellis family."

"I've had bloody Rosa's request."

"Quite a girl, isn't she?" said Georgiades. "All the same..."

◆   ◆   ◆

The phone call came through in the early evening. The offices were closed—the working day started at seven and finished at two because of the heat—but Owen had gone back to his office and was quietly working.

"I'll be right with you," he said.

Outside, it was already dark. The streets were filling again after the prolonged siesta. People sauntered up and down looking at the shops, the goods piled high on the pavement outside them and the stalls crowding into the street. Except in the really wealthy areas there was no glass frontage to the shops. They were open to the world and their light spilled out on to the streets and as you walked past you encountered a succession of smells: the pungent bazaar-smell of Egyptian leather, the more subtle but still heavy fragrance of sandalwood, the sharp, burnt smell of coffee, the different burnt smell of roasted peanuts, the various aromas of spices and perfumes, tobaccos and caramel.

The streets became narrower and darker, the shops smaller and less frequent. People were no longer promenading but sitting quietly talking on their doorsteps or gathered round the pumps in the tiny squares or forming animated groups outside the small cafés. For the most part the talkers were men. The women, almost indistinguishable in the shadows because of the blackness of their clothes, kept to the sides of the streets.

A few looked curiously at Owen as he went past. In the darkness and with his tarboosh on, however, there was nothing to mark him out from any other Egyptian.

When he reached the Sharia en Nakhasin he looked around for the little square and found it tucked away to one side. It was not much more than twenty yards across and was dominated by a huge lead pump around which a number of men were sitting. They looked at Owen as he came up and one or two of them muttered greetings. He stood quietly at the edge of the group, waiting.

It was not one of the men but a small boy. Owen felt his trousers tugged and glanced down to see a small urchin apparently begging for alms.

"You are the Mamur Zapt," said the boy, quietly so that no one else would hear.

"I am," said Owen, equally quietly.

"I have a message for you from the fat Greek."

"Yes?"

"He said you would give me piastres."

"I shall. Here is one now. The rest when you have told me."

"Go along the Sharia el Barrani to the Bab el Futuh. He will meet you there."

"Here is another piastre. Come with me and there will be another piastre when I see him."

As they walked along the boy said: "I have a friend who knows you."

"What is his name?"

"Ali."

"I know many Alis."

"This one lives in the Coptic Place of the Dead."

"I remember him."

"When I saw the fat Greek I remembered Ali and thought of you."

Cairo was a very personal city. The contacts and allegiances you made on one occasion carried over to others.

"What is your name," asked Owen, "that I may note it?"

"Narouz."

"Very well, Narouz. I shall remember."

He could see now, ahead of him, the massive bulk of the Bab el Futuk, one of Saladin's two great gates, and realized with a sudden shock of recognition that he was coming again to where he had been previously. To the right of the great Gate, outlined unmistakably against the night sky, were the square, pylon-like minarets of the Mosque of el Hakim.

A man stepped out of the shadows and said, "Effendi!"

"I am here."

"The Greek sends me."

Owen went with him, first giving the boy a piastre. Narouz slipped away but afterward Owen could see him following at a distance.

There were lights among the ruins where people had built their homes, and the glow of braziers where women were cooking. One or two of the workshops were still open. Owen could see the men bent at their serving machines.

They came as before to the liwan, the sanctuary, and its forest of pillars. For a moment Owen thought they were returning to the lamp store where he had come on that earlier, fruitless occasion. His guide branched off, however. They came to the far edge of the liwan.

Georgiades was waiting among the pillars.

"Thank Christ you've come!" he said. "I was beginning to think you would be too late."

"Who is it?" asked Owen.

"Someone from the house. One of the servants."

"I thought it might be the mother."

"No. One of the boys."

"Where?"

Georgiades took Owen's arm and pointed. His eyes were used to the darkness and perhaps it was not yet quite dark, for he could see the figure clearly, a slight, thin figure, walking away from the liwan.

"You would have thought they'd have met here. As before."

"Yes," said Georgiades, "but they haven't met. Yet."

The figure came to a high wall, hesitated and then

turned along it, bringing him back closer to Owen and Georgiades.

"You're sure?"

"We haven't seen anyone."

"What about the money?"

"It's in the bag."

"Where is the bag?"

"He's carrying it."

"I can't see it."

Georgiades looked.

"Bloody hell!" he said.

"For Christ's sake!"

"He had it. He's been carrying it all the time."

"Well, he's not bloody carrying it now."

"But—but—we've been watching him all the time!"

"Like bloody hell you have!" Owen was furious. "For Christ's sake!" he said. "This is bloody incompetent! What the hell were you doing?"

"He had it!" Georgiades appealed to the two agents by his side. "He was bloody carrying it, wasn't he?"

The agents were standing thunderstruck.

"He couldn't have given it to anyone. We've been watching all the time!"

"You've cocked it up. Again!"

Georgiades swallowed.

"He couldn't have met anyone," he said obstinately. "We'd have seen it."

"Where the hell's the bag, then?"

The thin figure reached the end of the wall and turned away again.

One of the agents looked at Owen.

"Yes," he said resignedly. "You'd better."

The agent slipped off in pursuit.

Again! It had happened again! Owen felt sick, furious. They had fooled him the first time. Now, they had done it again. And it wasn't even properly Zawia! Just some slip of a boy from the Tsakatellis household, told what to do, no doubt, by Zawia but quite capable on his own of pulling the wool over Georgiades's eyes. Georgiades! Christ, Owen had always thought he was good, about the only good one he had got. Two agents, too! All three of them, hoodwinked. Before their very eyes!

Before their very eyes. Just as it had been on the terrace when Moulin and Colthorpe Hartley had disappeared. Zawia seemed to make a specialty of it. They didn't want just to trick you, they had to do it in a way which would humiliate you. Well, they had certainly succeeded. He felt humiliated and he didn't like it.

"Christ!" said Georgiades. "Christ!"

The thin figure had all but disappeared into the darkness.

A great wave of fury swept over Owen. They were not going to get away with this.

"Get after him!" he said savagely. "Get after him! If you don't know what he's done with the bag, he bloody does. And he's going to tell me. Christ, he's going to tell me!"

The figure, clearly unfamiliar with the ground, came to a pile of huge blocks of demolished masonry and began to skirt around it. Georgiades, like Owen beside himself with fury, ran across to cut him off, moving with surprising speed for a bulky man. The two agents, coming up behind the thin figure, began to close in on it. They must have made a noise, for the thin figure looked back and then began to run. It disappeared behind some huge stones and Owen could hear it stumbling desperately on the loose rubble. Then it emerged again and ran around behind a rock—straight into Georgiades's hands.

Rosa screamed.

13

Rosa!"

The girl stayed for a moment in Georgiades's hands, then pulled herself away.

"What are you doing here?" she demanded fiercely.

"What are *you* doing here?" countered Owen.

"I told you to stay away!"

"This is not a place for someone like you," said Georgiades.

"I told you to stay away. Why have you come?"

"We did not expect to find it was you."

"It makes no difference. I told you to leave us alone. Why do you keep persecuting us?"

"I have no wish to persecute you," said Owen.

"Then go! Go quickly!"

"Tell me first why you are here."

"Why do you think?" She faced him defiantly. "They want more money. They want all she has. And then they say they will release him. Tonight. Please go!"

"What have you done with the money?"

"Left it. Left it where they told me."

"Where was that?"

She stayed silent.

"You had the bag with you," said Georgiades. "Or was that deceit?"

"Deceit?" She looked surprised. "I left it where they told me. They told me to put it down under a rock in a special place and then to walk around while they counted."

"You spoke to them?"

"No. This was in the message."

"You were to leave the bag and then walk around?"

"For half an hour. I have my watch." She showed it them, almost proudly. "Then I was to go back. And then I would find my father."

She began to weep.

Owen could see Georgiades looking at him in the darkness.

"We have no wish to hurt you or your family," he said gently, "nor to stop your father being released."

"Then you will go? Please go, in case they see you. Go now."

Owen hesitated. He could not make up his mind. He felt unusually at a loss.

"Why do you not go?"

"Is there no servant with you?"

"No. I came on my own. We were to tell no one. How did you find out?"

"Why did not your mother come?" asked Georgiades.

"I would not let her. She—she is not strong enough."

"Have you done it before?"

"No. We used Abou."

"Why did not you use Abou this time?"

"We were to tell no one. It was too important."

"Yet you knew your way."

"I came here this morning. In the light so that I could see."

"You should not be in a place like this," said Georgiades again. Owen realized suddenly that where the family was concerned Georgiades was still very much a traditional Greek.

"You must go!" Rosa began to cry again. "You will ruin everything!"

Owen made up his mind.

"Continue on your walk," he said to her roughly. "Keep to the time they set. Call out if you need help."

"You—you will not stop me?"

"No. Do as they told you. But we will be near."

Rosa turned obediently and started to walk away. Then she stopped.

"You will not interfere?" she demanded.

"We will be near. You may need help to take your father home."

"You do not think—?" she whispered.

"No. But he may be weak. It has been a long time."

"Very well," said Rosa. "But do not let them see you."

"I shall be near," said Georgiades.

Rosa considered him.

"I quite like that," she said softly. Then left.

"Follow her," Owen said to one of the trackers. "See that she does not come to harm."

• • •

The tracker came running back.

"I have seen Abbas," he gasped excitedly.

"You were told to stay with the girl."

"Yes, but I saw Abbas."

"He was the one who was with the donkey-boy," said Georgiades. "They were looking for that camel."

"I thought you would like to know," said the tracker, crestfallen.

"Well, yes, thank you. But keep with the girl."

"Where was Abbas?" asked Georgiades.

"By the liwan. He made signs that he would speak with me. But I came straight back to you," said the tracker, with an air of hard-done-by virtue, "that I might not leave the girl for long."

"Go back to her now. You have done well."

Appeased, the tracker sloped off.

"We'd better find Abbas. We don't want him breaking in on things."

Abbas had had enough sense to stay where he was. They found him and the donkey-boy sheltering among the pillars.

"Allah be praised!" said Abbas. "You are here!"

"We are here," said Owen, "but how do you come to be here?"

"I was looking for the camel," said the donkey-boy, "as you bid me. And, effendi, I have found it. I saw the track and I said, By God, that is the track of the camel I seek. So I followed the track and it brought me here."

"Where is the camel?"

"Over there, hidden among the stones." The donkey-boy pointed. "Effendi, there are three good riding camels with it. It came into my mind that those you hunt may be intending to flee. I felt, therefore, that you should know at once. But this man—" he looked pointedly at Abbas's direction—"would not go for you."

"How could I go?" objected Abbas. "I was bidden to stay with you."

"One of us had to go," said the donkey-boy, "and it could not be me, for if the camels moved, only I could follow."

"It could not be me," said Abbas, "for the effendi told me to stay with you and not leave you."

"Fortunately," said Owen hastily, "I am here so the

question does not now arise. You have done well," he said
to the donkey-boy.

The donkey-boy smiled with pleasure.

"The camel is in good condition, effendi, though I
would like to look at the legs. The left hind leg drags a
little. It may be nothing, just a habit of the beast. All the
same I would like to look, for it could slow them down if
they mean to travel far. But then, of course, they would
not be traveling together, for the others are true riding
camels whereas this is only a beast of burden. It is my
belief they used it to bring the prisoner."

"Prisoner?"

"Yes, effendi, they had a man with them who was
bound. Did I not say?"

"No, you did not say."

"The three riding camels came separately, I think.
When we saw them there were four men, and also the
one that was tied."

"Where are they now?"

"Two walked off across the stones. Two stayed with the
bound man near the camels."

Four men. They could not take them all at the same
time. They would have to take the two with the prisoner
first.

"Rosa will be returning at any moment," said Georgiades.
"We haven't got long."

•   •   •

The two men were squatting in a gap among the stones.
There was no light but Owen's eyes were used to the
darkness and he thought he could see a bundle lying a
little to the men's right. Tsakatellis would be bound and
gagged. If he were still alive.

The two men were talking in low voices.

A stone moved in the darkness and the men were suddenly quiet. There was no further sound and after a little while the men resumed talking.

Owen made no move himself. Georgiades and the trackers would do it better. It would have to be done quietly. The two men who had gone to collect the money would return at any moment. He had stationed himself where he could intercept them.

He wondered why Georgiades was taking so long.

Someone had made their home in the rubble. It was quite some way away but their brazier blazed up for a few seconds and he could see the two men clearly.

They both looked up together as if something had startled them. A dark shape suddenly appeared behind them and one of them fell sideways. The other two shapes merged.

Owen went forward.

The man Georgiades had hit lay inert. The other man was pinioned by the two trackers. One of them had his hand over the man's mouth.

Georgiades was bending over the bundle. The man was wrapped in a hooded galabeah. Georgiades pulled back the hood as Owen arrived.

The man was gagged but his eyes were open. And alive.

Footsteps approached, crunching slightly on the rubble.

Georgiades let the hood fall back over the man's face. He slipped quietly off to one side. One of the trackers, the one who did not have his hand over the man's mouth, slipped off to the other. Owen stayed where he was.

"Suleiman," called one of the approaching shapes softly. "Suleiman, where are you?"

The inert man suddenly groaned.

The two shapes froze. Other shapes closed in on them.

They had to do it from too far away. One of the shapes broke away and ran.

"Get after him!" Georgiades shouted.

The tracker ran off. Away in the darkness someone was scurrying and scrambling.

The first inert man, recovering, tried to get up. Owen put his foot on him.

There was a triumphant shout.

"I have him, effendi!"

It was the donkey-boy.

"I have him, effendi! Abbas, this way!"

Georgiades hauled the man he was holding over to where Owen was and threw him to the ground beside the other two. Then he went back for the bag.

Abbas and the donkey-boy came over the rubble supporting a man between them.

"I caught him!" said the donkey-boy excitedly. "Remember that, effendi, and let it tell in the scales for me. I caught him!"

Owen pulled the gag from Tsakatellis's mouth.

"It is the police," he said. "My friend, you are free."

•　　•　　•

They were just cutting his bonds when Rosa arrived. Georgiades took her gently by the arm and brought her to her father.

One of the men went with them to show them the house where Moulin was held. It was in one of the poorer quarters and some distance away and the donkey-boy proposed they use the riding camels. Georgiades, the complete city dweller, had never been on a camel before. Owen, however, had. When he had first come to Egypt and had been stationed with Garvin at Alexandria to learn the ropes he had spent some time with the drug patrols. He could not call himself an accomplished rider but he could ride without falling off and make the beast respond as he wished.

They took two camels only, the donkey-boy and the guide on one of them, the guide tied hand and foot and slung over the camel's neck. Owen and Georgiades on the other. Georgiades did not say much.

They stopped the camels at the end of the street and went the rest of the way on foot. The house, like the others in the street, was single-story. There was a solid wooden door, clearly barred on the inside, and heavy shutters on the windows.

They went around the back and found the outside stairs leading up to the roof. Two men were sleeping on the roof. They woke them and made them come downstairs and show them into the house. In one of the rooms they found Moulin.

There was a woman in the house but no other men. They made her light a lamp. When it was alight Owen looked at the men again and saw that one of them was Abdul Hafiz.

• • •

"Un brave homme," was Madame Moulin's judgment, as she prepared to make her departure. The Chargé bought two bottles of champagne, the first before she went, so that they could all drink Owen's health, the second after she had gone, to celebrate his own release.

The scheme to build a gambling salon on the other side of the river, alas, fell through. The Khedive decided, in view of the publicity, not to persevere with the idea. Abdul Hafiz and his associates were, therefore, able to go into prison with some sense of achievement.

The commercial interests Monsieur Moulin represented

were fobbed off with the award of the contract to build the masonry apron. Paul felt pleased with the establishment of the new principle that the usual greedy sods shouldn't have it all.

The Colthorpe Hartleys soon left for home, not so much for his sake as for that of his wife. Colthorpe Hartley himself had survived his ordeal remarkably well. "Damn donkey-boy!" he said with an amazed chuckle. "The fact is," said Lucy, "I think he had been a tiny bit bored with the holiday. He never did like shopping. Shall we be seeing you in England soon, Captain Owen? I do hope so." Returning to England had always seemed such a remote possibility that Owen had never really thought about it. However, on inspection the idea seemed to have merits. He did nothing about it, though. Some time later he received a letter from Lucy saying that she was thinking of coming back to Cairo next season as she had unfinished business. Gerald went to India.

The donkey-boys went to prison. That was inescapable. They received comparatively light sentences, however, in view of their cooperative attitude and after six months Owen had them transferred to police headquarters where he employed them as trackers. They all took to this with gusto and the one who had identified the camel stayed on after their sentence expired.

The other donkey-boys returned to their old pastures at Shepheard's, kept green for them by the help of sundry relatives and friends. Daouad's circumstances were, however, reduced to such an extent that the dowry Ali's family could provide no longer seemed so insignificant.

"Besides," he said to Owen, when he was inviting him to the wedding, "her face is like the moon and her eyes are like the stars. A true wife is better than a thousand piastres. Although, frankly, I would have preferred a thousand piastres as well."

Daouad's wedding was not the only romantic consequence of the kidnappings. One morning Rosa appeared
in Owen's office when he was talking to Nikos and
Georgiades.

"I wish to make a complaint," she said.

"You do? What about?"

"I have been assaulted."

"Assaulted?"

"Yes. By one of your men."

"Who? Who has—?"

"He has," said Rosa, pointing at Georgiades.

"Me?" said Georgiades, astounded.

"Georgiades!" said Owen and Nikos together, shocked.

"I have never even touched her," Georgiades protested.

"Yes you have."

"When?"

"That day. At the El Hakim Mosque. When you caught
hold of me."

"I am sorry that you should have been treated roughly
on that occasion," said Owen, "but—"

"He felt my breasts."

"Georgiades!" said Owen and Nikos, shocked again.

"I didn't feel her breasts! I thought she was a boy. And
then when she screamed, I—"

"There you are," said Rosa.

"I am very sorry this happened," Owen said to Rosa,
"but, you know, it is easily understandable."

Rosa stayed silent.

"Georgiades," said Owen, turning to the Greek, "you
should apologize."

"Apologize?"

"Yes," said Owen firmly.

"Very well, then," said Georgiades. "I apologize."

"I don't accept your apology," said Rosa.

"But what do you want?" asked Owen, bewildered.

"I look to you," said Rosa, "to see that my honor is protected."

"Well, yes, I'm only glad to. But..."

"He will have to marry me. He is not a man I would normally have chosen but in the circumstances..."

Owen tried to persuade her that this was not necessary. Rosa, however, was adamant.

"I cannot marry anyone else," she said, "not now that he has sullied me."

"I haven't sullied you!" protested the distraught Georgiades.

"My innocence has gone forever," declared Rosa.

"Anyway, you can't marry him," said Owen. "You are too young."

"I am fourteen," said Rosa with dignity.

"That's right. Too young."

Rosa's face darkened with fury.

"I shall speak to your lady," she said.

• • •

And did.

"Fourteen is quite old in Cairo," said Zeinab. "Most girls marry when they are thirteen. The men prefer it because it makes them more biddable. In Rosa's case I think that point has already passed."

"Georgiades is over twice her age," Owen pointed out.

"That is supposed to lead to proper authority in the household."

"I'll talk to her father," said Owen, "and get him to sort her out."

Tsakatellis was inclined to share Owen's view that his daughter was still too young to marry. This was to no avail, however, for his mother, the old Mrs. Tsakatellis, unexpectedly sided with her granddaughter. The other

Mrs. Tsakatellis, Rosa's mother, was not consulted in the matter.

Owen reported the deadlock to Georgiades.

"It's no good," said Georgiades. "They'll get me."

"What do you mean—'They'll get you'?"

"With a knife between the shoulder blades. You don't know the Greeks."

"Nonsense! Whatever are you thinking of?"

"Her relatives. It's a matter of family honor now."

"What nonsense!"

Georgiades, however, remained gloomy.

One morning he came into the office in a very agitated state. "It's terrible," he said. "They've sent a matchmaker."

"You don't have to agree," Owen counseled him. "You're a free man."

"Not any more," said Georgiades. "Not any more!"

•   •   •

First came two men carrying mirrors shaped like shields and mounted on long staves; then a band, playing strange Oriental instruments and mounted on camels with white shells on their bridles and shells and mirrors and tinsel on their scarlet caparisons. Then came masked jesters and banner-bearers, and a bagpipe band on foot, paid for by Owen. Last came the bride in a beautiful dark-wood palanquin borrowed for the occasion from one of the donkey-boys' clients.

The donkey-boys were naturally there in force. Owen caught sight of Daouad's beaming face among the throng and several of the faces behind the jesters' masks seemed vaguely familiar. Even the boys from the donkey-vous across the street had been allowed to join in for this special occasion. There was Ali marching proudly beside his new brother-in-law.

The procession passed directly in front of the terrace steps where Owen and Mahmoud were standing. The donkey-boys waved up and there was a splendid jingle of bells.

The snake charmer gave a violent start.

"There it is again!" he cried out in alarm. "Just as it was before!"

"Not quite as it was before," said Owen. "Or so I hope."